Return to Storyworld

By Alessandro Reale

Copyright © 2016 by Alessandro Reale
All rights reserved.

This is a work of fiction. Names, characters, businesses, places, events, and incidents are either products of the author's imagination or used in a fictitious manner. Any resemblance to actual persons, living or dead, or actual events is purely coincidental.

ISBN: 1539171647
ISBN-13: 978-1539171645

Thank you for joining me on another adventure.

Chapter 1

The Mystery of the Clockmaker

Giles Dickory dropped his brush into the bucket after adding the finishing touches to his latest masterpiece: a tall, freshly painted grandfather clock built from the finest oak in the region. It had taken the clockmaker more than five years to complete his project, and he couldn't help but marvel at how far he'd come since he first set up the large chunk of wood in the middle of his workshop. He had just finished putting a coat of varnish on the clock, giving it a beautiful sheen accentuated by the flickering lights from the fireplace.

It would take a while for the coat to dry, so Giles decided he could finally take a break after working nonstop for the past eight hours. He sat down at his bench and observed the workshop that had doubled as his second bedroom for the past several days.

Numerous clocks covered nearly every inch of the walls, from ground to ceiling. There were several dozen more clocks hanging from the rafters above, and one broken timepiece lying discarded on the floor. No matter where you turned, there was a clock to be seen, and no two clocks were exactly the same.

There was one piece that featured carvings of various exotic birds flying among wooden clouds, and whenever the clock struck a new hour, the birds would give a series of chirps that corresponded with the time. Another timepiece showed a carving of a pack of wolves with their snouts raised in the sky, howling at a wooden moon doubling as the clock's face. One of the clocks hanging from the ceiling appeared to be nothing more than two crossed wooden sticks, but Giles had specially designed it to always point to the correct time with its shadow.

Though Giles was renowned for his unique designs and extraordinary attention to detail, he decided to skip any ornamental designs or fancy mechanisms for his latest project. The grandfather clock remained simple and featured a more conservative, conventional appearance: a dark brown frame, a white face, a polished silver pendulum, and two large silver hands.

Perhaps it was fate that he finished the clock at six minutes to midnight. Both of its hands were already trained on the number twelve. All Giles needed to do was trigger the pendulum at the right moment. He figured he had enough time to grab a quick drink before setting the clock in motion.

The strong, permeating scent of paint and varnish filled the house, reminding the clockmaker to open the window and let the air exchange. There was a cool breeze tonight. It wafted in from the backyard and tickled his exposed belly. He shivered and shuffled away from the window, rubbing his blistered, bony fingers together.

As Giles made his way to the kitchen, he passed two large tables buried underneath mountains of tools, sketches, and discarded food remnants. With each step he took, a shiver slithered up his spine to the base of his skull. His work on the clock had taken its toll on his physical health, as well as his psyche.

Return to Storyworld

For the past five years, every evening, Giles adhered to the exact same routine: go to sleep, wake up from strange nightmares, work on the grandfather clock until sunrise, and then assemble or repair other clocks throughout the day. Never had a single project taken this long, but Giles knew it would be worth it.

The pain in his spine made him wince with each step he took, and he cringed his wrinkled gray eyes whenever his foot made contact with the floor. Another result of his nonstop work on the grandfather clock was his horrible aging. It was as if Giles was literally putting his own time into the project with each night he spent carving and chiseling away. The black hair once covering his head was long gone, and the thick beard shrouding the lower half of his face had turned almost completely gray.

His voice had grown hoarse to the point that he could've sworn he had more dust in his lungs than air. Whenever he shifted one of his limbs too fast, he would hear a light pop or crack. Most of the time, they were painless, yet he had a constant fear that one day he would hear the dreaded noise of one of his legs or arms popping out of their socket.

Giles trudged into the dark kitchen and lifted an enormous jug of rum from the shelf. Rather than pouring himself a glass, he chugged directly from the container. In the past, the rum would sting as it washed down his throat. Now, it was soothing and refreshing, like ice-cold water in the middle of summer. The true pleasure of the drink would take hold in minutes, once the alcohol kicked in. Giles was determined to get to sleep tonight, whether his body wanted to or not.

Return to Storyworld

A loud smacking sound caught the clockmaker's attention. He pulled the bottle away from his mouth so quickly he spilled rum on the ground. He swore quietly and went to investigate the source of the noise. It sounded as though something had fallen in the workshop.

When Giles reached his work area, he didn't notice anything out of the ordinary. The clocks ticked away with their hands at one minute to midnight. The fireplace crackled softly, casting dancing shadows around the room. The cluttered tables remained cluttered, and the empty food plates remained empty. The lone grandfather clock stood a silent sentinel in the middle of the room, untouched and unmoving, waiting to be set in motion. Nothing was out of place.

Giles was opening the grandfather clock's front panel when he saw that his window had shut. He rushed over to open it again as the heavy smell of varnish saturated the room. This time, he wedged a mallet under the frame to keep it open.

Suddenly, a deafening crash resounded throughout the room. Giles spun around and felt his heart sink to his stomach. The grandfather clock was on the ground with its body cracked into dozens of pieces. Seconds later, the clocks on the walls initiated their midnight chimes.

Giles only had a brief moment of remorse for his masterpiece's destruction when the fire went out, casting his workshop into near-total darkness. The half-moon poured through the window, illuminating the clockmaker and the shattered wooden pieces on the floor. The rest of the workshop remained pitch-black. Giles grabbed the mallet from the window and clutched it against his heart.

"Who's there?!" he asked into the darkness.

Return to Storyworld

From the depths of the workshop, amidst the ominous chiming of a hundred clocks, a high-pitched cackling was heard.

*   *   *

The Potts Theater erupted with thunderous applause. The guests sitting in the front row rose to their feet to give a standing ovation. The stage curtains opened to reveal the cast of *Legacy*, and the performers stepped forward to take a collective bow.

A skinny, pale gentleman with a pointed chin and slim nose approached the very front of the stage. The crowd cheered loudest for this man, for he was Benjamin Barker, a popular Himshire street performer who had portrayed the lead role in the show.

Benjamin beamed at the audience, drawing back his black cape and waving enthusiastically with both hands. *Legacy* had been a totally different experience for him. He had performed small acts for random passersby on the streets of Himshire for decades, but this was the first time he got to display his talent to such a large crowd at once.

"Thank you, my friends, thank you!" yelled Benjamin as the applause faded away. "My fellow performers and I would like to thank each and every one of you for coming out to this legendary event. As most of you are aware, this is the first step in our Literary Integration, and I can honestly say I wouldn't have preferred it any other way.

"However, we cannot take all the credit for this amazing performance.

Return to Storyworld

Tonight's success was due to the efforts of our latest Literary, whom I have had the pleasure of hosting for the past three months. I present to you, Lady Alayna Potts, Warrior of Haddonfield!"

The crowd cheered again as a brown-haired woman in a gold and white dress took the stage. She approached Benjamin and stood on her tiptoes to give him a peck on the cheek. Benjamin blushed and gently kissed her hand.

"Thank you very much, Mr. Barker," said Lady Potts, smiling widely. "I also want to thank everybody filling these seats tonight. You have no idea how much it means to be part of this. It's crazy to think how, a couple months ago, I was sitting at my desk at a low-grade investment firm in Jersey, and the next thing I know, I'm here in this Storyworld place. I mean, I never thought I'd meet people like Benjamin Barker, or the Phantom, or—"

A loud scream cut off her speech. Lady Potts frowned. She looked at the audience, where a woman was standing in her seat and pointing above the stage. Everyone's eyes went up to the catwalk stretching across the top of the theater. Perched on a rafter was a cloaked figure encased in shadows. The light from a nearby torch caught the glint of a metal blade in their hand. Before anyone could react, the stranger threw the dagger at the stage, striking Benjamin in the chest.

There was uproar in the theater as audience members rushed for the exits. The cast members hopped off the stage and followed suit, except for Alayna, who dove to catch Benjamin as he fell. The hooded figure leapt from the perch and used their billowing black cape to glide onto the stage. They landed yards away from Benjamin and Alayna and stepped into the torchlight.

Return to Storyworld

"We... we killed you," Alayna said in a quivering voice. She retrieved a dagger from the sheath around her ankle. "Don't you dare come near me us!"

The stranger didn't say anything, but gave a light growl from underneath their hood as they drew a thin sword from their belt.

"Halt!" Two men in long brown overcoats rushed into the near-empty theater and dashed toward the stage. "By Himshire law, you're under arrest!"

The cloaked stranger grunted angrily. They reached into their pocket and produced a handful of small gray pellets, which they tossed at the ground. A puff of thick smoke engulfed them, and when it cleared seconds later, they had vanished.

The two men vaulted onto the stage and approached Alayna. The man who had shouted was the taller of the two, with curly black hair partially concealed under a brown fedora. Pinned to the front of his jacket was a bronze badge that read, "Himshire Investigators - Agent Holmes". His companion was shorter and stick-thin, with a thick brown mustache and combed-over hair. He wore round-lensed glasses and a black bowler hat, and on his chest was a badge that stated, "Himshire Investigators - Agent Watson".

"Did you see where he went, Watson?" barked Agent Holmes.

"No, I think he might have got— THERE!" Watson pointed at the ceiling rafters as a shadowy form exited through the open window. "How did he get up there so fast?"

Holmes ignored his partner and bent down to examine the spot on the stage where the assailant stood moments ago. Watson went to check on Alayna, who had gone pale as a ghost and sobbed silently with Benjamin's head on her lap.

Watson placed his fingers to the side of Benjamin's neck and shook his head. "I'm sorry, Lady Potts, but he's gone. Holmes and I should've gotten here sooner."

Holmes was now gazing up at the window where the man had escaped. He then scanned the front row of seats closest to the stage.

"Was Councilwoman Jane here tonight?"

"Yeah, yeah, she was," sobbed Alayna. "She wanted to see Ben perform."

Holmes cursed to himself. "Watson, take Lady Potts to a safe location. I'm going after the Phantom before he reaches his next target."

Alayna looked up in horror. "You have to save her!"

The agent was already sprinting out the door before she could finish her sentence.

There was pandemonium in the streets of Himshire as citizens scrambled to get to their homes following the incident at the Potts Theater. News of the attack had spread rapidly across the city. The air was filled with the sounds of people crying and shouting, mixed in with doors slamming and bolting shut. The last time there was this much chaos was three months ago when the notorious Phantom first made his presence known in Himshire.

Antigone Jane ran down the street alone, holding her curly black hair out of her face with one hand and carrying her dress above her feet with the other.

Return to Storyworld

Every few seconds, she would nervously check over her shoulder and see people rushing into their homes. She had been sitting in the front row at the theater to see her lover Benjamin perform, but she was one of the first people out of the building the moment the Phantom revealed himself. While she was upset to see Benjamin murdered, she did not want to stick around and end up dead as well.

Turning onto Burrow Way, Antigone realized she was the only person left in the streets. Up ahead, she could see her home looming in the distance. Two more blocks...

Antigone felt an eerie sense of someone pursuing her. She glanced over her shoulder. There was nothing but an empty dirt road and rows of dark houses. When she turned back, there was a dark figure in the middle of her path. Antigone screamed and tripped over the trails of her dress, falling in front of the Phantom.

"No, please!" she pleaded. "I'm sorry!"

The Phantom slightly pulled back his hood, revealing a white domino mask that hid the top half of his severely scarred face.

"Sorry?" he grumbled through a gnarled, lipless mouth. "Sorry that you left me, or sorry that I'm about to kill you?"

"Please!" cried Antigone.

"You don't deserve my mercy," said the Phantom, unsheathing his sword.

Antigone whimpered at the blade shimmering in the moonlight.

"Don't do this," she begged one last time.

The large frame of a man sprinted out of an alleyway and barreled into the Phantom. Antigone looked to her savior and saw that it was Agent Holmes.

"Go home now!" he demanded.

Antigone didn't need to be told twice. She ran down the road without looking back.

"You will pay for that," said the Phantom as he rose.

Holmes pulled a pair of handcuffs from his belt. "I don't think so. Put these on and save me the trouble." He tossed them at the Phantom's feet.

The Phantom ignored his command. He stood rooted to his spot, silently glaring at the agent.

"Either you put them on, or I'll put them on for you, and I promise it won't be pleasant," said Holmes more forcefully.

With a loud yell, the Phantom charged. Holmes shifted to his left, allowing him to run past, then grabbed the back of his cloak and tugged it so hard that the Phantom was pulled off his feet.

"I told you it wouldn't be pleasant," said Holmes, retrieving his handcuffs.

There was a loud series of snaps, and the entire area was suddenly engulfed in thick gray smoke. Holmes squinted through the cloud, but all he could see was endless gray. The black figure appeared next to him and elbowed him in the head, sending him sprawling to the ground.

Holmes swiftly recovered and sprung to his feet. He couldn't see through the thick smoke, but he could sense the Phantom's presence nearby. He heard the flutter of a cloak behind him. Then to the right. Then in front. When Holmes felt the Phantom passing on his left, he snaked his foot out and delivered a swift kick to his shin. There was a loud howl of pain, and the black figure collapsed.

"Are you ready to cooperate?" asked Holmes, grabbing the man's wrists. As he was slapping the cuffs on him, the Phantom threw a handful of dirt in his face. Holmes yelled and reached for his eyes. The Phantom quickly delivered a knee into the agent's stomach.

Holmes collapsed, wheezing and wiping the dirt from his eyes. Through his tears, he saw the Phantom pick up his discarded sword and approach him.

There was another yell. The Phantom staggered to his knees, then turned around and stabbed at a second dark figure behind him. As the smoke cleared, Holmes spotted the body of Antigone Jane crumple to the ground with a large rock in her hand.

The Phantom chuckled as he wiped the blood from his blade. But as he turned back to face the agent, he was met with a stone-hard fist to the side of his head. Holmes threw another punch, this time at his ribs. The Phantom doubled over and feebly swung his sword in a wide arc. The agent leapt backwards out of the blade's reach, then dashed forward and attacked with a barrage of punches.

After numerous hits, the Phantom's face was bleeding, staining the edges of his domino mask with splotches of dark blood. In a last desperate attempt, he weakly swiped his sword once more. Holmes smacked it away and jumped at his opponent with his fist cocked. At the same time, the Phantom snapped the blade backward, cutting a long gash in the agent's knee. Holmes stumbled, and in that split-second of distraction, the Phantom punched him in the chin.

Holmes went tumbling to the dirt. The hit was so strong it blurred his vision and temporarily dazed him. He saw doubles of the Phantom bearing down on him with their swords raised. The agent forced himself to his knees and readied his hands. But before the Phantom could deal the killing blow, a gunshot rang out on the street, slicing through the air like the crack of a whip.

The Phantom paused as the sound faded away into an echo across the city. He looked down at the dark stain forming on his chest. With one last glare at Holmes, he dropped his sword and keeled over. Standing behind him was Agent Watson, a pistol clasped in his hand.

Holmes gave a sigh of relief. "Thanks, Watson, but I was handling him well on my own."

"Are you sure, Holmes? He was about to skewer you like a fish."

"I know how to take care of myself, thank you very much."

Watson rolled his eyes and pocketed the pistol. He helped Holmes up and said, "When do you want to commence the report?"

"Once the authorities arrive," replied Holmes, dusting himself off.

As if on cue, ten of Himshire's law enforcement officials rounded the corner of the street and approached the agents. The deputies sported the same uniform composed of brown boar-hide chest-plates, matching brown hoods, and thin gray sleeves and leggings. They carried the standard equipment: a short dagger, two pairs of metal clasps for binding suspects' hands, and a short bow and quiver full of arrows strung across their backs. Each deputy wore a polished silver badge on their chest.

One young female deputy with a black braided ponytail and the name

Return to Storyworld

"Griffin" stamped on her badge asked, "Did you catch the culprit?"

Holmes and Watson parted ways, allowing the deputies to see the two corpses behind them. Griffin and her fellow officials shared a somber look when they saw the body of Antigone Jane.

"Will the sheriff be arriving soon?" Holmes asked grimly.

"She's currently at the Potts Theater keeping an eye over Lady Potts. She told us to conduct the report without her."

Holmes nodded. "Very well, let us begin." He waited for Watson and Griffin to pull out their pads and pencils. Taking a deep breath, he stated, "Roughly three months ago, Himshire was visited by its latest Literary, a young woman by the name of Alayna Potts. She was summoned to protect the city from a mysterious assailant known as the Phantom, who seemed to have been inspired by a similar case many years ago. If you have any questions about said case, please refer to my notes entitled 'The Phantom of the Music Hall.'

"Several days later after the Literary's arrival, it became apparent that this new Phantom was targeting two particular citizens: Mr. Benjamin Barker, a street performer, and Ms. Antigone Jane, the town councilwoman."

"Hang on, hang on," said Griffin, catching up to the agent's dictation. Holmes was notorious for his unorthodox method of reporting, which often made it difficult for the deputies to keep notes. Once she had caught up, Griffin motioned for him to carry on.

"Within two weeks, Mr. Barker and Lady Potts defeated the Phantom and left him for dead in the Meyern Woods outside of Himshire. Though her mission was over, the Literary had requested to stay in the city to learn more about Storyworld. From that point on, she became the leading driver of the Literary Integration."

Watson cleared his throat. "By the way, you should include a note in your report about the Integration and its purpose of adapting our world to Literary practices. It's vital we incorporate that in our case files."

"Yes, thank you, Watson," said Holmes. "But back to the important part. After three months, Agent Watson and I deduced the Phantom was still alive. He'd been hiding out in the woods, calculating his next strike on his intended targets. It was around this time that Lady Potts and a dozen volunteers from Himshire had begun renovating the old abandoned warehouse at the crossing of Carriage Street and Maple Way. The building was restructured into the Potts Theater, where Himshire would soon hold its very first Literary Integration show, *Legacy*."

Watson and Griffin's hands flew across their notepads. Not looking up from his writing, Watson said, "I'm going to attach a copy of my notes from the night of the Phantom's first defeat as well. I'll get another copy to the sheriff's station in the morning."

"Thank you," said Holmes again. "Agent Watson and I came to the conclusion that the Phantom was planning to strike next during the show. Sadly, we didn't discover this until it was too late. We arrived at the Potts Theater at approximately midnight, when the show had ended and after Mr. Barker had been murdered."

"Sir," interjected another deputy, "why did the assassin wait so long to return? Didn't he have three months to kill Barker?"

"Mr. Barker wasn't the sole target in this story," commented Watson. "There was also Ms. Jane and Lady Potts. We assume the Phantom wanted his targets in one location so that it would be a quick and clean task."

"Also," said Holmes, raising a finger, "I believe the Phantom was very busy preparing for this mission. Following what Lady Potts and Mr. Barker had done to him during their previous encounter, he had to make sure he wasn't going to be foiled again. In order to do that, he needed the proper equipment."

Holmes strolled over to the corpse and lifted the Phantom's leg. Without any sense of delicateness or ease, he yanked off one of the boots. He also rifled through the Phantom's coat and pulled out a handful of gray pellets.

"I followed a set of unusual tracks from the Meyern Woods to the theater," Holmes said as he examined the boot. "I knew the prints couldn't have belonged to any traditional footwear, but what really intrigued me was how long of a stride there was between each step. The only way a normal person could've made these footprints was if they had legs as tall as trees, or if they hopped between steps.

"Now, if you check the bottom of this boot, you'll see these strange springs attached to the sole. They allow the wearer to propel himself into the air with each step. This explains how the Phantom traveled so swiftly and how he escaped the theater in seconds. I knew what we were dealing with when I found the same strange footprints indented in the theater's stage a few minutes ago.

"As for these smoke pellets, I think we now know who broke into the alchemist's lab last month. There was a report of half his ingredients being stolen, and I'm willing to bet my wages that those are the same ones used to concoct these little buggers."

"He really did plan this out well," remarked Watson.

"But as I was saying, we arrived at the theater as Mr. Barker was struck down by the assassin. Agent Watson stayed behind to tend to Lady Potts while I pursued the escaped Phantom. I knew his next target would be Ms. Jane."

"Shortly after my partner's departure," said Watson, intervening again, "three deputies arrived to escort Lady Potts to safety. Upon their arrival and once I made sure the Literary was safe, I followed Agent Holmes and the culprit."

"I confronted the Phantom as he was closing in on Ms. Jane on Burrow Way," continued Holmes. "I attempted to bring him in peacefully, but he resisted arrest and decided to attack me. We had a brief scuffle, during which time Ms. Jane made her escape. I tried to subdue the Phantom, but he got the upper hand and blinded me with these smoke pellets. In the confusion of the smokescreen, the Phantom murdered Ms. Jane, who had apparently come back to assist me in the fight. Agent Watson soon arrived and executed the Phantom."

Watson and Griffin finished the last of their notes and nodded. Holmes bent over and removed the Phantom's mask, revealing the horribly scarred and disfigured face underneath. He had no eyebrows or eyelashes, and the front of his hairline had been scorched away, leaving his severely burnt forehead exposed. The upper half of his face suffered from far worse burns than his lower half, though the scarring across his lips and chin wasn't minor by any means.

"Is that who I think it is?" asked Griffin.

"Just as I expected," said Holmes. "Let it be known that the identity of the Phantom was none other than Bertram Sansidin, a former model for Grothie's Robe Store. As you may recall, a fire decimated the store last year, resulting in multiple deaths and extensive injuries. Mr. Sansidin was one of the somewhat luckier victims who survived."

"Ms. Jane and Sansidin were once married, weren't they?" asked a deputy.

"Correct. Ms. Jane left him for Benjamin Barker, which sparked Bertram's desire for revenge, leading him to adopt the moniker of the Phantom."

"Now, I want this next statement emphasized in your report," said Holmes in a fresh tone. "From now on, we're enforcing a new policy among Literary hosts and Himshire law enforcement. Whenever a criminal is killed, they must be confirmed dead by a city physician. We can't leave corpses unattended and unchecked anymore. Thanks to your carelessness, we had two easily preventable murders tonight. Now get these bodies out of here and make sure Lady Potts is transported to her own world at once!"

The deputies frowned at one another. Griffin didn't say another word as she jotted down her final notes and then took off down the street. The remaining deputies collected the bodies of Antigone and the Phantom and escorted them to the town medical center. Watson and Holmes stayed behind at the crime scene, watching the officials disappear down the street.

"A little harsh, don't you think?" inquired Watson.

"Not at all," declared Holmes. "You know how I feel about our town's law enforcement. These deputies are as useless as a dull sword. It's a wonder there aren't killings every night in Himshire."

"You need to give them a break, Holmes. The deputies are doing their best to maintain order. Not everyone is as thorough as you."

"They're in charge of keeping this city safe, and they're doing a poor job at it," stated Holmes. The tone in his voice indicated the conversation was over. He tucked his hands into his pockets and walked up the street, Watson close behind.

The city was silent. Even though it was well past midnight, small groups of citizens were usually still roaming at this hour. It was eerie to see these streets so empty and lifeless.

Watson shook his head. "Some nights, I really hate this job."

"Some?" asked Holmes. "I feel that way *every* night. Do you think I like handling these kinds of cases? It's not supposed to be enjoyable, but it has to be done."

"I wish I was still a doctor," said Watson.

"Really? Was that any better?"

"When I was a doctor, there was always a chance to save my clients. As a detective, it's usually too late. We typically solve the crimes *after* there's been a death."

"Well, that's the life we chose, Watson. You and I are the only people in this town with the mental fortitude and intelligence to handle these cases.

Himshire would fall apart if we left everything up to those moronic deputies…"

"How do you do it, Holmes? How do you cope with the stress that comes with the job?"

"Did you forget about my little friend, cannabis?"

Watson muttered, "Of course I didn't forget. How could I?"

From the depths of his jacket, Holmes produced a curved smoking pipe and a small black velvet bag. He pulled clumps of a green and brown herb from the bag and stuffed them tightly into the pipe's bowl. With a snap of his fingers, Holmes conjured a tiny flame above his thumb, which he then held over the cannabis. A sweet smell and light crackling sound filled the air. The agent inhaled deeply, waited a moment, and then exhaled a large puff of smoke.

"You smoke too much," said Watson in a concerned voice. "If I was still practicing medicine, I would've diagnosed you with a physiological addiction."

"Impossible. You can't become addicted to cannabis. I've experimented with it for years and determined there aren't any addictive components. I know my herbs."

"It doesn't matter what's in it; you can still become addicted. You smoke every hour, on the hour. I can actually tell what time it is by how much you smoke. I'm guessing it's now one in the morning?"

"You're starting to annoy me, Watson," growled Holmes. "You asked how I handle stress. Well, this is how I handle it. Now leave it be! Good thing you're such a valuable partner, or else we would've parted ways after we moved out of Baker Street."

Return to Storyworld

Watson appeared slightly offended at this comment. Holmes laughed out another puff of smoke and slapped him on the arm.

"A joke, my friend! You know you're like a brother to me. In fact, you're more a brother than my actual kin. Your nagging annoys me to no end, but I wouldn't have it any other way." Holmes playfully slapped him again. "Come on. We should head to the sheriff's station for the debriefing."

The agents trekked down the street in silence. Holmes took three more drags from his pipe, then stowed it away. Rounding another corner, the agents ended up on Proctor Alley. They made it a few steps down the path when they froze in their tracks.

Halfway down the road, a team of deputies was huddled around the entrance of a building. Holmes recognized it as the home-workshop of Giles Dickory, the town clockmaker.

"What's going on here?" asked Holmes as he and Watson approached the scene.

"Another death in Himshire tonight," replied an older official holding a lantern. "One o' the neighbors flagged us down on our way to the station. Said they heard a crash inside Dickory's workshop a while ago. We went in and found the poor old bloke dead on the ground. I think he suffocated."

Holmes arched an eyebrow. "Suffocated?"

The deputy beckoned the agents to join him inside. Holmes recalled visiting this workshop long ago when Giles first moved to the city. Back then, the rooms were mostly empty except for large cobwebs strung across the windows and a solitary clock here or there. Since then, the place had transformed into a quaint little workshop with its walls shrouded in ornate timepieces.

"Smell that?" said the deputy, crinkling his nose. "That's varnish. The window and door were closed when we got here. The fool probably forgot the ventilation and choked to death." He gave a dry laugh.

The window was now open, allowing fresh air to circulate throughout the room, but the light smell of varnish lingered. The clockmaker was lying on the ground with his arms outstretched, his left hand loosely clutching a rubber mallet. But what caught the agent's attention were the shattered remains of an enormous grandfather clock near Dickory's body.

"We think he musta' collapsed into the clock when he passed out," said the deputy.

"If that were the case, then why did the clock fall toward him?" said Holmes.

Watson raised an eyebrow at Holmes. "Do you think there's foul play at work here?"

Holmes didn't answer. He was careful to never jump to conclusions, but he had a knack for seeing things others missed. The agent strode over to the fireplace in the corner, where three half-burned logs sat in the hearth. When he put his hand over the logs, he could feel warmth radiating from them.

"Was the fire burning when you arrived?" asked Holmes.

"Nope."

Holmes gazed around the room, taking in every detail, as Watson and the deputy watched. He took the lantern from the deputy and made his way into the adjacent kitchen, where he found a large jug on the countertop and a puddle of amber liquid on the ground. More ideas and theories floated across the agent's mind as he attempted to piece together a cohesive thought.

"Well, are you going to tell us what's going on?" shouted the deputy from the other room.

Once again, Holmes ignored the question. He approached the corpse and gently rolled the clockmaker onto his back. It had been a long time since Holmes had seen the man in person, but he recognized his face, though it was more gaunt and haggard than he remembered. His sunken eyes and hollow cheeks made him look like a skeleton with a thin slab of skin stretched over the bones. Time had not been kind to the clockmaker.

Holmes was about to stand up when his eye caught a small pile of yellow grains underneath Dickory's body.

"Sawdust, maybe?" asked the deputy. When Holmes didn't respond again, he angrily said, "Will you stop ignoring me and tell us what's going on?!"

The agent stood up. "There's a murderer loose in Himshire."

"What makes you say that?"

Holmes nodded at Watson, who pulled out his notepad and pencil. "The clues are around us. Why did the clock fall toward Dickory? Why is he holding a mallet if he had just applied a fresh coat of varnish on the clock? Who put out the fireplace if the clockmaker was dead? Why are there—"

"Whoa, whoa, slow down!" said the deputy. "Take it one step atta time!"

Return to Storyworld

Holmes rolled his eyes. "Here is my best prediction at what happened. Dickory had finished putting varnish on the clock and decided to take a break. Before he did so, he opened the window to let the air circulate. There is no way an experienced clockmaker would make an amateur mistake like leaving the windows closed when there are toxic fumes in the air, especially if there's a lit fireplace nearby.

"Then he went into the kitchen to have a drink. You'll find an open jug on the counter along with a puddle of rum on the ground. See the detail in Dickory's clock designs. He has the steadiest hands in the city, so it's very unlikely he would be careless and spill his drink, unless he was caught by surprise. He left the jug on the counter instead of putting it away, meaning that whatever happened required immediate attention. Most likely the window had slammed shut.

"When he came back into the workshop, he reopened the window; this time, he wedged that mallet of his into the frame to keep it from closing again. You'll see marks of white paint at the head of the mallet that match the window frame—"

"None of this sounds like a murder to me," grunted the deputy.

"These details are necessary for our notes," said Watson. "Now shut up and let him finish!"

Holmes was thankful that Watson intervened because his response would've been far less polite.

"While Dickory was putting the mallet into the window, the clock was tipped over and the fireplace was extinguished. At this point, the clockmaker must've realized he was not alone, which is why he pulled the mallet from the window in hopes of defending himself. Unfortunately, it didn't serve him well."

It took a moment for the deputy to absorb this information. "So what was the point of this? Why?"

"Maybe it was a thief?" suggested Watson as he jotted down notes.

"It's possible, but unlikely. This isn't a very wealthy district, and the clockmaker isn't swimming in riches. What treasures could he possibly have? And it seems the culprit was toying with him prior to the murder. Whoever it was, they had specifically intended to kill Dickory, and they went the extra mile to hide their tracks."

"How do you figure?" asked the deputy.

"Do you see any signs of damage to the corpse?" asked Holmes. "No stab wounds, no signs of strangulation, no blunt force trauma. The only other possibilities are poison... or magic.

"That being said, here is what I need you to do. Go to the sheriff's station and make sure the Literary Alayna Potts is sent home to the Literary world immediately seeing as there's another criminal on the loose. Once that's done, I want an alchemist to come scan the area for magical remains and to test the body for poisoning. In the meantime, this workshop is to be kept off-limits from everyone except authorized law enforcement personnel."

The deputy nodded and took off. Watson remained in the workshop to examine the corpse. Holmes had returned to scanning the room, keeping a close eye on the ground in an attempt to find footprints.

"What about this sawdust under the body?" asked Watson, eyeing the yellow substance.

"That's not sawdust," said Holmes. "It's sand."

Watson did a double take. "Does that mean someone from the shipyards could've done this?"

"No, if they did, there'd be sand everywhere. I can't find a single grain anywhere else. There's something very unusual about that particular substance. I think it might actually be a vital clue in our case." Holmes strutted to the window. "And isn't it odd how there aren't any footprints to be found? Not one sign of dirt or mud or anything. Whoever broke in must've cleaned their shoes. Maybe we should check the yard for footprints. What do you think, Watson?"

Holmes glanced at his partner and saw him scooping the sand into a glass vial. As soon as Watson touched the sand, he toppled over next to the clockmaker, with the same blank, expressionless face. Holmes ran to his side, but he knew it was too late.

Agent Watson was dead.

Chapter 2

Mark Bishop

Mark's hand was starting to cramp.

The author sat at a table surrounded by his fans and hundreds of copies of his novel, *Dodger's Adventure to Storyworld*. There was a line of people leading from the table, through the bookstore, out the doors, and halfway down the block. Most of the crowd had been waiting all morning to meet Mark Bishop. He couldn't let his fans down, so he tried his hardest to mask his discomfort. But he couldn't hide the grimace that crossed his face when the pain shot up his hand.

"Are you okay, Mr. Bishop?" asked a skinny boy with glasses pressed up against the table.

Mark flexed his fingers. He had been signing books for six hours straight and he was finally feeling it. The cramp made him accidentally smudge the signature on the book placed in front of him. He slid the copy out of the way and grabbed a fresh one from the pile behind him.

"Yeah, I'm fine. Sorry about the smudge. Here's a new copy, on me." Mark cracked the book open and began signing his name. "Who am I making this out to, buddy?"

"Can you write, 'To Steve Davis, my biggest fan'?" asked the child. His face lit up as the author wrote on the page. "Can I ask you a question?"

"Go for it."

"I know you probably hear this a lot, and it might be a dumb question, but how did you come up with these ideas for your book? What made you think of such a cool story?"

Mark chuckled. "Well, I had a huge imagination when I was a kid. Most of the time, I was daydreaming and playing video games, so my brain was filled with all kinds of ideas. I never limited my imagination, and neither should you. Just make sure you spend enough time studying for school. I wouldn't have made it here without a decent education."

Mark slid the book back to his fan and smiled. Steve squealed with delight and held the book out in front of him like it was a rare treasure. His father, standing behind him, nodded at Mark with an appreciative smile.

"You hear that, Stevie?" said the father, ushering his son away. "You have to study and do your homework if you want to be like Mr. Bishop…"

The next person in line stepped up and tossed his book carelessly on the table. He was an older teenager with a choppy hair and narrow eyes. He had on a very smug frown and appeared to be less than impressed with the opportunity to meet the author.

"How are you?" asked Mark, ignoring the teenager's rudeness. "Who can I make this out to?"

"You can write, 'To Tyler'. You don't have to get fancy with it. I don't want you cramping your hand again. It must be exhausting sitting behind a table and writing your name over and over and getting paid thousands of dollars for it."

A small smirk crossed Mark's face as he signed.

"I have a question for you too," said Tyler.

"Sure."

"What's with the characters in this book? Why did you borrow them from other stories?"

"Good question. Well, the whole point of the book is that the characters from Storyworld are what inspired our own fairy tales and folklore."

"I get that, but I mean, it's like you were really stretching for ideas," replied Tyler with a snide tone. "It's kinda lazy. Didn't you want to be original?"

Mark grinned. In the past, this kind of remark would've bothered him, but he had since played this game too many times, so he knew exactly how to respond.

"They're pretty original, if you ask me. I took existing characters and put my own spin on them. Like Humpty Dumpty. I made him a warrior instead of this goofball who fell off a wall. Then I made Rumpelstiltskin into an alchemist and Humpty's best friend. I think that's original." Mark closed the book and slid it across the table to Tyler, hoping he would leave, but he didn't move.

"But Humpty Dumpty, though? Couldn't you pick a better character? And what's with the name Storyworld? Were you even trying at that point?"

"Okay, kid," said the security guard behind Mark. "Stop causing trouble. You got your autograph and you asked your question. Let the next guest come up."

"How am I causing trouble? I'm pretty sure this is a free country and I can say whatever I want. I'm surprised anybody reads this crap anyway." Tyler picked up his copy and tossed it in the nearby trashcan. When the security guard approached him, he threw his hands up in surrender. "I'll leave, I'll leave. Not sure why you're defending this guy anyway. There's so much better stuff out there to read." He faced the crowd of people behind him in line. "You people don't know the first thing about good literature. Don't waste your time here."

"You seem pretty angry about something that doesn't affect you," said Mark.

Tyler spun around. "What's that?"

"I mean, I get it. You didn't like my book. Why do you care so much about what other people enjoy? You sound like a petty brat."

A few people in line giggled while Tyler blushed.

"It pisses me off that people like you can get away with creating terrible stories. There's so much better reading out there that deserves way more credit than this stupid book about Humpty Dumpty and Pinocchio. Your fans are a bunch of morons."

"Yet you're the one who waited in line for hours just to have this little rant." Mark glanced at the trashcan. "And you even threw out your copy of the book."

"Whatever," said Tyler, exiting the bookstore in a huff.

There was light round of laughter and applause. Mark smiled and beckoned the next person to come up for their autograph.

"Glad you took care of that, Mark," the security guard whispered in his ear. "I would've wrung the kid's neck, if I were you."

"The pen is mightier than the sword," quoted Mark.

The book signing went on for another five hours, way past the closing time for the store. The last person in line was a pretty dark-haired woman with glasses who left her phone number for Mark on slip of paper. As soon as she walked out the door, he crumpled the note and tossed it into the trashcan.

"Hey, I would've taken that!" said the security guard.

The manager of the bookstore thanked Mark for his time and walked him out to the parking lot. After *Dodger's Adventure* broke five hundred thousand copies sold, Mark had treated himself to a brand new sports car. He shook hands with the manager and the security guard, then peeled off down the street. The moment he was out of sight of the lot, he lit up the cigarette he'd been craving all day.

It was impossible for Mark to take a smoke break earlier as fan after fan came through the store. He was lucky enough to sneak away from his table for a brief bathroom break around noon, but he had to skip his lunch. All he had to keep him satiated throughout the day was the little bit of whiskey he had mixed into his thermos and a pack of biscuits an adoring fan had brought him. Mark's stomach grumbled loudly. Ten more minutes and he would be in his hotel room with a fridge stocked full of food.

Down the street, Mark could see the parking lot of New York City's World Hall, a newly constructed hotel rapidly becoming famous due to its accommodation of large-scale celebrities and global figures. *Home sweet home* thought Mark.

One of the great things about arriving at the hotel this late was that there were no reporters or cameras swarming around the entrance. Mark was already accosted earlier that morning by teams of newscasters and reporters who shoved microphones in his face while bystanders snapped pictures on their phones. He didn't mind the publicity as long as it was in moderation, but he also preferred his privacy now and then.

Flicking his cigarette into the ashtray, Mark handed his car keys to a valet along with a twenty-dollar bill and headed inside. It was almost midnight, yet the World Hall's lobby was bustling with activity. A group of men in suits surrounded a German pop diva whose name Mark couldn't remember as she chatted away with the concierge. Further down the counter was a senator from out west chatting with her assistant and security personnel. Mark flashed his keycard to one of the guards as he made his way to the elevator.

Within minutes, he was inside his suite. He dropped his bag on the floor and threw himself on the bed, savoring the sensation of the soft blankets that had been waiting for him. There was a pleasant lemon scent lingering in the room.

Despite only staying here for a week, Mark considered the World Hall to be more welcoming than his home back in Philadelphia. Next Saturday, he'd be packing up and heading back to his condo, before returning to New York City in a month for a guest appearance on a local talk show that had nominated *Dodger's Adventure* as its Book of the Year.

Return to Storyworld

Mark rolled onto his back and put his hands behind his head. His suite was so pristine and polished that it could pass for the cover of a home organization magazine. There was a suit hanging on the bathroom door and a suitcase propped open with clothes spilling out on the floor. Besides these small details, it was like nobody was staying in the suite. That's how Mark preferred it: minimal and organized.

His stomach rumbled again, reminding him of his intense hunger. He went to the refrigerator and grabbed the first thing in reach: a wrapped club sandwich he made last night but forgot to bring with him to the signing. He also grabbed a fresh bottle of whiskey to refill his flask. Mark unwrapped his sandwich and took a large, satisfying bite.

As he chewed, he absentmindedly ran his tongue along the inside of his lip, a habit he's had since he was a teenager with a lip ring. He could feel the tiny needle-sized scar that never healed. *What a stupid idea* he thought. Although it was hardly noticeable, he was self-conscious about the scar, but he figured he could always grow his goatee a little thicker if he wanted to hide it.

Mark found it funny how, aside from the missing lip ring, his appearance hadn't changed much in ten years. He had the same brown eyes, thick nose, and bony cheeks. He was practically the same height and build, but he had developed a belly in the past few months. The only major difference was his hair. He no longer had a shaggy mane covering his head like when he was a teenager. After college, he kept his hair fairly short and swept to the side, coming dangerously close to a comb-over. If his teenage self could see him now...

Return to Storyworld

Returning to his bed, Mark devoured the last of the sandwich and grabbed his planner to review his schedule for the next month. He had two more book signings scheduled this week. One was tomorrow on the other side of Manhattan, and there was another one on Friday in Times Square. The rest of the week was for Mark to enjoy, except for Wednesday, when he was meeting with a team of executives who wanted to discuss the possibility of a movie adaptation for *Dodger's Adventure*.

While Mark hated traveling, he didn't regret this lifestyle. Luck had been with him for the past ten years, helping him become one of the most popular young adult authors in the country. He leaned back and closed his eyes, reflecting on everything that led up to this moment.

Mark's entire life changed when he was seventeen, on that one fateful night when he ventured through the magical doorway into Storyworld, a realm filled with monsters, magic, and mayhem. When he came back from Storyworld, he developed an intense passion for literature and storytelling and began writing a chronicle of his adventures. Before he left for college, he decided to change his major to English Literature so that he could continue his work. He made it his mission to tell the world about his journey.

Life at Temple University was a drastic change for Mark. In high school, he considered himself a friendless wimp and pushover. Once he returned from Storyworld, he was a changed man who refused to stand down from confrontation. On his first night in his college dorm, Mark proved he wasn't going to take any more abuse.

Return to Storyworld

It was the Friday right before classes began, and the students were celebrating their newfound independence. Mark's roommate had convinced him to go to a party down the hall, where he immediately felt out of place considering he had never been to a real party in his life. It got worse when his roommate left him to go play a drinking game with his friends. It wasn't long until Mark decided this wasn't the place for him. He decided to make a break for the door.

On his way out, he passed a guy with a buzz cut and a red letterman jacket with the name "Barry" stitched into the back. Mark noticed he was standing in front of a nervous redheaded girl who looked uncomfortable (even more uncomfortable than Mark). Every time she tried to move away, Barry would sidestep to block her.

"Hey," Mark called out, prodding him in the shoulder. "Is there a problem?"

Barry glanced over his shoulder. "Get lost," he grunted, throwing his empty cup into Mark's face and laughing loudly.

Mark stepped back, wiping the remnants of beer off his face. The redheaded girl tried to sneak away from Barry while he was distracted, but he stuck his arm out to block her. As he made another attempt to flirt with her, Mark shoved him on the shoulder.

"Leave her alone."

"Get outta here," Barry said with a smirk.

Mark refused to move. "Leave her alone. Now."

"Come on, then. Do something," Barry said, shoving Mark.

Several nearby partygoers watched the confrontation unfold. Mark cocked his fist as Barry sloppily put his hands up.

"Hey," said the redhead, standing between them and holding up two cups of beer. "Don't worry about him, babe. Why don't we go into the other room?"

Barry gave an enthusiastic nod as he put his arm around her.

Mark shook his head, dumbfounded, and made for the exit. As he walked out the door, he heard a rousing "Oooooo" from the party guests. He looked back as the redhead was holding the now-empty beer cups over Barry's head and shoving him out of the way. She briefly caught Mark's eye as he left the dorm.

Mark was walking to his own room when he heard the door behind him open then close. Assuming it was his roommate, he turned around and said, "I don't feel like stayi—" He was interrupted by the redheaded girl giving him a hug.

"Thanks," she said in his ear. "I really appreciated that."

"I didn't do anything. That was all you," Mark said with a grin.

When she stepped back from the hug, Mark was awestruck at how beautiful she was up close. She had light green eyes that matched the bow in her hair, and there were dozens of freckles peppering her cheeks and forehead. She smiled widely, revealing pearly white teeth.

"I'm Amy."

Mark introduced himself and invited her to his dorm, where they spent the entire night talking. Right away, they sensed a strong connection to one another. Like Mark, Amy grew up with a rough home life and very few friends. She told him how she too had come to Temple to leave her past behind and to turn her life around. Mark was thrilled to hear that she was an English major as well, and that they shared several classes together.

The pair developed a close bond over the next couple of weeks, and it wasn't long until they were officially dating. The two remained together throughout college and beyond graduation. Once they had finished school, Mark became an editor for one of Philadelphia's publishing houses while Amy went on to teach English as a Second Language. Two years after graduation, Mark proposed.

Mark couldn't believe how much things had changed in those few years. The same lonely, bullied boy who used to spend his evenings in his room listening to his parents fight was now a grown man with an amazing wife, a great job, and an overall amazing life. But despite all this, there was one thing still missing.

Mark had spent three years writing about his adventures in Storyworld. He began the project in his final months of high school, but he had put the novel on hold to focus on his education and his relationship with Amy. He resumed his writing shortly after his wedding and committed himself to concluding the story. Mark wanted to make sure he gave an exact recounting of his adventures and properly recognized the heroes he met in Storyworld. It was up to him to give them the recognition they deserved.

After completing the first draft of *Dodger's Adventure to Storyworld*, Mark was hesitant about submitting it to publishers. He honestly didn't think anyone would accept such a cliché story filled with pre-existing characters. Fortunately, Amy discovered the manuscript when he left his computer on one night, and the next week, she told him how much she loved the story and that he should definitely submit it to an agent for consideration. The one suggestion she had was that he added a little more explanation regarding the overall setting of Storyworld.

It took another year for Mark to flush out the background of the world he had visited. Drawing from his memories, he did his best to elaborate on everything he knew about the magical realm.

According to his knowledge, Storyworld was a planet similar to Earth that existed within a magical, parallel universe. The people of Storyworld were characters from famous fairy tales and myths, such as Red Riding Hood, the Headless Horseman, Peter Pan, and more. Throughout history, random people had been transported to Storyworld to assist its inhabitants with missions and quests. These visitors, dubbed Literaries by the Storyworld inhabitants, were assigned to hosts who were in charge of guiding and assisting them on their adventures.

Nobody knew how or why Literaries were summoned to Storyworld. Mark was told that certain alchemists and wizards could predict where and when they arrived, but they couldn't figure out why certain people were chosen.

Once Literaries finished their mission, they were sent back to their own world, where they would succumb to a strange force of habit: they would be compelled to write stories about the characters and places they encountered during their stay in Storyworld. Notable Literaries from the past included Edgar Allan Poe, the Brothers Grimm, J.M. Barrie, and more. Upon his own return, Mark had followed his predecessors' example and created a book based on his adventures.

Return to Storyworld

After facing rejections from a handful of agents, Mark eventually found a publisher who was enraptured by the story. Within two months of publication, thousands of copies were soaring off the shelves and into readers' hands around the world. It became a particular favorite among young adult readers, and it was soon recognized as a hallmark of a new stream of literature that was reintroducing teenagers to reading. Older audiences also enjoyed the story for its innovative plot elements and unique take on classic characters.

Pinocchio the Wooden Soldier was the leader of the Neverland Military Arm, and the fearless warrior Humpty Dumpty was his second-in-command. Rumpelstiltskin was the kingdom's immature yet brilliant alchemist and leader of the Neverland Science Arm. These characters were loyal subjects of Neverland's Princess Tinkerbell, who eventually became a queen when she chose to marry Humpty Dumpty at the end of the story.

Captain Hook was a despicable villain whose intention was to rule over Storyworld by becoming immortal and omniscient; a feat he could achieve by killing the protagonist of the story, a seventeen-year-old Literary named Dodger. In order to carry out his plan, Hook hired the double-agents Hansel and Gretel to lure Dodger into an elaborate scheme that ended with a full-on battle within Neverland Castle.

Dodger's Adventure to Storyworld was praised for its fast pace and unique premise. Readers loved joining Dodger and his companions as they encountered vicious bounty hunters, mischievous giants, a troll under a bridge, and many more interesting characters along the way. However, while there was praise to be had, not everyone was a fan of Mark's story.

Despite the book being rated for young adults and the indication that there were mature themes, many parents were unhappy about the fact that Mark had taken beloved children's story characters and made them into soldiers and killers. Established literary critics called Mark's story unoriginal and uninspired. One significantly harsh review stated the book was a "sloppy mash-up of popular fictional characters lacking real depth and meaning." There was another literary group that commented on the list of inconsistencies and supposed plot holes plaguing the book. Why did Hansel and Gretel become ash when they died? Why did Humpty Dumpty transform into a human at the end? How exactly does magic work in Storyworld?

Mark found himself caught between a rock and a hard place when it came to addressing these issues. How was he supposed to explain these strange quirks of Storyworld when even *he* didn't understand them? He just told his readers that he intentionally left it a mystery so that fans could fill in the gaps with their imagination.

The most criticism was directed at the main character of the story. While many people thought Dodger was a fun and relatable protagonist, there were those who denounced him as "painfully pathetic," or as one critic put it, "a Gary Stu suffering from a severe inferiority complex that made him incredibly annoying." Regardless of this, Mark did his best to not let the comments get to him. In the end, his fans outnumbered his detractors.

Mark opened his eyes and stretched his arms. Rolling on his side, he glimpsed at the alarm clock on his nightstand that read 12:01 AM. Next to the clock was a framed photograph of him and Amy on their wedding day. Both of them were so young and happy, ready to embark on a long life together. Neither of them knew how, in a few short years, this picture would be nothing more than a painful memory. Mark knew it was a bad idea to bring the picture around with him everywhere he went, but he felt like it was the last real connection he had to his wife.

"I miss you so much," he whispered, a tear sliding down his cheek. Amy's smile always melted his heart. He would give anything to see her one more time. No matter how hard he tried to move on, there was nothing that would ever make him get over the pain. The most he could do was keep himself distracted, and the best way to do that was to think about business.

Reaching for his cigarettes and flask, Mark got out of bed and walked out onto the suite's balcony to have a smoke. The air had gotten much colder since he was outside a half-hour ago. This didn't bother him much except for the minor goose bumps. Other than that, the cold air boosted Mark's spirits because it indicated that summer was almost over and fall was on the way. This meant that libraries and schools would be buying more copies of his book for students' leisure reading. His agent had told him that fifty copies were already heading out the door tomorrow.

Mark had just lit up a cigarette when he heard the phone ring. Cursing to himself, he flicked his cigarette over the balcony and went inside to answer it.

"A little late for room service, isn't it?" he said in an annoyed tone.

"I'm sorry for the late call, Mr. Bishop," came the concierge's voice on the line, "but I have urgent news. Do you happen to know a woman by the name of Inga Hansson from Northside, Pennsylvania?"

The name was slightly familiar to Mark. It took him a second to recall it. "Yeah, she was my neighbor when I was a kid. Haven't heard that name in forever. What's going on?"

The concierge's tone sounded uncomfortable. "Ms. Hansson phoned the hotel asking for you and left a message. I'm very sorry to tell you this, Mr. Bishop, but... your parents were in a car accident."

Chapter 3

The Literary Companions

As soon as he hung up the phone, Mark checked out of the hotel and set off for his hometown. It was three in the morning by the time he reached Northside Police Station and met with an officer.

Mark barely heard anything the officer was saying, except for the words "freak accident." At one point, the officer asked him if he could identify the bodies from a series of pictures, but Mark couldn't give him an answer. He didn't *want* to give an answer.

"It's okay," said the officer. "I'm gonna go grab a coffee. Take as much time as you need." He got up to leave, but he left the envelope full of pictures on the table. Mark stared at the envelope as thousands of thoughts coursed through his mind.

The Bishop family had always had a strained relationship. Throughout Mark's childhood, he always felt like he was the root of his parents' problems. Whenever his mom and dad weren't fighting with each other, they were directing their anger toward him. He had endured their abuse for years, but he refused to let it break him as it became tougher with each passing day. Things finally changed once he came back from his adventure in Storyworld.

The morning of his return, Mark stood up to his parents and said he was tired of their abuse, and that he was no longer going to be the target for their anger. He told them how they were just miserable people who only knew how to take their anger out on each other and him. That wasn't going to happen anymore. He was done with it. He'll never forget the looks on his parents' faces as he walked out the door that morning.

For the next two months, there was an uneasy silence in the Bishop household. Mr. and Mrs. Bishop acted like children who had been scolded for spilling milk. Nobody in the family yelled anymore. In fact, the only time anybody talked to each other was the occasional "goodnight", and even that ended three weeks later. When he moved out on his eighteenth birthday, Mark didn't say goodbye to his parents. All he did was grab his backpack and suitcase and walk out the door without a look back.

Mark tried not to dwell on his past and attempted to move on each day. During the school year, he lived in his college's dorms, and in the winter and summer, he would either spend his break at a friend's place or take up monthly leases at his apartment. Mr. and Mrs. Bishop didn't make any effort to contact their son during his college career, and vice versa. His parents didn't even call him when his book became a best seller. The connection among the Bishop family was gone…

It was too much to handle right now. Mark was going to break down if he sat at the police station much longer. Staring at the door, he imagined running far away and never looking back. Who cared about being rich and famous? Who cared about selling thousands of copies of a book? None of that mattered at this point. Mark had lost his wife, and now he lost his parents. He was alone in the world. There was nobody there for him anymore.

"I need to get out of here," he said to himself.

The moment Mark was out the door, he retrieved his flask and took a deep swig, allowing the alcohol to burn his pain away. As the whiskey swished down his throat, a memory flashed across Mark's mind: Humpty and Rump sitting on either side of him in the Fallen Timber Inn. Around the table sat Hansel, Gretel, Jack, Jill, and Pinocchio. They were laughing and cheering about their last adventure where they competed in a series of trials against the giants living in the sky. Mark smiled briefly at the memory, until it was replaced by another, more sinister recollection.

A board of nails swung down from the ceiling and impaled Geppetto in the back. Mark was lying on the floor, staring up at the corpse, whose image was forever etched into his mind. Hansel was looming over him, pointing the rifle at his face. The memory then flashed to Captain Hook towering over Mark, his rusted hook high in the air, ready to strike.

Mark shrugged off the chills fighting their way up his body. He soon found himself back in his car, driving down his childhood street. In the middle of the avenue stood his old home. It looked almost the same as when he left, except there were new curtains in the window and a little garden by the front door.

Please let this work, Mark thought, heading up the walkway and fishing for his old house key in the depths of his wallet. He had held onto it as a memento of the place he called home for eighteen years, even if it reminded him of unpleasant times. Saying a silent prayer, he inserted it into the lock and flushed with relief when he heard the door click open.

The inside of the home looked the same as it did when he left, aside from a fresh coat of paint and minor furniture rearrangements. The kitchen was slightly unkempt; there were dishes piled up in the sink and empty grocery bags scattered near the refrigerator, but what caught Mark's eyes was a brown folder on the table. According to the papers inside, his parents had been seeing a marriage counselor for the past four years. They had also been taking medication for depression for the last nine. Mark couldn't help but feel that his departure had left a huge emotional impact on his parents. He decided to go upstairs to see what was left of his old room. The moment he opened the door, his jaw dropped in utter shock.

Everything was exactly the same as how he had left it; the bed with the same sheets, the old dresser with the lopsided legs, the nightstand with its broken drawer, and the small table at the foot of the bed holding the fossils that used to be his television and video game system. Everything in the room was coated in a layer of dust, as if it hadn't been touched for years. Mark couldn't believe that his parents had left his room the same all these years.

As Mark came face-to-face with his closet, his heart leapt into his throat. The door was slightly ajar, like when he first saw the entrance to Storyworld, but this time, there was no light coming from beyond the doorway. Slowly, he pulled the door open, only to find an empty closet. It was strangely disappointing. He decided to close the door and open it again. Then he did it again. He couldn't explain why he kept doing it, but it was almost as if everything would be okay if he opened the door the right way. But he wasn't opening it correctly, and each time he did it wrong, he was getting further and further away from what he wanted.

Mark opened and closed the door faster and faster, until eventually, his eyes started to water. He angrily slammed the door shut a final time. That was when he caught his reflection in the old, dusty mirror hanging on the door. He hated the person staring back at him. It was his fault his family fell apart, and he didn't even try to fix it when he had the chance. He was a coward, just like the boy who saw himself in that mirror ten years ago. He yelled loudly and punched the mirror as hard as he could.

The sound of the glass shattering was so loud that it probably woke up the whole neighborhood. Mark cussed loudly and slumped next to his old bed. His knuckles were bleeding, but the pain didn't hit him yet. All he could feel was the tight sensation in his chest, like his heart was in a vice.

You're a coward, he thought to himself. *It's your fault.*

All of a sudden, there was a loud thumping. Mark quickly stood up, thinking it was coming from the front door downstairs. But who would be coming by at this time of night? After several more thumps, he realized it was actually coming from inside the closet. Mark's entire body went numb.

It was impossible.

The thumps stopped, but there were now muffled voices coming from the closet. Mark froze with his eyes glued to the door. After a couple more seconds of the voices, the door finally opened, ejecting two men onto the bedroom floor. Mark's mouth cracked into a wide, unbelieving grin.

"Humpty?! Rump?!"

Although it'd been ten years since he had seen either of them, there was no way Mark could forget his old friends. They both looked almost exactly the same as when he departed Storyworld.

Rumpelstiltskin was a little man with dark wrinkly skin, thick black hair, and kind brown eyes. He wore a short black robe that covered most of his torso, but left his wrinkled arms and knees exposed. When he fell out of the closet, his horned helmet had toppled off his tiny head and rolled away, revealing a small bald patch at the top of his skull. Wrapped around the alchemist's chest was a bandoleer of test tubes and vials filled with multicolored liquids, and chained to his belt was a short silver mace with dull spikes around its head.

Humpty Dumpty, once a walking, talking egg, was now a tall, skinny human with brown hair and big brown eyes. He shared the same black outfit as Rump, except he wore a layer of polished chainmail underneath to protect his thin arms and legs. His black shirt was adorned with the image of a wolf holding a scroll in its mouth: the royal crest of Neverland. A curved sword and dagger were strapped to either side of his belt, and he wore a halo-like crown made of intertwining silver and gold wires.

"I told you the spell would not work, Rump!" yelled Humpty.

"What are you talking about?" replied the alchemist. "We made it to the

Literary world, didn't we? Honestly, you shouldn't get your undergarments in a bunch."

"You transported us into a closet!" fired back Humpty, blushing.

"Oh, loosen up, Humpty! Sometimes, I think you're too uptight."

"And sometimes, I think I should order you to call me *King* Humpty!"

Before the two could go on with their bickering, Mark jumped in and said, "Guys! Can't you at least say hi?"

The two men spotted Mark and their expressions changed from anger to pure shock.

"Sir Dodger? You've… you've changed!" exclaimed Rump.

"Why are you bleeding? Have you been in battle?" asked an alarmed Humpty.

Mark had forgotten about his hand. It was throbbing slightly, but his adrenaline nulled most of the pain. Rump produced a vial of green liquid from his belt and poured it on Mark's wound, making it close up in a matter of seconds.

"Good as new!" said the alchemist, patting Mark's hand and smiling broadly. "Now that that's settled, Sir Dodger, you must tell us why you look so different!"

"Well, it's been ten years since I came to Storyworld. And you can call me Mark now."

Humpty took a step back. "Ten years and you've changed this much?"

"Is that weird?"

"To be frank, this is the first time either of us has ever seen a Literary at two different time periods," admitted Rump. "Apparently, your people age quite differently than ours. Ten years is practically the blink of an eye for us."

"How old are you now?" asked Humpty.

"I'm twenty-eight, but don't change the subj—"

"Twenty-eight?! You're an infant! I don't think I was even speaking at your age! Does that mean…" Humpty covered his mouth in horror. "We must have met you when you were fresh from birth! How could we put an infant in that kind of danger?!"

Rump clapped his companion on the shoulder. "It's not nice to tease people, Humpty. Don't be jealous that he's in his younger years. How old are you now? Eight hundred? Nine hundred?"

"I am six hundred and ten, thank you very much. I am hardly older than you!"

"My mistake, *Your Highness*," replied Rump, putting a sarcastic emphasis on the last two words and bowing deeply.

"Stop changing the subject!" Mark demanded before Humpty could throw another fit. "Can you guys just tell me how and why you're here?"

Rump blushed. "Our apologies. He's a bit grumpy," he said, nodding at Humpty, who responded by huffing and rolling his eyes. "I learned how to reconfigure the potion that allowed us to send Literaries to their home world. With a little tweak, we were able to use it on ourselves, thus letting us travel beyond the reaches of Storyworld."

"And how did you find me here?"

Return to Storyworld

"We don't have time to explain the details," said Humpty, placing his hands on his hips. In an official-sounding tone, he declared, "Sir Dodger, we need your help."

"Wait, what? Why?"

"There has been a mysterious murder in the town of Himshire, and we believe a dangerous assassin is on the loose, so—"

"Nope! Not happening!" said Mark, shaking his head. "Sorry, guys, but there's no way you're taking me back, especially when there's a killer out there. I'm not going through that again. If Himshire needs help so badly, how come they don't get their own Literary?"

"They've already sent their last Literary home," said Rump. "There isn't enough magic in their region to support another summoning." When Mark responded with a confused shrug, Rump sighed and continued. "You know how Literaries are summoned to areas that have a special magical presence, yes? Various places, such as Neverland, have a higher concentration of this presence than smaller locations, like Himshire. Whenever a Literary arrives, they utilize a bit of this magic, and the area has to 'refuel', if you will. That magic is crucial to the survival of Literaries. It's what allows your people to live in our world, breathe our air, digest our food, speak and understand our languages, and so on. Imagine it as a magical aura of sorts."

"Then how am I supposed to come with you if there isn't enough magic to support a Literary?"

"You've been to Storyworld already. You still have the magic residing inside you. You've adapted to our environment."

"But why me? There have to be other Literaries out there who could probably do a better job."

"On the contrary," interjected Humpty. "You are the top candidate. You were an excellent companion when you worked with us, even if you were practically a fetus. Since then, your reputation has spread across Storyworld. You're now known as the man who defeated Captain Hook. In many regions, you've been dubbed 'Dodger Hook-Slayer'."

Mark rolled his eyes. "That's cool and all, but that doesn't explain why I'm the one that has to come back."

"Well, given the unusual circumstances surrounding the murder, Himshire believes that we need the best and the brightest to solve the case. Plus, the city believes we owe them a favor, hence why Rump and I have gotten involved in the first place."

"What favor?"

"Do you remember the sentry captain, John Tell?"

Mark frowned. He definitely remembered him; he watched the man die right in front of his eyes. It was another memory forever burned into his mind.

"Yeah, I remember him."

"He was a former sheriff and local hero in Himshire. When the town learned of his death, they didn't take the news lightly. They held Neverland responsible and declared that we owe a debt to them. In light of the recent murder, they've demanded we work with their law enforcement to catch the perpetrator."

Return to Storyworld

Mark rubbed his face in his hands and gave a frustrated groan. "What exactly happened in Himshire that's making them ask for your help?" Rump and Humpty exchanged optimistic smiles, but Mark raised his hands. "This doesn't mean I'm definitely coming. I just want to know what's going on over there. Tell me the details."

"The town's clockmaker was murdered, along with one of the investigating agents at the crime scene," explained Rump. "The city's chief investigator is under the impression that there are grand motives behind the crime."

"We will not be alone on this mission," Humpty added quickly. "We've assembled a team called the Literary Companions. It will consist of us three, General Pinocchio, Robin Lox, Himshire's sheriff, and the Himshire Investigators."

"All that for a clockmaker being killed?" asked a baffled Mark.

"It seems like much, but as we mentioned, the investigator believes in a larger agenda. Seeing as we're indebted to Himshire, we have no choice but to comply."

Mark didn't answer right away. Rump and Humpty glanced at each other nervously.

"I know you are hesitant, but it would mean a great deal to us if you would join the mission," said Rump. "At the very least, you will be clearing Neverland's name of its debt."

Rump and Humpty stared at the Literary with a shred of hope in their eyes. Mark rubbed his face again. There were other things that he was more worried about, but he couldn't help feeling guilty about Neverland being dragged into this mess.

Sighing heavily, Mark said, "Fine, I'll go."

It took ten minutes for Mark to grab his bags from the car and to prepare for the journey ahead. There wasn't much he wanted to bring with him except his jacket, his flask, and his notepad for jotting down ideas in case he wanted to pen a sequel to *Dodger's Adventure*. The items in his suitcase consisted solely of spare clothes, copies of his book, toiletries, and leisure reading, so he decided to leave it behind. Mark thought it was a good idea to travel light, though he was half-considering bringing his pillow to Storyworld after his horrible sleeping experience last time.

Mark also decided to bring the Hunter's Dagger, a legendary artifact given to him by Princess Tinkerbell during his previous visit to Storyworld. The durable blade once belonged to King Gabriel of Neverland, until he went into exile and vanished from the kingdom. Tinkerbell had bestowed it upon Mark to assist him on his quests, and he had held onto it long after his journeys were over. He brought it with him every time he traveled as a good luck charm and as a reminder of his journeys.

The dagger sported a foot-long, razor-sharp blade that had taken down bounty hunters, pirates, and a Jabberwocky, and it came with an enchanted sheath for Mark to wear around his shin. The sheath was half the blade's size, but the magic woven into it allowed for it to fully conceal the weapon. Mark hoped he wouldn't need the blade for this latest mission, but he'd rather be safe than sorry.

Strapping the dagger around his shin, he stood up and saw Humpty sitting on his bed, rifling through the pages of a book. Upon a closer look, Mark realized it was a spare copy of *Dodger's Adventure* that had been sitting in his opened suitcase. Humpty was entranced by the text and didn't seem to notice anyone entering the room.

"Some light reading?" asked Mark.

Humpty jumped. "My apologies, Sir Dodger. This is absolutely fascinating; an actual Literary account of our adventures. I have never read such a story." Perusing through the pages once more, he asked, "May I bring this with us to Storyworld?"

"Go ahead. It's a great read."

"Are we ready to go?" asked Rump, emerging from the hallway. "Sorry, I was using the washroom. It's very clean and tidy. I was a tad confused as to why the washing basin was so low to the ground, but I did enjoy making the water swirl by pressing that metal tab."

Mark contained his laughter and decided it was best not to tell Rump he had washed his hands in the toilet.

"So, how are we getting to Storyworld?"

Rump's response was to pull a vial from his bandoleer and empty its silvery contents into the closet's doorway. The second the liquid touched the ground, it created a thick swirling cloud of white smoke that engulfed the closet.

"Onward and outward!" shouted the alchemist, hurtling into the smoke.

Humpty tucked the book under his arm and ran in as well. Mark checked his jacket one more time to ensure his flask was stowed away in his pocket, and then followed his friends.

At first, he half-expected to collide with the back of the closet, but he kept running and found himself in a dimly lit underground tunnel. Up ahead, Humpty and Rump were running toward a light at the end of the path. The tunnel was narrow and short, forcing Mark to keep his head bowed and his arms pinned to his sides. There was already a stinging pain growing in his lungs as he was losing his breath. When he was a teenager, he wouldn't have had a problem with running, but the past three years of smoking hadn't been kind to his lungs. Each step was like a jab in his chest. The added claustrophobic feeling of the tunnel didn't help either.

The trio exited the tunnel and arrived on a cobblestone path in the middle of a quiet city. The low sun, cold air, and light mist meant that it was early morning. There was no activity in the area aside from the lone citizen shuffling by and the sounds of a carriage wheeling down a side alley.

Mark noted the serenity of the city and how much it reminded him of the eerie aura of Sleepy Hollow. The houses were packed closely together and made out of a mixture of gray stone blocks and wooden planks. Every building had a similar, uniform appearance: a dark roof slanting down toward the street, a single door flanked by a pair of windows, and a wooden fence enclosing a small lawn on the side of the property. The cookie-cutter imagery of the town made it creepier.

Return to Storyworld

A sense of nostalgia washed over Mark as he breathed in the Storyworld air. It was partially comforting to be back in this realm, as if he belonged here. He was about to ask Humpty and Rump where to go, when they took off down the street. Mark stayed close behind them as they ran toward a large landmark in the distance.

Once they came closer to the monument, Mark realized it was a lifelike bronze statue of John Tell, with a stone bow and quiver strung across its back, and its hand pointing toward the sunrise. The statue stood on a metal plaque that read:

JOHN TELL

- SHERIFF OF HIMSHIRE -

- CAPTAIN OF THE NEVERLAND SENTRIES -

DEATH BY THE HAND OF CAPTAIN HOOK OF BARBARIA

MAY HIS SOUL REST IN PEACE AND HIS COURAGE LIVE FOREVER

"I didn't realize he was that big of a deal here," muttered Mark upon reading the plaque.

"Such a shame," said Rump in a saddened tone. "He was a good, brave man. Unfortunately, fate decided to take him away prematurely. John Tell died a hero."

"He didn't have to die if it weren't for Neverland's carelessness," declared a nearby voice.

Mark, Humpty, and Rump swung around to see a woman approaching the memorial. As she got closer, Mark noticed how she much she resembled John Tell: a surly face with a thin nose, hazel eyes, wavy brown hair tied in a ponytail, and an authoritative demeanor. She wore a chainmail suit underneath a brown animal-hide breastplate, and at the top corner of her armor was a gold badge with the word "Tell" stamped on it. A quiver full of arrows and a large wooden bow were strapped across her back.

"John was the heart and soul of Himshire," said the woman. "He was a brave soldier, and thanks to Neverland, he died a petty guardsman."

Humpty cleared his throat and said, "John came to us requesting the position, Sheriff. I am sorry for the loss of your brother. He was indeed a very brave man, and he remained that way up until the moment he died. Neverland recognizes John Tell's heroism."

The woman narrowed her eyes. "King Humpty Dumpty, right? You're not how I imagined."

"Then it would be wise not to make unfounded assumptions," said Humpty coldly. "Sir Dodger, this is Sheriff Wilma Tell, one of our partners for the upcoming mission. Sheriff Tell, these are my companions, Lord Rumpelstiltskin, Head Alchemist and Magicker of the Neverland Science Arm, and Sir Dodger, Literary of Philadelphia."

Mark sighed. "I told you, my name is—"

"DODGER HOOK-SLAYER!" called out another voice.

Two more people came up the street. The one who shouted was a slender man wearing a green hooded cloak that cast a shadow across the upper part of his face but exposed his light brown beard, grinning mouth, chipped teeth, and rounded chin. His green cloak was partially draped over a silver breastplate emblazoned with the Neverland crest. Like Sheriff Tell, he was also an archer equipped with a quiver of arrows and a small bow.

Accompanying this man was a person made entirely out of wood. Everything about him, from his rounded feet and knobby legs, to his tree-trunk-like torso, thick arms, and spherical head, was made out of lumber. He wore a torn and tattered black shirt featuring the Neverland crest, and hanging off his back was an enormous bronze war hammer.

"You've grown a bit, boy," exclaimed the man in the green hood, lowering his hood to reveal large blue eyes.

"Ten years can really change a person, Robin," replied Mark, shaking the archer's hand.

"Oh, I know that's true. I was made part of the Neverland Military Arm. Once I heard you were going to be part of this mission, I begged King Humpty to let me join."

"And," added the wooden man, "when I heard Robin was going to be part of the Literary Companions, I decided to come along as well to keep an eye on him. Can't be too careful with this one…"

"Oh, shove off, Pinocchio! You know I've changed since then. I'm not the same trouble-maker you're used to."

"Do you think it's a good idea for all of you to be away from Neverland?" asked Mark. "We have the king, the general, the second-in-command,

and the top alchemist here. Doesn't Neverland need protection?"

"Fear not, Hook-Slayer," said Pinocchio. "The Neverland Military Arm and the kingdom's defenses have improved tenfold since your last visit."

"Not to mention Queen Tinkerbell is a far superior ruler than I," admitted Humpty. "She is perfectly capable of overseeing the kingdom without me. If anything, I tend to be a bit of a distraction."

When Robin noticed Wilma, he stood up straight with his shoulders arched. He extended his hand to the sheriff and said in an unnaturally deep voice, "You must be the sheriff of this fine town! Sir Robin Lox, Second-in-Command of the Neverland Military Arm, at your service!"

"Wilma Tell, Sheriff of Himshire," said Wilma, stone-faced and ignoring the outstretched hand.

Robin's smile evaporated as an awkward silence fell on the group. "Oh, er…"

"Yes, you know that John Tell was my brother. Correct me if I'm wrong, but you two weren't on the friendliest terms many years ago."

"Well, it's complicated…"

"Now I remember," said the sheriff, putting her finger on her chin. "He out-shot you at the Arbonox Archery Tournament, and you attacked him. Who won that fight again?"

When Robin didn't answer, Wilma smirked.

"Embarrassing, I can imagine. Must have humiliated you. I hope you had nothing to do with John's death."

Robin's expression shifted from embarrassed to slightly offended. "What are you implying?"

"I'm not implying anything, Lox, but I *am* telling you to watch yourself. Rumor has it you spent years robbing people in Neverwood Forest. If I find out you had any part in my brother's murder—"

"Sir Robin has redeemed himself in the eyes of Neverland, and he was instrumental in the defeat of Captain Hook," said Pinocchio, stepping between the two. "He's now a trustworthy soldier and a reliable companion. He had nothing to do with John Tell's death. I am willing to stake my name on it."

Wilma glared at the wooden man. "Pinocchio the Wooden Soldier. If you didn't have such a respectable reputation, I'd think twice about trusting you. If you truly think Lox is innocent, then so be it." She said no more on the matter, but she continued to glare at Robin, and he returned the gesture.

An awkward silence lingered, prompting Mark to speak up. "Are we meeting anybody else here?"

"No, not here. Come with me. We're going to the scene of the crime to meet the Himshire Investigators."

Wilma steered the Literary Companions around a corner and down a narrow alley, which directed them to a side street populated by more uniform buildings. They stopped in front of one particular house that was slightly different from the rest. This cottage had one window next to its brown front door and another peeking out the side, providing a wide view of a lush green lawn. In the center of this yard was a tall oak tree whose leaves were turning brown and falling off.

Standing in front of the cottage was a lean, middle-aged man wearing a dirty, weathered fedora and a long brown overcoat. Though his wrinkled face and gray-flecked black hair showed evidence of his older age, the man's young and alert eyes indicated he was still in the prime years of his life. The collar of a white button-down shirt could be seen hiding underneath the coat, and there was a bronze badge pinned to his chest that read, "Himshire Investigators - Agent Holmes."

Behind Holmes stood a shorter man with a full head of dark brown hair combed to the side and a pair of long sideburns that crawled down to the bottom of his jawline. He wore a gray suit overtop a white button-down shirt and a pair of sheer black gloves on his large hands. A pair of thinly framed glasses sat in front of his tiny eyes, which were currently entrenched in a thick book. As the group approached, Mark noticed how this man's eyebrows seemed to be permanently arched, as if he was in a constant state of worry.

"You're late," said the man in the fedora curtly. "Agent Holmes, Himshire Investigators." Motioning to the man behind him, he stated, "This is my new assistant: Himshire's top alchemist and medical doctor. We've come to know him as 'Doc'."

The man in the gray suit slammed his book shut, smiled at the Literary Companions, and nodded.

"Nice to meet you, gentlemen," said Humpty. "I am—"

Holmes held out his hand. "Please, I know who you are. I could deduce your identities from a mile away." The agent studied Mark with an unimpressed smirk. "And this must be the famous Hook-Slayer."

"Mark Bishop," said Mark, attempting to match the agent's tone.

"I don't think it really matters what your name is. Hopefully, we can solve this case before I get to know too much about you."

Mark immediately felt an intense dislike for the agent.

"Pretty cocky, aren't you? You know, you're kind of a big deal in my world, but I'm wondering if you're really that great of a detective."

"Is that so?" asked Holmes.

"Well, you needed our help to solve this murder case, so..."

Mark smiled, knowing he had struck a nerve with Holmes. The agent's smirk shifted into a smug frown.

"A Literary with an attitude! That's new. I admire your nerve, but you should know, I am indeed an accomplished detective."

"Prove it, then," said Mark, crossing his arms.

The agent went silent. His eyes poured over the Literary, carefully examining him from head to foot.

"You're an habitual drinker and smoker, although you seem to be cutting down on these vices, you're a writer, and you were once married. Also, you haven't slept in about a day-and-a-half."

Mark tried to hide the surprise in his face, but Holmes grinned in satisfaction.

"That's what I thought. Your breathing is much heavier than that of your companions'; years of smoking can do that to you. Your bloodshot eyes and slight slouch indicate you haven't gotten proper rest in quite some time, but obviously you have a bit of energy. Your hand is slightly contorted, as if it's gotten used to holding a writing utensil for a long time. You also have a bad habit of rubbing your ring finger, where I can see the slightest indentation of a wedding band. Is that a fair assessment?"

"Yeah, it is," Mark admitted sourly. "But how did you know I was cutting back on my drinking?"

"That was mostly a guess based on your attitude. I'd be a miserable ass too if I had to quit drinking."

Mark balled his fist, but Humpty stepped in front of him.

"Enough, agent! We get your point! You are a fine detective! If you don't stop with the attitude, then we will have a big problem."

"Fine, fine, I was only having fun," said the agent. "But let it be clear, King Humpty, that you will be going by my lead. I heard about what happened with those double-agents in Neverland. Frankly, it concerns me that nobody found out their ruse from the beginning. You will be listening to my orders. My word is final."

"That's fine with us, as long as you cut down on your sass," said Humpty.

Not another word was said on the matter. Mark's doubts were growing stronger by the second. So far, both Wilma and Holmes had gotten on his bad side. All he could hope for was that this mission was over sooner rather than later.

"So, where do we begin the investigation?" asked Humpty.

Return to Storyworld

"It began a week ago," said Holmes, nodding at the cottage behind him. There was a banner across the door that read DO NOT ENTER in large black letters. "Last week, my partner Watson and I were leaving another case when we came across this scene. According to the clues, someone had broken in and murdered Mr. Giles Dickory, the town clockmaker. While we were searching the area for further evidence, we seem to have come across the murder weapon." The agent held up a glass bottle with a yellow dust-like substance inside.

"Is that sand?" asked Rump.

Doc adjusted his glasses and spoke in a soft voice. "More or less. It's special, magical sand that apparently has the ability to kill anyone who touches it with their bare skin. Unfortunately, Agent Watson became the latest victim." His eyes quickly glanced uneasily at Holmes. "I was able to analyze the sand and found that it works similarly to an Asher spell, if you happen to be familiar with that kind of dark sorcery."

"Asher…" Mark remembered that word vividly. "That was the spell on Geppetto's house. It kills anybody who touches it except the person who cast it, right? So does that mean that sand can kill anybody except who made it?"

"That's my theory. The main difference here is that an Asher spell is cast as a defensive spell. This sand, however, might have been intended for use as a weapon. Like you said, the caster should be able to touch the sand without being harmed. Therefore, we need to track down the alchemist who formulated it."

"Have you spoken with any other magickers or alchemists in town?" asked Rump.

"No need." Doc thumped the large book in his hand. "My research tells me of a lone hermit with a reputation for magical sand."

"Who's that?" asked Mark, although a small part of him assumed he already knew the answer.

"The aptly named Sandman," declared Holmes. "He lives on the Isle of Twilight south of here. The Literary Companions are going on a voyage!"

Chapter 4

The Sandman's Isle

Himshire was much larger than Mark imagined. The Literary Companions descended from a high hilltop at the edge of the city and headed to the shore. As they walked, Mark noticed how the city was built on a slight incline leading toward the sea, similar to Neverland. A dense forest circled the higher end of Himshire, cutting it off from the rest of the mainland. The lower part of the city slanted toward a coastline that stretched for roughly a mile. Both ends of the coast sloped back upward and into the encircling forest. Himshire resembled a large funnel pouring into the ocean.

Agent Holmes led the group to the beach where a dozen ships were moored against the docks or resting on the sand. The ships ranged in size from petite fishing vessels with two-man crews, to long, covered cargo ships the size of airplanes. No two ships were the same, which was a stark contrast from the solidarity of the homes that populated the city.

Out in the middle of the bay, about a mile from the shore, three ironclad towers sat several yards apart from each other, leaving enough space for one or two ships to pass between them. Each of these towers was equipped with an array of long cannons protruding from their sides. It appeared that nobody could enter the bay without passing these sentinels.

The Literary Companions walked onto the beach, passing by crowds of sailors sporting aggressive scowls and unfriendly demeanors. Some of them stared at Mark and whispered to each other behind their hands. A skinny man with a sun-damaged face and a massive shark tattoo on his chest sat on a long piece of driftwood in front of a small hut. He was eating pieces of raw fish from a tray next to him, and every couple of chews, he'd spit a piece of fish into a bucket by his side.

"Wharf-master?" Holmes asked the man.

The man nodded and continued eating.

"We seek passage. Do you have any boats we can take?"

The man kept chewing. He casually nodded at a nearby boat bobbing about in the water. The Companions watched as a man with light brown skin, a red sash wrapped around his bald head, and a body covered in scars emerged from below the boat's deck carrying an enormous crate over his shoulder. He threw the crate onto the sand and soon noticed everyone staring at him.

"Can I help you?" he asked in a rumbling voice.

"We're hoping to buy a ride to the Isle of Twilight," replied Holmes.

"Why's that? Nothing to find there except strange tales and stranger happenings."

"Maybe we're seeking a strange time?" asked Rump. Humpty smacked him on the back of the head with the copy of *Dodger's Adventure*.

Return to Storyworld

"Be that as it may," said the sailor. "It'll cost you two silver pieces per person to get you there, another two to get you back. There's also an extra gold piece in it for precious cargo."

"Precious cargo?"

The man nodded at Mark. "I'm shipping the Hook-Slayer overseas. If we run into trouble, you can bet there'll be a fight for his life. An extra gold for the trip."

"Fine, we'll take it," said Holmes. He dumped a handful of coins in the sailor's outstretched hand. "I threw in a little extra. We're in a hurry."

The sailor pocketed the money and gave an affirming nod. "You can count on a quick and safe trip with me. My name's Conrad, and I'm the Captain of the *Titan*."

Mark thought the name of the *Titan* was inappropriate considering the ship's small size. It was a thin banana-shaped vessel with two short masts popping out from the deck; one at the front and one near the back. The white sails were adorned with a large image of a fist clenching a cannonball. The same insignia was sloppily painted on the deck as well. There was a thick railing wrapped around the edge of the ship, with wide gaps every few yards. Each of these gaps was occupied with a giant black cannon on a swiveling platform.

When the last passenger stepped onto the boat, Conrad wound a crank at the rear of the ship, hoisting the anchor up to the deck. The *Titan* drifted away from the shore and gently floated into deeper waters. Within minutes, they were out into the bay and sailing past the three enormous iron towers.

"We've got a bit of a journey to the Isle of Twilight, even with the strong wind at our backs. Should be there by tomorrow afternoon at the latest," said the captain.

"Have you taken many passengers out this way, possibly within the last week or two?" asked Holmes.

"Never. I told you that place is a den of strangeness. Most people are smart enough to stay away from the island. Speakin' of which, what business do you lot have there?"

"There's been a murder in Himshire, and we're going to solve it."

Mark was on the ground, crawling away from Geppetto as he advanced on him with a hammer in his hand. Now he was staring up at the barrel of the Hunter's Rifle as Hansel pointed it at his face. Then, a board of nails swung down and impaled Geppetto in the back.

Now, a hooded figure carrying the rifle chased Mark through a forest.

Finally, Mark was standing at the front door to his apartment, saying goodbye to Amy as he left for a book-signing, kissing her for the very last time.

Mark jolted up from his bunk, breathing heavily and drenched in sweat. His head spun from sitting up so fast. He closed his eyes, desperately trying to steady his breathing. The dreams were projected on the inside of his eyelids and played as clearly as if they were a movie. It made him feel sick. He shook his head vigorously to rid himself of the nausea.

Return to Storyworld

The gentle rocking of the ship made the dizziness worse. Mark swung his legs over the edge of his bed and squinted through the darkness. He was sitting in one of a dozen bunks below deck of the *Titan*. The bed across from him had previously been occupied to Holmes, but he was nowhere to be found. The other bunks belonged to Rump, Doc, and Wilma, who were sound asleep.

Whiskey was good for nightmares. Mark grabbed the flask from his jacket and took a swig. It was half-full when he put his lips to the container, and it was empty by the time he set it down. Usually, he felt better after filling his stomach with a nice drink, but this last draft combined with the rocking of the ship and the loud crashing of the waves made him more nauseous. Taking another deep breath, he stumbled his way to the stairs leading up to the deck.

It was a calm and fairly quiet night, except for the sounds of the modest waves sloshing against the *Titan*. There wasn't a single cloud in the sky, and the stars were shining brightly around the moon. Aside from the waves, the only other sounds penetrating the silent atmosphere were the hushed voices of other people on deck.

Holmes conversed with Conrad at the front of the ship, the captain gripping the large wooden steering wheel. The agent seemed to be showing him a small object in his hands. Robin was seated against one of the masts, restringing his bow and humming to himself. He smiled and nodded when Mark stepped on deck. Humpty sat against the other mast with his knees curled up and *Dodger's Adventure* propped open in front of him. Mark chose not to disturb him and instead headed for the rear of the ship.

Return to Storyworld

The ocean was beautiful under the pale moonlight. There was nothing beyond the ship except for more water and sky. The salty sea air was soothing and made Mark feel much better. His stomach may have been sedated, but his mind was now reeling in a state of worry.

He was out of alcohol. He could kick himself for failing to bring any more with him. The same went for his cigarettes. It would be days, if not hours, until the withdrawal and anxiety set in. Storyworld did indeed have alcohol, and most likely tobacco, but Mark wasn't sure if it was as strong or as potent as the kind he preferred.

Mark did a double take. He rubbed his eyes and shook his head, wondering if he had imagined what he had just seen. He was so absorbed in his own thoughts that he wasn't paying attention to his surroundings, but he could've sworn there was a face beneath the waves. Maybe it was his reflection?

The face appeared again, this time breaking the surface and emerging from the water. Mark was now staring at a beautiful young redheaded woman who bore a striking resemblance to Amy. When she smiled, she revealed tiny dimples and pearly white teeth that matched her pupil-less eyes.

"Hi, stranger," said the woman. Her voice sounded like a crowd of girls speaking at once.

"Hi," replied Mark in a trance.

The woman giggled and retreated into the water. Mark frowned and leaned forward to see where she went. There was another splash as the mysterious woman escaped the water and leapt high into the air, performing a backflip and returning to the ocean's depths. In the instant she was in the air, her silhouette against the moon revealed that the lower half of her body was a shiny, fish-like tail.

"Mermaid," whispered Mark. He bent further over the railing to get a better view. He could hear loud creaking coming from the wood, but he didn't care. All that mattered now was that he saw the mermaid again. She came to the surface once more and beckoned him with her finger.

"Dodger!"

Robin appeared behind Mark and grabbed him by the back of his collar. The railing broke away with a loud crunch as it fell into the ocean. The mermaid disappeared, her echoing screams resonating from the waters.

"Damn sirens!" said Robin. "You're lucky I got here in time!"

Mark felt confused and lightheaded. "What happened?" He could barely recall what occurred in those last fifteen seconds.

"Come, you're going back to bed. You need your rest."

Mark agreed with him, especially now that he was feeling sick again. The archer led him to his bunk below deck. Wilma was now awake and sitting next to Holmes on his bed. They were both talking in low voices while huddled over a small object.

"You're going to stay here the rest of the night, understand? The last thing we need is for our Literary to get lured away by those sirens."

Robin stomped upstairs, leaving the ashamed and confused Mark sitting on his bed.

"Hah! The sirens almost got you?" asked Holmes with a smile.

Mark ignored him. The last thing he needed was Holmes giving him a hard time about such an embarrassing incident. His head was swimming. He instinctively reached for his flask, but forgot it was empty. Mark angrily tossed the container to the floor and cussed to himself. Holmes eyed the flask and chuckled.

"It's not funny," Mark said hoarsely.

"Oh, but it is. I was a fan of the ale back in my day. But alcohol is too juvenile."

Mark buried his face in his hands. "Please, shut up," he murmured.

Holmes snapped at Mark. "Hey! We need you to be in top form for this mission. A sick Literary is a useless Literary. Come here."

Mark joined Wilma and Holmes on the bed. Holmes held up the mysterious object he was inspecting earlier, which turned out to be a wooden tobacco pipe. The bowl was packed with a grainy, brownish-green herb that gave off a sweet and vaguely familiar scent.

"Is that weed?" asked Mark. Though he had never tried pot, he wasn't unfamiliar with it. His college roommate used to smoke by the window of their old dorm room.

"Cannabis," explained Holmes. "A recreational drug found in the deepest parts of the Meyern Woods, outside of Himshire. It's known to carry traces of chemicals and compounds that, in well-measured doses, can induce tranquility and relaxation."

"Yeah, I know what it is. We have it in my world."

Return to Storyworld

"What a coincidence." The agent winked and finished packing the cannabis into the pipe. He then snapped his fingers, and a little flame popped out of his pointer. Holmes inhaled deeply as he stuck the flame into the bowl. Crackling sounds and a sweet smell issued from the pipe.

Holmes held his breath and passed the pipe to Wilma, who repeated the practice. Once she was done taking a drag, they both exhaled clouds of smoke at the same time, followed by coughing and clearing their throats. Mark hesitated as the sheriff offered him the pipe. Figuring he had nothing to lose, he took it and inhaled as Holmes lit the bowl. Three seconds of breathing in and he sensed a burning in his throat. He coughed forcefully as Holmes thumped him on the back.

"It might be a bit stronger than what you're used to. I've been experimenting with a more potent batch recently."

Mark coughed harder and blinked tears out of his eyes. The cannabis was burning his lungs and throat. He wondered how people found pleasure from this. It was worse than when he first smoked cigarettes.

In a flash, the burning sensation was gone, and Mark felt his lungs clearing up. A sense of euphoria washed over him, wiping away his anxiety and nausea. An aura of positive energy now radiated from inside.

"Whoa," said Mark, his voice sounding light and airy.

The next thing he knew, he was laying in his bed, which had turned into a soft cloud, and all was well with the world as he closed his eyes.

"Land ahead!" Conrad yelled around late afternoon the next day.

Return to Storyworld

The Literary Companions assembled on deck and watched the Isle of Twilight draw closer. The island was tiny from a distance, but as they neared the shores, they saw how it spanned for miles in both directions. Several steps from the shoreline, the beach turned into a thick forest, denser than either of the woods surrounding Himshire and Neverland. Further inland, a group of short mountains poked out of the treetops.

"They call it the Isle of Twilight 'cause of the darkness that shrouds the area. Once those trees swallow you up, it practically becomes nightfall," said Conrad.

"It's a big island," noted Wilma, scanning the trees. "How long do you think it'll take to find this Sandman?"

"Tracking him shouldn't be difficult. I suspect he lives toward the center of the island, as far away from peeping eyes as possible. We should make our way to those mountains," said Holmes.

"So what's the Sandman's deal? What does he do?" asked Mark.

Doc raised an eyebrow. "You've never heard of the Sandman in your world? I was sure at least one or two Literaries had encountered him in the past."

"I've heard of him, but he's probably nothing like the stories in my world. Literaries think the Sandman is this magical guy who goes around at night and sprinkles sand into kids' eyes to make them fall asleep."

"Ah, if only it was that innocent of a tale," said Doc, peering at Mark over his glasses. "Legend has it the Sandman was once an alchemist who earned his moniker from his extensive use of sand in his magic. Not much else is known about him except for a bunch of hearsay. It's been said that he committed a heinous crime and was about to be arrested, until he fled town and escaped to the abandoned isle."

"What did he do?"

"Alas, we don't know. This happened many, many, many years ago, and the details remain a mystery."

Conrad steered the *Titan* up to the beach and dropped anchor.

"Do you want me to come with you?" asked the captain, eyeing the forest suspiciously. "I think you'll need all the help you can get in there."

"It'd be best if you stayed here with the ship," said Holmes.

"You sure? I've tangled with monsters in the past. I wouldn't say no to another adventure—"

"Honestly, I insist you stay here with the ship. Not to be rude, but we can't risk anything happening to you, or we'd be stranded here without a captain."

Conrad looked offended. "You think I can't handle myself in a bunch of trees? This is nothing compared to my past adventures."

Holmes was about to respond, but the captain grumbled something about changing his mind. He handed Pinocchio a satchel full of provisions and then tossed a rope ladder over the edge of the ship's railing. The Companions descended the ladder, and Conrad yanked it back onto the ship without a word.

Doc and Holmes set off into the forest, and the rest of the Companions followed. Mark took one last glance behind them as Conrad, the *Titan*, and the entire coastline disappeared beyond the foliage.

The forest was thick and very dense. The vegetation clumped so close together made the air thick and humid, and venturing through the trees was an exhausting endeavor. Mark had to take his jacket off to stop himself from succumbing to the heat.

In addition to the intense humidity, the forest was also very dark, to the point of almost being pitch-black. Holmes and Rump both had to conjure small flames in their hands to lead the way. The flames didn't help much, illuminating a few extra feet around the Companions. The treetops and their leaves wouldn't let the smallest bit of sky poke through. What made matters worse was that Mark couldn't shake the feeling that someone was watching them from afar.

The Companions traveled for hours until Holmes called for a break. Mark plopped himself on the soft dirt and tried to cool himself down. Thankfully, the air had gotten significantly colder over the past hour, meaning the brush was thinning out, or that it was finally nightfall.

"What time is it?" asked Mark, his throat bone-dry.

"I would say around nine o'clock. We're due for a much-needed break," said Doc, shedding his overcoat.

The Companions set up camp. Wilma and Robin were stationed on the lookout while Pinocchio and Mark collected firewood. They gathered a respectable number of logs and piled them in the center of the clearing. Holmes lit the lumber with his finger-flame.

Once the fire was going, the Companions sat down and enjoyed a meager dinner of fruit and water from Pinocchio's satchel. They sat in silence and ate their meals without a word, but once they filled their stomachs, the mood lifted and they began talking. Mark chewed on an apple as he floated between conversations.

"It's very simple," Holmes was saying to Rump. The agent snapped his finger and another tiny flame popped out. It faded away when he clenched his hand into a fist. "I collected a specific type of phosphorus that grows unstable when exposed to oxygen. All it takes is a little friction, such as snapping my fingers, and the phosphorus ignites. I've coated my hands in a wax composite that sustains the flame."

"Most impressive," admitted Rump. "But I'm curious about whether you can do anything else besides make your finger into a candle."

The alchemist sipped from one of his vials and produced an entire fireball in his palm. Similar to the agent's finger-flame, this magical fire was extinguished once he closed his hand.

"Well, we have our different uses for the flame, Stiltskin. It's good that you can create fireballs since you use your magic for combat. This little trick I learned is for… other tasks." The agent winked at Mark.

Mark grinned and went over to join Humpty, who was deep within *Dodger's Adventure*. It took a second for him to realize Mark was sitting next to him. When he noticed him, he jumped.

"Oh! Sorry, Sir Dodger. I did not see you. This story is very entrancing."

"It's okay. And I told you I go by Mark now. How far are you into the book?"

Return to Storyworld

"We have just crossed over the bridge and defeated the troll! I have to tell you, it is fascinating to finally read one of these Literary stories we have heard so much about, and a story featuring myself, no less! But I have to ask, was I really this much of a nuisance on our last adventure?"

"I wouldn't say you were a nuisance or annoying or anything. You were really cut-and-dry and wanted to get down to business. You got us from point A to point B. We needed you to keep us in line."

"Those are kind words, but I am getting very flustered reading about myself. Aside from that, it is a thoroughly enjoyable tale. Another question: why did you not elaborate more on the background of Storyworld?"

"You guys never really told me about it," said Mark. He retrieved the pencil and notepad from his pocket. "Why don't you tell me now? I can put it in the sequel. What's the deal with Storyworld? How did it come together?"

Humpty laid the book down and steepled his fingers under his chin. "Rump is far more knowledgeable about this. There is such a rich and complex background, but I guess I can give you a summary.

"Everything goes back to the First Being, who we refer to as the Builder. He was the one who 'created' existence, if you will. It was he who lit the stars, ignited the sun, illuminated the moon, constructed the world, and so on and so forth. He eventually came across a dilemma: he couldn't make living creatures. It takes a lot of effort to create life, even for such a supreme being as the Builder. In order for him to do this, he had to sacrifice himself, which led to the birth of the first walkers of Storyworld: the humans, the giants, the dwarves—"

"Wait, how did his sacrifice do all that?" asked Mark.

"It is a most ancient and legendary form of magic that draws upon the power of our very own existence. Basically, every living being has a life-force within them. This life-force consists of their attributes, their personalities, and other details. When a Storyworld inhabitant dies, their life-force dies along with them unless they can magically channel it into someone else.

"The Builder was such a great being that he was able to spread his life-force into the dwellers of Storyworld. The traits that exist in us are believed to have been passed down from the First Being: the bravery of warriors, the knowledge of wizards, the evil of murderers, and much more."

"Wow," said an astonished Mark as his hand flew across his notepad. "Is this kind of magic popular in Storyworld? Like, can people learn how to channel life-force?"

"Oh, no, no, no. It was decided a long time ago that this magic should neither be learned nor taught. Most places have outlawed the practice, and anyone caught attempting such a spell is severely punished. The ability to control a person's life-force is too powerful. It can be deadly if it falls into the wrong hands. Regardless of the restrictions and taboo of the spell, there are adept wizards who have secretly attempted to teach themselves the art. I know of only one magicker who could even come close to unlocking the power."

Mark's head snapped toward Rump, who was flicking sparks at insects buzzing around his head, but Humpty shook his head.

"No, not him. Rumpelstiltskin is indeed brilliant, but I am talking about his former mentor, a sorcerer named Prospero. He was King Gabriel's Chief Advisor. Now *he* was an accomplished spell-caster.

"Now, I would love to talk more, Sir Dodger, but I really want to finish my book." Humpty didn't say another word and dove back into the pages.

Mark was irritated with the king's familiar curt attitude. *And he wonders why he's such a pain in the book,* he thought. He decided to make his way over to Pinocchio and Robin, who were bickering over weapons.

"Nothing compares to a bow's distance," Robin said fiercely.

"Nothing compares to a hammer's brute force!" countered Pinocchio.

"A hammer is for hammering; a bow is for fighting!"

"You clearly don't know a fine weapon when you see one. This hammer has slayed hundreds of enemies over the years, and it once belonged to the infamous Midnight Marauder himself!"

"The who?" asked Mark.

"The Midnight Marauder. He was the leader of a band of mercenaries that assisted us in the Battle of Neverland. A legend, he was."

"What was this guy's real name?" Mark asked with his notepad and pencil back in his hands.

"We do not speak his name aloud, for he committed a major atrocity in Neverland," said Pinocchio quietly. "However, I will admit he was a fantastic warrior and possibly the greatest combatant I had ever seen. He singlehandedly held off a hundred pirates with nothing but this hammer at his side. Like I said, quite the fighter."

Robin scoffed. "Obviously he wasn't that great of a fighter if he died. I mean, who *can* be a great warrior with such a primitive weapon."

Pinocchio's wooden eyebrows swiveled in circles, signaling to Mark that the conversation was about to escalate. He escaped the verbal line of fire and went to join Doc and Wilma in their discussion. Doc was showing off a brown leather flask with a gold trim.

"It's a personal concoction of mine that I made when I hosted a Literary. Here, have a taste. Be careful not to drink too much, or else you will make the same mistake I did," he added with a chuckle, passing the flask to the sheriff.

"Aye, these things happen," said Wilma, popping the top off the flask. Taking a deep draft, she said, "You know, when I was a host, I drank so much I tried to shoot an apple off my Literary's head."

"So *you* were the one who did that?" interjected Mark. When Wilma raised an eyebrow at him, he said, "Sorry, in our world, the story talks about a guy named William shooting an apple off someone's head."

Wilma frowned and took another swig. "Why doesn't that surprise me? I guess my Literary thought he was a better character for their tale." She took another drink. "William was my father. Me and him never got along. John was his favorite. Dad was raising him to be a champion tourney shooter like him, but John went into law enforcement and became a sheriff. I told my father to train me instead, but he said I'd never be fit to carry a bow. To him, I was just a dainty little flower."

"Is that why you became a sheriff?" asked Doc. "To prove him wrong?"

Return to Storyworld

Wilma drank. "No. It's always been in my blood. I was born to be a warrior. While the other little girls were dreaming of marrying heroes, I dreamt of becoming one. I might not have a bunch of medals to prove my skill, but I'm doing something with my life, and I still get to prove I'm the best damn archer this side of Storyworld. I could've easily shot the apple off that man's head, even if I was a wee bit drunk. The only thing stopping me was that I cranked my crossbow's arms too hard and they snapped right off."

Wilma gently rubbed her current bow. "This belonged to John when he was the sheriff. After he passed, I took it as my own. I prefer crossbows, but I figured I could get used to a regular bow."

"The far superior weapon," said Robin, joining the conversation.

"I wouldn't agree with that. These standards are toys compared to crossbows," commented Wilma.

Robin scoffed. "I think you're complaining to hide your lack of skills. Not like you need a lot of skill to shoot a crossbow…"

Mark sensed this was the wrong thing to say when Wilma's eyes narrowed and her nostrils flared. The sheriff stood up and loaded her bow. For a moment, it looked like she was going to shoot Robin, but then she aimed her weapon toward Mark and fired. The arrow struck the apple core out of his hand and pinned it to the dirt.

"Are you crazy?!" yelled Mark, grabbing at his chest.

Wilma bowed and waved her hand with a smirk. Robin clapped twice, then ripped an arrow from his own quiver and swiftly shot it into the dark forest.

"That was an excellent shot, if you were aiming for open air," remarked Wilma.

Robin didn't respond. He slung his bow over his shoulder and trudged off into the darkness in the direction where he shot his arrow. Moments later, he came back carrying a massive black boar over his shoulder, the arrow implanted between its eyes.

"Shall we eat?" asked the archer, tossing the carcass next to the fire.

Robin and Pinocchio cooked the boar over the fire and served it to the group. Everyone carried on their small conversations as they feasted (except Wilma, who ate in bitter silence, and Pinocchio, who didn't eat at all). Once the last morsel was gone, they sprawled out on the soft forest floor to rest.

Mark laid on his side with his back to the fire and his front facing the trees. The heat on his shoulders was soothing, but there was a sense of unease plaguing his mind. More than once, he thought he saw eyes out in the darkness, but when he blinked, they disappeared. It was the same eerie sense that Mark felt when they were walking earlier that day.

He sat up. Holmes was lying next to him, using his overcoat as a makeshift blanket. Mark crawled over and tapped the agent on the shoulder.

"What?" Holmes asked in an annoyed tone.

"Sorry, I'm having trouble sleeping. Any chance we could have a quick smoke?"

Holmes huffed quietly. He rolled over and pulled the pipe from his coat.

Return to Storyworld

As he prepared the cannabis, Mark cast one glance at the forest. No eyes in sight. He could've sworn they were out there. But maybe it was just his imagination.

The Literary Companions were awoken the next morning by the sounds of violent retching. Mark sat up and rubbed the grogginess from his eyes. As his vision cleared, he looked past the smoldering fire pit, where Wilma was vomiting on the edge of the campsite.

"Sheriff, are you all right?" asked Humpty, running to her aid.

Wilma retched again as Humpty, Pinocchio, and Rump went to her side. Doc and Holmes were nowhere in sight. It was still fairly dark in the forest, yet the glowering ashes in the fire pit gave off enough light to illuminate the concern on everyone's faces.

"I feel t-t-terrible," sputtered the sheriff between heaves.

"What do you think happened to her?" Humpty asked Rump.

"Food poisoning? Maybe the boar was undercooked?" replied the alchemist.

"Then wouldn't we all be sick?" said Mark.

"Here, take this."

Rump popped the cork stopper off one of his potion bottles and handed it to Wilma. She took a deep breath and sipped the drink. A few seconds later, she vomited again.

Rump frowned. "So much for the healing potion."

Wilma continued vomiting as Holmes and Doc entered the campsite. The duo stopped talking when they spotted the Companions huddled around the sheriff. Doc knelt next to her.

"Are you all right? What happened?"

"We were hoping you could tell us," said Mark.

"Food poisoning?" suggested Doc. "It is possible that later night din—"

"Can't be. Why is Wilma the only one who's sick? We all ate the boar."

Wilma caught her breath long enough to point at Robin, who had just woken up.

"You did this, Lox!"

"Did what? What are you talking about?"

"You poisoned me!"

"Why in the world would I do that?!" asked the archer.

"He did not have anything to do with this, Sheriff," said Pinocchio.

Wilma did not (or could not) respond and resumed her heaving. Rump patted her on the back and held her ponytail out of the way of her sickness. The Companions shared a concerned glance with one another.

"I hate to come off as insensitive," said Holmes, "but we *are* on a time-sensitive mission."

"I can barely stand!" groaned Wilma.

"You go on ahead and I'll stay with her," said Rump.

"No, no, Lord Rumpelstiltskin," said Doc. "It is best if I stay with her. I do not believe she is gravely ill, but I'm going to see if I can concoct a remedy from the local plant life. You go on. We will be fine."

Return to Storyworld

Mark didn't want to leave a sick Wilma behind, especially given the strange presence he'd been feeling since they first set foot on the island, but Holmes was right; they had a job to do.

The Companions said their farewells and walked off into the forest.

"You know I had nothing to do with Sheriff Tell getting sick," claimed Robin.

"Of course," said Pinocchio, his eyes straight ahead, avoiding the archer's gaze. "You know better than that, I hope."

Robin raised an eyebrow. "Wait, what do you mean by tha—"

"All I am saying is that I defended you, Robin. Do not make me regret it." Pinocchio stopped and stared Robin in the eyes. "You might be my second-in-command, but so help me, if I find out you're intentionally trying to do us harm, I will lock you away in the dungeons and make you my new practice dummy for weapons training!"

Robin went silent. Although Mark believed he was telling the truth about not poisoning Wilma, he could understand the need for Pinocchio's words. Given the long-standing feud between the Tells and Robin Lox, he couldn't blame anyone for being cautious.

When Mark first came to Storyworld ten years ago, Humpty had explained to him how Robin was once the head of the sentries for Neverland. But instead of guarding his post, Robin often spent his time in the taverns, drinking and gambling. He was eventually fired and replaced by John Tell. Robin and his gang went and sought a new home in the Neverwood Forest, where they spent their days robbing and harassing travelers.

Robin had since made up for his actions. During Hook's takeover of Neverland, he and his Merry Men joined forces with Mark and the Royal Guard of Oz to take back the castle. If it wasn't for them, Hook may have never been defeated. Robin was allowed to return to Neverland Castle with a full pardon; however, given his criminal past, it's not unreasonable for Pinocchio to be suspicious of his new second-in-command. Even Mark decided it'd be best to keep an eye on Robin as well.

The Companions went deeper into the forest, until Holmes signaled them to stop. They had arrived at the edge of a wide clearing, untouched by any trees and coated in a layer of sand. A thick beam of sunlight poured through the gap in the treetops and illuminated the area.

In the center of the clearing was a tall dome made out of hardened sand. Its exterior was unusually smooth and perfectly rounded, like a giant ball that had fallen from the sky and buried itself halfway into the ground. There was a gap in the side of the dome, revealing the first steps into a dark cavern.

"This is it," said Holmes.

Before anyone took another step, Mark spoke up. "Wait, what if this is a trap? Shouldn't we get clearance?"

"I can check for an Asher," suggested Rump. He retrieved another vial from his belt; this one filled with white smoke, and hurled it against the side of the dome. The glass shattered, unleashing a thin cloud of grayish-white. The smoke flooded the clearing and crept up to the entrance to the cavern. There was no fire, indicating no Asher was in place.

"Nothing," commented Holmes.

"So he must be home, then, right?" asked Mark.

His answer came in the form of a loud cough that cracked through the air like a snapping twig. A man appeared at the cave entrance so swiftly it was as if he came out of thin air. He wore a tan cloak that resembled an oversized piece of sandpaper with scuffmarks all over. Almost his entire body was hidden within the folds of this cloak, leaving only his chalk-white feet, fingers, and face exposed. Two tufts of gray hair popped out the sides of his hood and trailed down his cheeks. His beady red eyes and thin grainy lips were unsettling, and they made the hair on the back of Mark's neck stand up.

"Hello," said the Sandman in a voice that sounded like two pieces of sandpaper scraping together. "It is not often I get visitors on my isle. What brings you here?" He let out a series of hoarse coughs.

"Murder brings us here," said Holmes, stepping forward. "We want answers. Someone on the mainland was killed the other night, and we've traced his death to you."

"Me? How was it me? I never leave my island, especially to meddle in the affairs of you folk." He coughed again.

"Your magic sand was found at the crime scene. Explain yourself."

The Sandman stifled a cough and glimpsed at the trees above as he spoke. "I have many varieties of magic sand, so I am not sure what you speak of. This murder is a mystery to me, as it is to yo—"

"Don't lie to us!" Holmes said in a stern voice. Behind him, Robin loaded an arrow into his bow and took aim.

"Well, I can tell you he is not the first Literary to traverse these shores," said the Sandman, pointing at Mark. "My isle's been visited by his kind in the past. That is all I will say." He retreated into his cave, coughing lightly.

Holmes whispered to Robin. The archer loosed his arrow, which zipped through the air and tore through the Sandman's cloak, tearing a sliver above his shoulder. The piece of cloak fell to the ground and dissolved into sand.

The Sandman spun around. He gave a very eerie grin as he spoke. "You think it wise to threaten me, sir?"

"Perhaps I should've been clearer," said Holmes, his voice becoming more intense by the second. "There were actually *two* murders in the city of Himshire, and one of them was my closest friend and partner. Your sand was responsible for taking his life. You're going to tell me why it was in Himshire, and I promise you, I will take drastic measures to uphold justice."

"I sense," said the Sandman," that you are an honorable man. You must be, if you are so dedicated to avenge your fallen companion. As a fellow honorable man, I shall propose to you a deal."

"No deals! Just answers!"

"Let me finish, let me finish. I will gladly tell you everything you need to know, as long as you can defeat my personal guard." The Sandman clapped his hands twice and waited.

Return to Storyworld

Nothing happened at first; then Mark heard the rustling of leaves and the creaking of branches. The Companions looked up at the trees. Something was coming.

There was a loud yell as a behemoth of a man came swinging around a nearby treetop on a thick vine and hurled himself into the center of the clearing. He was as large as Hansel, making Mark wonder if he was another Stronghand. He wore a brown loincloth around his waist and a brown rag around his forehead to keep his long brown hair out of his face. His arms were like hairy tree trunks ending in enormous fists that left deep craters in the ground when he landed. As he faced the Companions, Mark recognized his yellow eyes as the same ones that were watching him through the campsite the previous night. The guard let out a thunderous, ape-like roar.

"As I was saying," said the Sandman, "this will be one-on-one combat. If you can get past him, I shall relinquish any information you desire."

The wild man grunted loudly. Mark's eyes were locked on that haunting yellow gaze.

"Is anyone up for a fight?" asked Rump.

"Maybe we can rush him and take him out together," Mark whispered.

"No need," said Holmes, shedding his coat. "I've handled bigger."

The guard slammed his chest with his fists as Holmes approached. Mark expected the agent to prepare himself in some way, but when he took his position in the center of the clearing, he simply folded his hands behind his back and waited.

Return to Storyworld

Without warning, the guard charged. Holmes dipped to the left and swung his elbow around, hitting his opponent in the nose. The wild man collapsed with a bloody nose.

It was a strong blow, but not strong enough to keep him down. The guard dashed again, this time swinging his fists erratically. Holmes ducked and dodged every punch nimbly. Mark was amazed at how he smoothly pivoted and maneuvered, as though he could predict his opponent's moves before they happened.

The wild man eventually seemed to be getting tired and frustrated. As he threw more punches, his breathing became ragged and hoarse. He swung his left arm too wide and threw himself off balance. Holmes sent an uppercut directly into his jaw. There was a loud crack, and the guard stumbled to his knees. Holmes delivered a kick so fierce it must've broken his opponent's ribs. There was a wheeze and a groan, and the guard crumpled to the ground a final time.

Holmes wiped his brow. "Would you look at that? I broke a sweat. Good spor—"

"He's escaping!" yelled Robin.

The Sandman scrambled back into the cave, but he fell when Robin's arrow caught him in the leg. The Companions surrounded him. Mark unsheathed the Hunter's Dagger and held it up to the Sandman's chest.

"You owe us answers! Tell us why your sand was in Himshire!"

The Sandman breathed heavily and cringed when he moved his leg. In a quivering voice, he uttered, "Someone… someone trespassed upon my isle weeks ago. It was in the middle of the night when I heard a strange laughter." He coughed violently. "When I went to confront the intruder, it was too late. He had stolen a pouch of my experimental new sand. My guard scoured the entire island to find him, but he came back alone. I did not see the trespasser, but I did see his silhouette when he escaped. He was demon-like, with a shocking head of hair that sprouted out in a mane, and he had a noticeable hunch. His laugh was especially unsettling. It sounded like numerous men cackling at once."

"All he took was some sand that killed people? That's it?"

"Some sand that killed people?" repeated the Sandman indignantly. "That sand can defy the barrier between life and death. It was a major breakthrough in science and magic!"

"What kind of breakthrough?"

There was no answer. Holmes shouldered Mark out of the way and grabbed the Sandman by the collar of his cloak.

"Tell us what you know!" said Holmes, shaking him so hard his hood fell off, exposing his bald, gray head.

Mark grabbed the agent's shoulder to tell him to ease up when he saw a glint of silver in the Sandman's hand. "Watch out!"

Before Holmes could see what was happening, an arrow pierced the Sandman's chest. His red eyes sprung open in shock, and his body went limp.

Holmes rounded on Robin. "Why did you shoot him, you dolt? We needed more information!"

"It wasn't me!" replied the archer, his bow still loaded with an arrow.

Mark looked past them to see Doc and a revitalized Wilma entering the clearing. The sheriff was holding her bow by her side.

"Not a bad shot, if I say so myself," said Wilma. "You're lucky I got better so fast or else…" Her words trailed off when she met the Companions' glares.

"We were interrogating him, you idiot!" said Holmes.

"He was about to knife you!" replied Wilma.

The Sandman's violent coughing and loud wheezing interrupted them. He pointed a gnarled white finger at Wilma with a horrified expression, and then gave one last raspy cough as the life left his eyes.

As he died, his body withered away into heap of sand. There was a rumble, and his entire home collapsed into sand as well. Soon, the Companions were left standing among nothing but piles and piles of sand.

Chapter 5

A Slight Detour

There was little conversation as the Literary Companions headed back to the ship. Holmes and Pinocchio were leading the way, having a hushed discussion among themselves. Everyone once in a while, one of them would stare back at Wilma, who walked with her head down and her bow slung over her shoulder. Rump, Mark, and Doc walked behind her, and Humpty and Robin followed at the rear of the group. Humpty had his head buried within the pages of the book again, squinting through the darkness to read the words.

Rump whispered, "Tell me, Sir Dodger, did you notice anything strange at the Sandman's lair?"

"Stranger than any of the other stuff I've seen in Storyworld? Not really."

"Didn't you see how he pointed at Wilma as he died?"

"She shot him!" hissed Mark. "How else do you expect him to react?"

"It's very odd, is all I'm saying. And it's another part of this case that has sparked my curiosity. Also, I'm wondering what the Sandman meant when he told us about his magic sand."

The Companions had sifted through the remnants of the Sandman and his home to find any potential clues to the case. Unfortunately, everything had disintegrated upon the Sandman's death. All they found was sand upon sand, and the body of the unconscious bodyguard. The Companions thought it best to head back to the ship before he woke up and found what had happened to his master.

Holmes slowed down to join Rump and Mark's conversation. "He mentioned that it was a major breakthrough in science and magic, and that it could defy the barrier between life and death, whatever that means." The agent held up the vial of sand from his pocket. "There must be something special to it."

"But what else can you really do with it?" asked Mark. "Only the Sandman can touch it without dying. Kind of pointless, if you ask me."

"I'm afraid I'm also stumped. I wish we could've gotten more information out of the Sandman, but the damned sheriff had to interfere."

"It was a mistake. You can't blame her for—"

"I will blame her," said Holmes acidly. "Because of her, we're at a dead end. All we can do is go back to the scene of the crime and pray we find a new clue." The agent trudged away, leaving Rump and Mark in bitter silence.

Tensions ran high until nightfall, long after the Companions had returned to the *Titan* and set sail. Wilma was a pariah among the group, but everyone had isolated themselves once the ship was out to sea. Nobody seemed to be in the mood for a conversation. Conrad sat quietly at the helm, his gaze uneasily shifting from one person to the next.

The ocean was calm and quiet again, amplifying the awkward silence onboard. It was becoming unbearable for Mark. He leaned against one of the cannons with his arms crossed as he thought of ways to break the stillness. Luckily, Robin took the initiative and finally approached Wilma, striking up a conversation about the best wood to craft arrows. Almost instantly, the tension broke and a sense of ease washed over the ship.

"It's a start," Rump said quietly as he approached Mark.

"Good. I can't handle this kind of awkwardness. This is worse than the time my roommate broke up with his girlfriend while we were at a concert. Worst car ride home ever."

"Speaking of which, how has life treated you, Sir Dodger? You haven't filled us in on any details about the past ten years."

Mark smirked. "Well, I can tell you that my life's changed a lot since the last time I was in Storyworld."

"Indeed. You look sadder," Rump said, nonchalantly gazing at the water.

"I — wait, what?"

"I can read emotions as well as I can read spells, Sir Dodger. When we met you ten years ago, you were a bright young man, despite your difficult past. I could sense a certain purity and optimism in you."

"Purity and optimism?" said Mark with a dry laugh. "Please, Rump. I was a wimp with a lip piercing and goofy hair. I nearly got us killed a bunch of times. Remember the troll under the bridge? Or the trials with the giants? Back in my world, I was what we call a 'loser'. I'm a lot happier now. I'm a best-selling author. I've got a sports car, a nice condo in the city, a vacation home in Europe. Life is good."

"And what of your love life?" asked the alchemist.

"No offense, Rump, but that's not really any of your business."

Rump gave the tiniest smile. Mark sighed.

"Okay, I met this girl, Amy, in college. She was amazing. Sweet, funny, smart, drop dead gorgeous. She was the definition of perfect. I knew I was the luckiest guy in the world when we got married a couple years ago, but…"

"What happened?"

Mark paused. "I messed up."

There was suddenly a loud crash. The entire ship trembled so violently that everyone fell over. Conrad grabbed onto the helm as Mark helped Rump back up. The Companions gathered along the side of the ship. All they saw were large waves sloshing against the hull.

"What the hell was that?" asked Mark.

"Did we hit something? Maybe a reef?" said Doc.

"No reefs along this route," barked Conrad, joining the Companions at the railing. "We didn't hit something; something hit us!"

The ship was struck again, but everyone managed to stay upright this time. Conrad squinted into the water as they all clung to the railing. The ocean was becoming rougher as large waves were thrown at the ship's hull.

"Hang on!" said Conrad.

For the third time, an incredible force struck the *Titan*. That was when Mark saw it: a tall, corroded fin gliding past the ship and disappearing under the waves.

"Sea monster!" roared Conrad. "Man the cannons!"

The Companions split up among the cannons around the deck, except for Pinocchio. Mark approached him and saw a look of pure horror on his face.

"Pinocchio, you need to get to a cannon!"

"No, no, I cannot..."

"What? Why not?"

"I... sea monsters..." Pinocchio slid to his knees while clutching the railing, a blank expression on his face.

Conrad issued another order, and Mark regretfully left Pinocchio so he could arm a nearby cannon, while Doc, Holmes, Conrad, and Humpty did the same. Wilma and Robin waited at the front of the *Titan* with their bows at the ready. At the rear of the ship, Rump guzzled down a vial of blue potion. By the time he conjured up an orb of cackling blue energy in his palm, dark storm clouds had formed in the sky, accompanied by loud thunder and flashes of lightning in the distance.

"There's ammo in those chests by your feet!" shouted Conrad over the rising sound of the storm.

"How do we shoot them?" asked Mark.

"What the bloody hell do you mean 'how do we shoot them?' It's a cannon! Put the ammo into the barrel, aim it, then yank that big lever at the back!"

Mark kicked open the nearby chest to find a small stack of black iron balls the size of his head. He and the other Companions started loading as the waves became more violent and aggressive, reaching up to the deck and splashing the crew. The sea monster hadn't attacked for a while. Mark prayed it had changed its mind and swam off.

Just as this thought crossed his mind, Conrad fired his cannon. The air was filled with a monstrous roar that shook Mark's bones. The sea monster didn't ram the ship this time, but the water became so rough it pushed the *Titan* sideways, coming dangerously close to toppling it over. Mark held onto his cannon for dear life.

A spout of water and air erupted near Mark, prompting him to peek overboard. The sea monster had risen to the surface, and it was now glaring at the ship with one of its ominous black eyes. Two stubby white horns protruded from the creature's head, and in between these horns was a small blowhole that gurgled and moaned as it spouted more drops of water.

Pinocchio gave a horrified gasp and collapsed to his knees. Mark wanted to check on him to see if he was okay, but Conrad ordered him to fire his cannon. In a panic, he yanked the lever without properly aiming. The cannonball soared over the sea monster's head and landed harmlessly in the ocean. Before he had the chance to reload and fire again, the sea monster submerged, leaving behind more rippling waves.

"I think it's coming around the other side!" said Mark.

His prediction turned out to be true. Doc and Holmes both fired their cannons. Mark heard one of the cannonballs miss its mark and land in the water. The other one made an odd thudding sound, which was accompanied by an ear-shattering roar.

Return to Storyworld

"Reload and keep firing!" ordered Conrad.

Robin, Wilma, and Rump came to the side of the ship and joined in the assault with Doc, Holmes, and Conrad. While this was going on, Mark and Humpty attended to Pinocchio. He was conscious, but his eyes appeared to be glazed over.

"What's wrong with him?" asked Mark.

"He is frightened," murmured Humpty.

"What? Pinocchio's scared? Of what?"

"You never heard of his terrifying ordeal with the sea monster?"

Mark stared in disbelief. Out of all his companions, he never expected Pinocchio to ever show fear. He was always so brave and stoic, never backing down from anything. But now, here he was, frozen with fright.

"It's coming 'round the other side!" said Robin.

Humpty and Mark jumped back on the cannons as the sea monster emerged from the water. This time, Mark waited to aim before tugging the lever, and he was thrilled to see his cannonball hit its target. There was another roar, this one the loudest of them all. Humpty fired his own cannon, scoring another hit and forcing the monster to retreat to the other side.

Eventually, it began to rain. Lightly at first, then picking up in a matter of seconds and transitioning into thick droplets that pounded on the deck. Bursts of thunder trailed flashes of lightning almost instantly.

"It's no use!" Conrad yelled over the pouring rain. "The skin is too tough. Blasted beast won't go down without a fight. The cannons aren't doing enough damage, and my ship won't last much longer!"

As he said this, the sea monster rammed the *Titan* again. There was a loud splintering sound from below deck. Mark ignored it and reloaded his cannon. He was having trouble forcing the cannonball into the barrel. He cussed loudly and kicked the base of the cannon out of frustration.

"There's gunpowder around the lip!" Conrad called out, pointing at the black buildup on the edge of the cannon's barrel. "Clean it off. You don't wanna clog it. If there's a clog, you build up pressure and bust the cannon!"

Mark cleaned off the residue with his jacket sleeve. Out of the corner of his eye, Holmes fell into a sort of trance. The agent looked at the cannon, then over the railing at the sea monster.

"Get back to your cannon! He's coming to this side!" shouted Conrad..

"That's it!" said Holmes, holding up a finger. "I know how to beat the monster! We need to aim for the blowhole between the horns. If we can get a cannonball in there, we could plug up the beast's windpipe and suffocate it. Aim for the blowhole!"

The sea monster rammed the ship over and over. The Companions responded by firing the cannons nonstop, aiming for the blowhole per the agent's orders, but not a single cannonball could reach the target. Even when Robin and Wilma took up the cannons, they were unsuccessful. Soon enough, they were down to a handful of ammunition.

"It is no use!" said Doc after firing his lost round.

Mark's spirit sank. He had run out of cannonballs, as did Humpty.

Return to Storyworld

Everyone was soon out of ammunition, except Conrad, who had one shot left. The captain loaded it into his cannon and prepared to fire.

"Pray this works!"

As he yanked the lever, the sea monster rammed the ship again. The cannonball went far left and missed the target completely. Conrad swore to himself. He ran to the edge of the stairs leading to the bunks below deck.

"The hull's been breached! The *Titan*'s taking on water! Get ready to abandon ship!"

The Companions scrambled to their bunks to grab their belongings. Mark almost followed until he remembered the catatonic Pinocchio. He shook the Wooden Soldier by his shoulders, shouting his name loudly.

There was a crack of thunder, and a bolt of lightning struck the deck of the ship at the base of the front mast. The wood splintered and the tall beam fell toward Mark and Pinocchio. Someone grabbed them by their collars and pulled them both out of the way. The mast fell over onto the deck, crushing a portion of the railing.

"That was too close!" panted Robin.

The Companions reassembled on deck. Holmes was carrying a small barrel over his shoulder.

"What're you plannin' to do with that?" asked Conrad.

"This should be the right size to plug up the blowhole and stop the monster once and for all."

"How do we do that? Throw it?"

"No, it's too risky a shot. I'm going to do it by hand."

Before anyone could say anything, Holmes hopped onto the railing and walked across the fallen mast as it protruded beyond the ship. Mark and Humpty went to stop him, but he was already halfway over the water.

The rain fell faster now, and the lightning and thunder were striking more frequently. The Companions gathered to watch Holmes move further and further up the mast until he was at the very edge. He wrapped his legs around the beam and dangled from it upside down, with the barrel hanging from his fingertips. The sea monster's fin appeared from the underside of the boat, but it then sunk underneath the waves and swam past where Holmes was hanging. It moved further away from the *Titan*, and for a moment, it seemed to be gone for good.

Then the ship trembled as the monster's tail snapped at the hull.

And the barrel slipped out of the agent's hands and fell into the water.

Despite the deafening roar of the storm, Mark could hear Holmes unleash a barrage of swears as he clung to the mast. The corroded fin emerged from the water and spun around as the monster made its way toward the ship. Holmes shimmied down the mast, but the monster was rapidly drawing closer.

Conrad grabbed Mark by the shoulder and said, "If I don't come back, head north and you'll eventually reach Himshire."

The captain vaulted over the railing and dove into the sea. Mark watched him swim up to the barrel as it bobbed around in the tumultuous waves. Holmes climbed safely onboard the *Titan* as Conrad crawled onto the monster's head with the barrel tucked under his arm.

"You think you scare me, you ugly brute?" Conrad's voice could still be heard over the storm and the sea monster's roars. He lifted the barrel over his head and threw it into the blowhole.

A flash a lightning, a clap of thunder, and the monster ceased its attack. The barrel vanished down its windpipe. The sea monster's roars turned into a deep sputtering and rasping sound. It thrashed its head up and down, side to side. Conrad held onto one of the horns for dear life.

"Get back on board!" shouted Holmes.

Mark couldn't tell if Conrad had heard or not. He appeared to be yelling at the Companions, but it was impossible to hear his words.

Another bolt of lightning struck the *Titan*'s other mast, cracking it down the middle. The two halves of the mast fell away from each other, tearing the remaining sail to shreds. A large piece of wood broke off and careened through the air. The debris flew directly into Conrad's face, throwing him into the water. The sea monster quickly swallowed him up.

"No!" shouted the Companions in unison.

The monster continued its panicked rampage. It was beating the side of the *Titan* with its tail and knocking more shards of wood loose. The sputtering from the blowhole sounded more intense and frantic.

"Jump off the other side," commanded Holmes, "and swim as far away from the ship as you can!"

Nobody needed to be told twice. Mark threw the immobile Pinocchio over his shoulders, then sprinted across the deck and leaped over the railing.

Return to Storyworld

The water was freezing. It felt like an icicle had pierced Mark's windpipe the moment he sank under the waves. Fortunately for him, Pinocchio's wooden body kept him above the surface. The rough waves threatened to drag him under, but he tried with all his might to keep his head above the water. Rump and Humpty were straddling the broken piece of the mast like a makeshift canoe and managed to rope in Mark and the rest of the Companions.

As the current hauled them further out into the ocean, they watched as the *Titan* sank below the waves. The lifeless body of the sea monster followed.

For hours, the Companions floated through the sea. The thunder and lightning had stopped, but the rain didn't end. The clouds refused to break, and without the sun to guide them, it was impossible for them to know which way was north. There was nothing in sight for miles except for more water and white skies.

Pinocchio came around just as the rain finally ended. He had a mild bout of panic until everyone told him what happened.

"That was very irresponsible of me," he said, embarrassed. "I am sorry."

Mark wanted to tell him it was okay, but he wasn't feeling well. His head was pounding and his stomach was churning from the waves. The cold weather wasn't helping either. He was also slightly annoyed.

Humpty revealed he had saved a rucksack from the *Titan* before it sank, but all that was in it was his copy of *Dodger's Adventure*. Mark wanted to ask why he didn't grab a compass or provisions or any other useful items, but he could barely find the energy to talk.

Return to Storyworld

It was late morning when the fog dissipated and the group spotted land. They washed up on the shore as the last of the clouds dissolved, revealing a shining sun that bathed the beach in ample light and warmth; a refreshing change of pace from the frigid ocean waters.

Holmes claimed they had drifted west, miles off course. There was little debate as to what to do next: they needed to find a nearby town and acquire transportation to Himshire. Doc suggested they head further west, chasing the sun as it soared toward the horizon.

Leaving the beach, the Companions ventured inland, trekking across barren fields filled with lush green grass and interesting rock formations. The sloping hills, although pleasant to gaze at, enhanced the exhaustion in the adventurers. They were tired, hungry, and anxious, yet it was crucial they didn't stop. According to Holmes, time was of the essence, and the shipwreck had set them incredibly behind schedule.

Mark's nose was stuffy, and he had developed the chills when they reached the shore. The cool air didn't mix well with his soaking wet clothes. He abandoned his wet jacket, realizing he felt much better without it.

"How're you feeling?" he asked Pinocchio in an attempt to keep his mind off his growing feverish condition.

"Ashamed, very ashamed. My actions on the ship were inexcusable. But how are you? You do not sound too well, Sir Dodger."

"I've felt better. Hope I'm not catching anything. You might want to keep your distance."

Return to Storyworld

"What do you mean?"

"I don't want to get you sick." Mark sniffled. "Actually, can you even get sick? Does your body work like a regular human's?"

"I am afraid I do not understand."

"How exactly does your body function? Are you like a human in a wooden body? How are you... what you are?" Mark cringed at his failed attempt to phrase the question more appropriately.

"I figured you knew my story already."

"I only know your Literary's version, and I have a feeling that's not the true story."

"Probably for the best. My story is not pleasant, nor is it brief. I was essentially created by Geppetto to be his servant. When his old slave died, his life-force was channeled into this body and—"

"Wait a minute, you mean that life-force stuff is real?"

"You didn't believe me?" asked Humpty, walking behind Mark.

"I thought you said nobody knew how to do it anymore!" objected Mark.

"Incorrect. I said the channeling of a person's life-force was forbidden, which it is. That does not mean that certain sorcerers did not figure out the process on their own."

Mark pondered for a moment. "Does that mean Geppetto was this powerful wizard who could transfer life-forces?"

"Geppetto was as magical as a horse's fart!" said Pinocchio, prompting Rump to giggle. "But someone very close to Geppetto was adept in spell-casting."

Return to Storyworld

Mark took two steps and it dawned on him. "You mean the Forever Witch?!"

One of Mark's first adventures in Storyworld involved an encounter with the Forever Witch, a shape-shifting monstrosity that almost seduced and killed him had it not been for the intervention of his friends. Humpty and Rump had mentioned how she was an ancient being with magical talents and murderous tendencies, but Mark never figured she would have the ability to transfer people's souls into other bodies.

"That blasted Forever Witch, yes," answered Pinocchio. "As I was saying, Geppetto's slave died, and I guess he wanted a new servant who could work forever and never tire. So he carved this body out of a pine tree and had that witch bring me to life. Her magic made me as human as possible without actually making me a human. I can eat and drink, but I'll never go hungry or thirsty. I can breathe, but I'll never become exhausted. Geppetto and the Forever Witch created me to be the ideal servant.

"For years, I toiled under their servitude, until I eventually escaped and made it to Neverland, where the gracious King Gabriel took me in and trained me to become a warrior. As it turns out, the aspects that made me the perfect slave also made me into the perfect soldier. In a grim way, I owe my thanks to Geppetto.

"But I should also be thanking Geppetto's original servant, whose life-force I now possess. He might have had an unfortunate life as a slave, but I can tell he was exceptionally brave."

"Until faced with a sea monster," Holmes remarked off to the side.

Return to Storyworld

Both Rump and Mark gave Holmes a disgusted glare. Even Wilma scoffed at him. Pinocchio frowned and bowed his head in shame. Mark looked to Humpty, expecting him to chastise the agent for his rude comment, but his face was again buried in the book.

"What about you, Humpty? Where did you come from?"

Humpty peeked over the edge of the book. "Well, first off, 'Humpty' is not my birth name. When I was a young boy, I was named Hubert Dumpty. "

"You mean you weren't always an egg?"

"Of course not!" said Humpty in an offended tone. "I was a normal human such as yourself, born to a single mother who was a horse-breaker. When she passed on, I became an apprentice to a wall-builder, the same wall-builder responsible for creating Neverland's fortifications, mind you. Later on in life, I joined the Neverland Military Arm and worked my way up the ranks until I became a high-ranking official."

"And where exactly did the egg part come in?"

Humpty frowned. "I am... unsure of whether to tell you about that. I would not want it to end up in more Literary works." He flipped a page in the book.

"I lost my notebook during the shipwreck," admitted Mark. "I doubt I'll be adding any of this to my stories."

"Fine, fine, I will tell you. In my adolescence, I was a bit... promiscuous. I had relations with many women, and one of those women was a witch who didn't really approve of my liberal love life. Long story short, she bewitched me into an egg. A thrilling tale, is it not?"

"Oh, I remember that!" said Rump. "You came to me for help. I couldn't stop laughing for a good hour."

"The laughter sure ended when you discovered you could not reverse the spell!"

"True, true. That witch knew her magic. At least I deduced the one way to change you back, which was—"

"A kiss," concluded Mark, remembering how Tinkerbell's kiss had transformed Humpty into a human being.

"True love's kiss," corrected Humpty. "The witch wanted to teach me a lesson, and she sure did. As for the name 'Humpty', that came about after my infernal Literary and I were walking along the walls one night and he pushed me off in jest. Insult to injury at its finest! If I could see him now, oh, how he would be sorry!"

Mark and Rump caught each other's eyes and stifled their laughter.

Luck was with the Literary Companions that afternoon. They arrived at a settlement tucked away in a valley in the middle of a small canyon. The plains had partially obscured the view of the town, and they would've missed it had Holmes not detected footprints and wagon tracks nearby. The group traveled down a sloping road, passing by a decrepit wooden sign that bore the city's name: Bunkertown.

The aggressive wind that had been berating the Companions all morning calmed down by a considerable amount once they entered the valley. The canyon's walls partially blocked the sun's rays so that there was a light shadow cast over Bunkertown. There were no walls protecting the city, which Mark found odd, but there was a series of towers lined up across the valley. Each of these towers was topped with an enormous silver bell, big enough to house three grown men. A lone guard sat next to each bell, wielding a long wooden mallet. Holmes called up to one of the guards as the Companions attempted to enter Bunkertown, but he did not say anything back. He simply smacked the bell once with his mallet, then nodded for them to keep walking.

Little attention was paid to the group as they journeyed through the city. The hundreds of people milling about shared the same somber expression, apparently too concerned with other matters to notice the adventurers. There was an overall depressing aura emanating from the citizens, as if an important figure had died.

Similarly to Himshire, the streets of Bunkertown were lined with uniform housing made of stone and wood. Every house was exactly the same, with the exception of a window placement or a differently colored painted roof. Each home's roof was lined with small silver bells, and whenever a breeze drifted by, they would utter a soft, unsettling tinkling sound.

Once the Companions arrived at the main street, they encountered a booming marketplace filled with carts of food and merchandise. The somber townspeople walked from merchant to merchant, conducting silent business transactions. Again, nobody paid attention to the Companions. Mark found the environment creepy and unsettling. It was as though they were walking among oblivious ghosts.

Sticking to the busy main street, the group eventually happened upon a grand building that must have marked the center of the city. Mark had to crane his neck to see the top, where a flag waved the city's crest: two enormous silver bells.

Holmes steered the Companions to the foot of the building where two spear-wielding guards guarded a pair of tall wooden doors. The guards crossed their weapons in front of the entrance as the group approached.

"Your name and place of origin," said one of the guards automatically.

"Agent Holmes of Himshire," replied the agent, flashing the badge on his chest. "Is this the capitol building?"

"What is your purpose here?"

"We've suffered from shipwreck and are currently seeking passage home. We're not here with hostile intentions."

The guard nodded to his fellow, then rapped his fist against the door. The entrance creaked open, allowing the Companions to enter.

Another guard led them down a dimly-lit hallway lined with torches on stone pillars. To their left, the wooden walls were decorated with portraits of past Literaries. On the right, there were landscape paintings of epic battles and amazing feats. Dozens of doors lined the hallways as well, but the guard led the Companions past them, to the very end of the hall. The humid atmosphere in the building reminded Mark of the Isle of Twilight. It made him feel claustrophobic.

They arrived at the end of the hallway and entered through another pair of double-doors. This new room was dark, lit by a single candle within a tarnished bronze brazier dangling from the ceiling. A solitary bronze throne sat at the opposite end of the room, with three armed guards on either side. Occupying the throne was an elderly man with a protruding belly, large enough for him to rest his elbow on as he stroked the graying whiskers on his chin. He wore a navy blue robe down to his shins, leaving his bare feet exposed. Shockingly white hair popped out from odd angles on the man's head, and he had a beak of a nose with a disturbing wart on the very tip. He was hunched over and reading from one of the dozens of scrolls scattered about his throne.

"Mayor Thaddeus Scrooge of Bunkertown," announced the guard.

The man in the throne continued reading the scroll without noticing the visitors. Holmes bowed and nodded to everyone to mimic his gesture. Mark clumsily dropped to his knees, ignoring the pain on the side of his head, the pressure building up in his sinuses, and the scratchy feeling in his throat.

"Excuse me, Mayor Scrooge," said Holmes in the same annoyed tone he often picked with the Companions. Scrooge ignored him and kept reading. Holmes repeated his statement louder. No response again. Finally, he practically shouted, "Mayor Scrooge!"

Scrooge acknowledged him with a glare. "What? What do you want? Can you not see I—" He froze when he saw Mark.

"We're sorry to intrude, Mayor Scrooge, but time is of the essence. We were recently shipwrecked during a mission out east. We drifted onto your shores this morning and came here seeking passage back to our homeland, Himshire."

Return to Storyworld

Scrooge stood up, causing his bodyguards to shift uneasily. He waved them off and approached the Companions. His left leg was bent at an odd angle, giving him a heavy limp.

"Are you the Hook-Slayer?" Scrooge asked hoarsely.

Ignoring the pressure in his head, Mark wheezed, "Yes."

"Did you hear what I said, Mayor?" asked Holmes, even more annoyed now. "We need—"

"I will give you every single ship in the land," said Scrooge. "I will let you have your weight in gold. I will grant you every weapon, every relic, every treasure within Bunkertown, but only if you and the Hook-Slayer assist us."

This was the last thing Mark wanted. His head was ready to explode, but the tone in Scrooge's voice made it through his sickness. It sounded serious, like he had lost something dear to him.

"What is it that you need?" asked Holmes.

"It is a long story. Please, just help us."

"We need to know everything before we lend our services. Tell us everything."

Scrooge sighed. "Fine." He reseated himself on his throne. "As strange as it may sound, our troubles all began when Bunkertown was suffering from an infestation of rats. This was not one or two rats hiding in a cupboard, or a lone rat prowling down the street. There was literally an army of rats overrunning our city.

"My father was Mayor of Bunkertown in those days. He was ready to order an evacuation, until a stranger named Peter came to the city, claiming he could rid us of our pest problem. Using a magic flute, he fulfilled the promise, and within the hour, the rats were gone."

"The Pied Piper," said Mark. For a moment, frustration overtook his sickness. "Let me guess, your dad didn't pay him for clearing out the rats, so he took the kids?"

Scrooge frowned. "My father was a miserable, greedy man. You are correct. He refused to pay Peter for his services, so he used his magical pipe to lure the town's children away. Our Literary arrived just in time to rescue most of the children, but many of them disappeared with Peter, never to be seen again."

"And?" said Holmes.

"A week ago, a strange music sounded throughout the town. It was an eerie, piercing sound, like when you scrape a blade against an anvil. I remembered it from when I was a young boy, but when I had last heard it, it was a pleasing melody. I knew what it meant: Peter had returned.

"Scores of the town's children began to leave the city, children of all ages. Even the babes attempted to crawl out of their cribs, but we were able to stop them, at the very least. The older children, especially the ones nearing adolescence, couldn't be stopped. They fought tooth and nail to follow the music. Nothing could stop them; much like how nothing stopped the children the last time the music played.

"I was one of the children hypnotized by Peter during his first visit. My leg slowed me down and prevented me from keeping up with the others. Who would've thought a lame leg would save my life?" Scrooge let out a hoarse laugh.

"But now that you and your Literary are here, I am begging for your assistance. The children were led to the Adrictan Mountain, roughly a mile south down the canyon. You must save them."

"Do you not have any soldiers to seize the mountain? That might be more effective than sending our small troop," said Pinocchio.

"I sent ten of my best guards to retrieve them a month ago, along with a trained mercenary. None of them returned. The only armed forces we have left are twenty-some guardsmen, and I cannot risk leaving the city entirely unprotected. We haven't received a Literary, and we are desperate. My… my own daughter was one of the many children taken." Scrooge stared directly at Mark. "Please help us, Hook-Slayer."

Holmes seemed to be fighting his annoyance, but he also had a sympathetic gleam in his eye when Scrooge mentioned his daughter. After getting an affirming nod from the rest of the Companions, he turned to Scrooge.

"Fine. We'll rescue the children."

Chapter 6

Under the Mountain

The Literary Companions hastily set off on their mission. They walked to the other end of Bunkertown and exited into the valley, where they descended a steep slope that led into the depths of the canyon.

The further they distanced themselves from the town, the darker the area became. As the land sloped further downward, the canyon's walls rose higher, until the sun's rays hardly penetrated the valley. The Companions eventually found themselves in an ominous shadow.

It was a surprisingly short journey. At the very end of the canyon, they came face-to-face with the towering Adrictan Mountain sprouting from the rock face. The peak was higher than the canyon walls, so high that clouds obscured the top. On the left side of the mountain was a sprawling forest covering half the base and climbing to the top of the canyon. Between the right side of the mountain and the adjacent canyon wall, there was a pathway sloping down and out of sight.

Holmes detected footprints leading down the right-hand path. The Companions agreed to split up so half of them could stay close by to watch for any signs of the Piper. Wilma and Robin took up hidden positions next to the path while Mark, who was feeling worse by the second, sat down against a tall boulder.

Humpty also decided to stay behind, presumably so he could catch up on his reading. Everyone else walked down the path.

Mark was hot and thirsty. The scratching in his throat felt like he was swallowing gravel, and his temples pounded furiously. His nose was stuffed up and his body was covered in chills. This was undoubtedly a fever, or worse, the flu. Robin took notice of Mark's worsening condition and slid down the mountainside to check on him.

"Is everything okay?"

Too weak to respond, Mark simply shook his head. Each movement made the pounding in his head worse. Robin pressed his hand to Mark's forehead and recoiled in horror.

"You're hotter than a dragon's egg! You need medicine! I'll fetch Rump."

Robin sprinted down the path, past a bewildered Wilma. Next to her, Humpty remained oblivious to his surroundings, deeply engaged in *Dodger's Adventure*.

The burning in his throat made it hard for Mark to talk, let alone scream for help. He took out the Hunter's Dagger and laid it on his lap. A fever was not going to make him forget to protect himself, especially in unknown territory.

The area had become disturbingly quiet, similar to the previous night, prior to the sea monster's attack. The difference now was that there was no soothing sound of water lapping against the ship's hull and no refreshing wind blowing through the air. All Mark heard was the blood pounding in his ears. The environment was hauntingly tranquil and hypnotizing. His vision grew hazy and disoriented as he slowly lost consciousness. The last thing he saw as he blacked out was a small figure hobbling behind the trees.

It had been a long day for Mark. He had just finished another book signing at a small bookstore in Philadelphia called the Rabbit Hole. The store opened recently, and most authors would've passed on such a small venue, but the owner, Becky, was an old college friend of Mark's. She had called him to come by as a favor to attract new customers. Word had spread around the city about Mark's appearance, leading to a successful turnout.

It was late, and Becky was locking the doors to the Rabbit Hole while Mark waited for her at the curb. She was an athletic girl with thin black hair, sweet eyes, and a permanent smile on her face. Even though he was with Amy throughout college, Mark wouldn't deny he used to be attracted to Becky.

Once she clicked the lock shut, Becky gave Mark a big hug. "Thank you so much for your help today. You have no idea how much it means to me."

"It's no problem, Beck. You know I'm always happy to help."

"I still can't believe you published a book! It's so cool knowing a real author."

"You sound surprised that I turned out successful," Mark said with a grin.

"Well, I was a bit caught off-guard. I remember you being the quiet kid in creative writing workshop. I didn't think you really cared about writing. Honestly,

I figured you were some burnout taking the class for an easy A."

"I kept to myself! I didn't want to stand out. I wasn't a burnout or a slacker or anything."

"Oh, I know that now," Becky said defensively while grabbing Mark's arm gently. "Don't get me wrong. I meant that you were so... isolated. Remember when we exchanged papers for our first peer review and you let me read the draft of Dodger's Adventure? I was blown away! It was pretty good for a freshman who said he never wrote before."

"I had a lot of inspiration," said Mark, shrugging.

"And I'm not gonna lie. I used to have a bit of a crush on you," replied Becky, biting her lip gently.

Mark hesitated. "Yeah, okay."

"I did! What wasn't there to like about you? You were smart, cute, not cocky, a great writer. I bet you had girls fighting over you."

"Not exactly," said Mark, motioning to his car. He suddenly felt very nervous. As he went to put his key in the door, Becky slid in front of him, a wide smile on her face. Mark paused.

"Um... hello?"

Becky closed her eyes as she leaned in.

"Ouch!"

Someone slapped Mark across the face so hard he was wrenched out of his stupor. It took a second of forcefully blinking his eyes for him to regain focus.

Return to Storyworld

Rump, Robin, and Pinocchio were kneeling in front of him with looks of concern. Aside from the stinging in his face, his entire body felt hot and achy; he was on the verge of passing out again.

"He's sick," whispered Rump, peering into Mark's eyes.

"Do you think it's serious?" asked a worried Robin.

"Doubtful. Probably just a combination of exhaustion and dehydration. It's a strong fever, but... here, drink this, Sir Dodger."

Rump pressed a vial of bubbling green liquid to Mark's lips. It had a familiar lemon-lime effervescent taste. Mark recognized it as the trusty healing potion he drank the last time he was in Storyworld. As the last of the contents slid down his throat, he lost consciousness again.

"We cannot go in until he wakes up. I refuse to leave him here, Agent Holmes."

"We're on a tight schedule. We can't sit around waiting."

"I would rather let my body crumble to dust than leave Sir Dodger behind. We either wait for him to wake up, or we carry him on our shoulders. That decision is final."

Mark's eyes snapped open. The Literary Companions were huddled around him. Pinocchio and Holmes faced each other, locked in intense glares. Wilma and Robin had their bows aimed at a little man lying on the ground with his hands pinned over his head. This stranger bore a slight resemblance to Rump; he possessed the same dark, wrinkly skin, and short stature, and he also had tufts of black hair on his head and chin. Lying next to his head was a sky-blue conical hat that matched his heavy wool robe.

"What happened?" asked Mark.

Everyone jumped when they heard his voice. Rump knelt next to Mark and put his hands on either side of his face.

"Are you okay? Don't move too fast."

"What happened," Mark repeated.

"I gave you medicine. You should be good as new in no time."

Mark rubbed his eyes and stared at the little man on the ground. "Who's the guy in the robes?"

"He's our new friend," said Robin, nudging the hostage with his foot.

"This dwarf was found lurking in the trees not too far from here," explained Holmes with his arms crossed. "He was planning to ambush us." He nodded at a broken spear by his foot. "It took a little unconventional negotiation, but he generously agreed to escort us into the mountain. We think he's in cahoots with this Piper character."

"Go bite a rock, you idiotic high-top!" squeaked the dwarf. As he lifted his head to yell at the agent, he revealed a swollen black eye.

"No need to be hostile. It's not making it any easier for you," said Holmes.

"*No need to be hostile. No need to be hostile*," repeated the dwarf in a mocking tone with his face scrunched up. Robin pressed the heel of his boot into his back to stifle him.

Return to Storyworld

Mark rose so fast his head spun. He closed his eyes to focus on holding his balance. Thankfully, the hot and painful throbbing in his head was gone. Aside from the minor weakness, he felt infinitely better than he did a short while ago.

"There is no need to rush, Sir Dodger. We can go when you are ready," said Pinocchio, casting a scowl at Holmes.

"I'm fine, Pinocchio. Let's get into the mountain." Mark hated going against the general's decision, but he had to agree with Holmes. There was no time to spare, and the sooner they found the missing children, the faster they could head back to Himshire. "How do we get inside?"

"We were about to ask our new friend," said Holmes. He bent down so that he was eye-to-eye with the dwarf. "My dear associate, would you mind opening the entrance for us?"

The dwarf huffed loudly, his cheeks swelling with anger. Mumbling and groaning, he dragged himself to his feet. Mark could've sworn he saw his eyes shift, as if he was planning to make a run for it. Robin tugged on his bowstring. The soft twanging sound made the dwarf twitch. From the sleeve of his robe, he conjured a short blue flute. He hesitantly placed it to his lips and began playing a string of different pitched tones.

For a moment, Mark wondered if the dwarf was truly going to help them get into the mountain or if he was mocking the Companions. It was then he noticed something strange occurring to the mountainside: a collection of symbols appeared in the stone. They started out as misshapen lines and squiggles, then took on more defined forms as the dwarf's tunes became more pleasant and melodic.

The symbols glowed with a pale blue light, which became brighter as the music went faster and faster.

The dwarf yanked the flute away from his mouth, abruptly halting the music. The entire area shook with a tremendous rumble. The Companions struggled to remain standing while the dwarf kept his footing with little effort. Mark was sure he had led them into a trap, until the mountainside transformed. A section of the rock face melted away like a thick liquid, and in seconds, there was a dwarf-sized hole in the side of the mountain.

"Most impressive," commented Rump. "I'm not accustomed to this type of magic. Do remind me to research it—"

"Not the time," said Holmes curtly. "Now, dwarf, take us to the infamous Piper we've heard of. We'd like a word with him."

The confined innards of the Adrictan Mountain were so narrow that the Literary Companions had to walk in a single file line with their heads bent. The dwarf led the way with Wilma and her loaded bow close behind. Mark was at the back of the line, trailing Humpty.

"It's so cramped in here," Mark whispered. "I wonder why the Piper picked this place for whatever he's doing." Humpty didn't respond, possibly because he couldn't hear him. Mark raised his voice slightly and said, "You know, I was supposed to go cave exploring for this geology elective I took in college, but I ended up missing the bus the day of the trip. I was so mad. I guess this makes up for it."

Return to Storyworld

Humpty again chose not to speak. Mark assumed the king was distracted with the mission, so he decided to avoid any further conversations.

It was a long trip through the mountain. Each step the Companions took made Mark more and more uneasy. He was having difficulty breathing, and he wasn't sure if it was the claustrophobia or a general sense of panic. What he wouldn't give for a cigarette.

Through winding passages and intersecting routes they traveled, further descending into the heart of the mountain. The dwarf easily navigated the maze of tunnels despite there not being any torches or other sources of light. Holmes and Rump had conjured tiny flames to guide the group, but they could only do so much in the constricted space.

At one point, the tunnel opened wide, allowing the Companions to stand up straight and spread out. They were now walking along a passage filled with dripping stalactites hanging from the ceiling and little pools haphazardly scattered along the ground. Twice the dwarf stopped in his tracks, only to be prodded in the back by Wilma's arrow to keep going. Mark remained cautious about where he was leading them and thought it would be a good idea to stay on his guard. The Hunter's Dagger was in his hands, ready to strike in case of an ambush.

Finally, a white light shone at the end of a distant tunnel sloping upward. The dwarf quickened his pace and ascended the path with the Companions on his tail. Mark thought he could hear noises coming from the tunnel's opening. It sounded like a mix of people shouting, metal clanking, and a massive object hissing and whistling.

Return to Storyworld

The dwarf made a dash for the opening. Wilma grabbed him by the collar of his robe, yanking him back so forcefully that his hat fell off his head.

"Ah, ah! You aren't going anywhere yet, dwarf," said Holmes. "Lox and Pinocchio, you will go up ahead and scout the area."

"I want to go too," said Mark. He felt uneasy around the dwarf.

Pinocchio nodded. "Fine. You two, with me. Everyone else, stay here with this nuisance."

The Wooden Soldier led Mark and Robin up the long, steep incline toward the light. When they reached the end of the passage, they were met with a tremendous sight.

They were standing on a ledge overlooking an enormous cavern that had been hollowed out and resembled a massive stadium. At the center of the cavern's base was a miniature factory of sorts, with conveyor belts carrying chunks of metal scraps to and fro, giant gears moving at a slow but steady pace, webs of thick ropes wrapped over pulleys and hauling more metal scraps, and hundreds of chains swinging up and down, side to side.

An ominous white light emanated from the walls of the cavern and illuminated the grisly mechanical features of the factory. There were numerous covered walkways intersecting with one another, connecting little metal huts strategically placed around the cavern. Hundreds of workers carried chunks of metal on their shoulders or dragged them in little carts and sleds across the ground. Most of these workers were taking the metal and dropping it at the top of long slides that led into the center of the factory, into an area hidden from view under a wide bronze ceiling and tall bronze walls.

"What's going on?" asked Mark, astonished.

"I'm not sure," said Robin grimly, "but I think we might've found the Bunkertown children."

Mark did a double take. He couldn't believe what he was seeing. The workers dragging the scraps of metal around were actually children. They ranged in age from younger tweens, grouped together in teams of three or four to carry larger chunks, to older adolescents, struggling to push carts filled to the brim. Mark watched as they continued gathering the metal from an opening at the other side of the cavern.

Pinocchio struggled with his words for a moment. "This is not right. We need to stop this. I want you to stay here and keep watch in case there are any changes. Sir Dodger and I will go report our findings."

The two of them retreated down the slope. Pinocchio seemed at a loss for words. Mark found the sight disturbing as well, but he managed to speak up.

"I think the Piper is controlling them with his flute. Maybe we should split up to find him?"

Pinocchio was about to reply when he halted in his tracks and took up his hammer. "That may not be necessary."

Mark followed his gaze and quickly armed himself as well.

Wilma, Holmes, Humpty, Rump, and Doc were kneeling with their heads bowed and their hands behind their backs. Standing behind them were seven identical dwarves, including their former hostage, armed with axes and spears (and one with a torch). Each dwarf wore a different colored robe: red, orange, yellow, green, blue, indigo, and violet.

To the far left of the dwarves stood a slender man with very thin legs and arms, resembling a frail skeleton with pale skin stretched tightly over his bones. The bulbous eyes, toothy grin, and greasy black hair gave him the appearance of an overgrown child. He wore a button-down shirt and matching puffy trousers with multicolored vertical stripes, each color corresponding with a different dwarf's robes. He also wore a shockingly orange beret that clashed with the rest of his outfit.

"Hello, friends," said the Piper in a tone as greasy as his hair.

"Let them go," demanded Pinocchio.

"Let them go?" repeated the Piper, frowning slightly. "But that's no fun. Why let them go when there's so much work to do?"

"I will not ask again," said Pinocchio, his hands tightening on his hammer.

"What do you want from us?" asked Mark.

"Now *that* sounds appealing," said the Piper. "What do I want? Oh, I want many, many things. When I was a child, I wanted a pet basilisk. When I cleared Bunkertown of its rodent infestation, I wanted payment. But that was long ago. Who knows what I want now? Hm…"

"Oy, Peter!" called the former hostage dwarf. "How about what we want? I spent the last hour being jostled and prodded by these arrogant instigators, and I want my dues."

"Hmm, that sounds fun," said the Piper thoughtfully. "Anyone in particular you fancy?"

The dwarf's eyes lingered on Wilma, but then they wandered to Holmes. He smiled and approached the agent while rolling the axe in his hand.

"There's no need for this!" stated Pinocchio. His voice sounded calm yet stern, as if he was giving a final warning.

"Your Literary asked what we wanted. This is what we want. Fair is fair."

The Piper smirked and nodded to the dwarf. As he raised the axe above the agent's head, several things happened at once.

There was a quiet yet distinct sound of glass shattering. Rump jumped from his knees and slammed both his fists to the ground, causing the entire mountain to quake so hard that the dwarves and the Piper fell over. At the same time, Pinocchio flung his hammer at a stalactite hanging from the ceiling. The stone dislodged from its base and almost fell on the Piper, who rolled out of the way at the last second.

The Companions scrambled away from their dwarf captors as Rump punched the ground again. There was another minor earthquake that shook more stalactites from the ceiling. They came crashing down around the area as the tunnel began collapsing in on itself. Pinocchio threw himself over Mark's head to protect him from the cloud of dust and gravel shrouding the area. Mark could hear more yelling amidst the sounds of shifting rocks and the rumbling mountain.

As the quaking subsided, Mark peeked out from under Pinocchio's arms. The tunnel was nearly pitch black, except for the slight glow coming from the embers of the dwarf's discarded torch. Mark could faintly see a wall of rocks obstructing the tunnel where the dwarves and the Piper had been moments ago. The silhouettes of the Companions were hunched over and coughing through the dust cloud. Mark and Pinocchio went to help them up. Their enemies were nowhere to be seen.

"That was a little too close for comfort," admitted Holmes. There was a small gash across his cheek, and his jacket was covered in scuffs and tears. "Was that a trick of yours, Stiltskin?"

"Experimental, yet effective," said the alchemist. He nudged his head at Pinocchio and said, "Well done, General. That was a superb throw."

"I owe it all to luck and quick thinking," said Pinocchio, retrieving the hammer. "Unfortunately, we are relying too much on luck rather than strategy. We need to plan better in the future."

Mark held his arm out to Humpty to help him up. Humpty briefly glanced at his outstretched hand, then turned away. He picked up *Dodger's Adventure* and went to join the other Companions. Mark scowled.

Pinocchio nodded up the slope. "There is a large factory beyond that tunnel. The children of Bunkertown have been working for the Piper. Sir Dodger believes they are possibly being controlled by dark magic. Rumpelstiltskin, can you find out what is going on with them?"

"That might not be necessary," called out Robin as he came down the path. "Is everyone okay? I thought the mountain was imploding!"

"We are fine. What do you mean it is not necessary?"

Return to Storyworld

"The children, they're acting differently. Come see for yourselves."

Robin led the Companions up the path. When they reached the ledge, he pointed to the bottom of the cavern, where the children were no longer in their mindless trance. The younger ones were screaming or crying while the older ones looked around, confused and terrified. The shrieks reverberated off the cavern walls and produced an unbearable echo.

"What happened?" Pinocchio asked Robin.

"I was keeping an eye on them, like you said, and then when the tunnel collapsed, they just stopped." Robin scratched his head. "Do you think that had to do with it?"

"Of course it did," said Holmes, reaching into his pocket. He fished out a fragment of a black, glossy tube and held it up for the Companions to see. "I found this near the rubble. It's part of a flute. When it was crushed in the collapse, it must have broken the spell."

One of the children called out and pointed at the Companions up on the ledge. Silence swept over the crowd as heads turned toward them. The cries were now hushed whispers and occasional sniffles, as if the children knew they were safe. More of them came out from inside the enclosed spaces of the factory. The youngest child couldn't have been more than four years old.

"We need to get them out of here," stated Mark.

"How do we do that? The tunnel is blocked off from the cave-in," said Wilma.

"There!" said Robin, pointing at the opening on the other side of the cavern. "There were children bringing in scraps of metal from that tunnel. Maybe it leads to another way out of the mountain?"

The Companions descended a nearby metallic staircase that spiraled down the walls of the cavern and exited at the bottom. The crowd of children gathered at the foot of the walkway, their faces scared and apprehensive.

"Well, are you going to say anything?" Pinocchio whispered to Holmes.

"I-I never was good with children," admitted the agent.

Mark rolled his eyes and stepped in front of the crowd. "Don't worry. We're here to help you."

The number of children the Piper had been holding captive was incalculable. Mark assumed it was well over a hundred. The youngest of these children had a difficult time trying not to cry hysterically while their older peers attempted to settle them down.

All of them looked worn and haggard. Their clothes were torn and coated in dirt, grime, and the occasional splotch of blood. Mark grimaced at the children with their arms and legs hastily patched up with makeshift bandages. This past week must have been torture for them.

The tunnel Robin had pointed out led through the lower portions of the mountain, where the air felt warmer and windier. A draft was coming from somewhere that Mark hoped was an exit. As the formation made its way through the tunnels, they found more spell-broken children hiding in small groups here and there. The crowd grew larger at every turn.

Return to Storyworld

Mark felt a rush of relief when they finally emerged from the mountain and into the fresh air. It was sunset. Robin and Wilma ran to the top of a nearby hill to scan their surroundings while Mark looked around the area. He had no idea where they could be. All he recognized was the Adrictan Mountain at their backs. Beyond where they stood, he saw open fields and a wide forest hundreds of miles away.

"We're on the wrong side of the mountain," called out Wilma. "We'll have a bit of a walk, but it can't be that long of a journey. I think we can make it by nightfall."

"Let's hope so. I don't think these kids will want to be out here when it gets dark," Mark whispered to the other Companions.

"Then let us make haste!" declared Pinocchio.

According to Robin and Wilma, the Companions would have to skirt the base of the mountain, walk along the side of the cliffs, and then re-enter the canyon like they did earlier that morning to get to Bunkertown. They set off immediately.

The region surrounding the mountain consisted of barren dirt fields with little vegetation. Every couple of yards, a dead tree sprouted from the ground, its gnarled branches devoid of life and resembling charred skeletal remains. Aside from these small landmarks, there was nothing but more rolling hills and empty plains as far as the eye could see.

The wasteland appeared harmless and low key for the most part, but it was important to make the children feel protected and safe. Pinocchio walked at the front of the crowd with his hammer in hand. To his right was Robin with his bow drawn, and further back was Doc. On Pinocchio's left was Wilma, followed by Humpty (reading his book). Rump, Holmes, and Mark brought up the rear, overseeing the congregation.

Mark noticed a straggler at the edge of the group: a young girl with a large pointy nose, prominent chin, and short brown hair that stood out at odd angles all over her head.

"What's your name?" asked Mark.

"Bara. Bara Scrooge."

Mark smiled. "Your dad misses you a lot."

"Really? You mean he's not mad?"

"He sent us to come rescue you. Why would he be mad? You didn't know what you were doing."

"Actually, sir, I did a little bit."

Holmes tilted his head at Bara. "You mean you knew what was happening when you were in the mountain?"

"A little bit," repeated the girl nervously. "It's a really strange feeling. A part of me knew I wasn't home, but it *felt* like home in that mountain. I thought I belonged there."

"Do you remember anything important, like what the Piper or his dwarves discussed?" pressed Holmes.

"Not really, no. I'm sorry. I remember the dwarves yelling a lot. They'd tell us to work harder and faster. They were really mean. Peter never yelled, though. He was always happy. Really happy. And one time, someone visited us, and that made him happier."

"Who visited?"

"I... I didn't hear a name, but I remember his shadow on the wall. He was a hunchback, and he had a lot of hair around his head, like a lion. And his laugh was really scary."

The agent's eyes suddenly popped wide open. He shot a glance at Mark.

"Bara," said Mark, "did you know our friend Rumpelstiltskin is a magician? Why don't you ask him to show you his fun tricks?"

The girl's face lit up with joy. Rump, overhearing the conversation, raised his eyebrows at Mark, but donned an excited smile when Bara ran over to him. As the alchemist occupied her with a series of sparks he shot out of his fingertips, Mark addressed Holmes in a low whisper.

"You thought of something, didn't you?"

"A hunchback with a mane and a penchant for laughter? Remember how the Sandman described the intruder who stole his magic sand? He said they had a large mane of hair and a noticeable hunch.'"

"Yeah, but what are the odds they're the same person? Are you sure it isn't a coincidence?"

"I've seen stranger things in my time. You'd be surprised at how well everything in this world fits together."

"But it's still a stretch..."

"Fine, keep thinking so narrow-mindedly," said Holmes impatiently, "but won't you at least humor me? Let's say it *was* connected. Let's believe everything stems from this one case."

"Okay, okay. I'll play along," said Mark.

"Good. So, starting from the top: Giles Dickory was murdered in his workshop by the magic sand. We can assume the person who took the magic sand from the Sandman was the same hunchback mentioned by the Scrooge girl."

"If you say so…"

"Now, on the other side of the board, we have to decide what the Piper and the dwarves were doing in the cavern. It required the labor of hundreds of servants and a huge stockpile of metal. What if they're building something?"

"What could they be building?"

"Buggered if I know. These are merely deductions. I'm more concerned about how the hunchback plays into this grand scheme. Why did he need the magic sand? Why did he kill the clockmaker? And what connection would he have with the Piper?"

"That's what I've been asking you! Are you sure this isn't one big coincidence?"

"There are coincidences, and then there are connections. Storyworld works far differently than your Literary realm. Almost everything is connected in one way or another."

The crowd made its way around the mountain and up the canyon's edge after an hour of walking. The sun was now almost fully tucked behind the horizon, and near-darkness had settled on the region. Pinocchio urged the children to pick up the pace if they wanted to get to Bunkertown soon. They still had to walk up the remaining length of the canyon, turn around at the opening, and then take the slope down the valley to Bunkertown. Mark agreed with Pinocchio and advised the children to hurry if they wanted to get home to their families sooner. These words were hardly effective. The children were too tired and weak to quicken their pace.

Fortunately, the length of the canyon ended up being much shorter than anticipated. The group reached the opening at the perfect time. The sun was gone, and a dense cloud had already hidden what little portion of the moon was in the sky, throwing the land into pitch-black darkness. Mark couldn't see his own hand in front of his face, but he could hear the hundreds of children whimpering at the onset of darkness.

"Sir Dodger, come here," said Rump, somewhere to the left of Mark. A light sparked to life. It was coming from a large fireball Rump had conjured within his hand. The children stared at the fire in awe and ceased their whimpering.

Rump scooped his free hand into the fireball. When he pulled it away, he was holding a separate, smaller ball of flame, which he dropped into Mark's outstretched palm. The sensation was odd. It was like holding a baseball that had been sitting in a pot of boiling water. Rump passed the spell around to the other Companions, until all of them wielded a fireball in their hand, powerful enough to illuminate the surrounding area.

Return to Storyworld

The bright lights of Bunkertown loomed in the distance. The city couldn't have been more than a mile away at this point. The children rejoiced, and some sprinted in the direction of the lights. The Companions shouted at them to slow down, but they might as well have been trying to halt a stampede of wild animals. The children yelled and cheered as the lights drew closer.

All of a sudden, a large boulder the size of an elephant rolled down the middle of the canyon. Screams erupted from the crowd as the children stopped yards away from the landslide. Wilma and Robin tossed away their fireballs and took up their bows.

"What's going on?" Mark asked, rushing to the front of the crowd with his fireball held high. He couldn't hear an answer over the cries of the children.

Wilma loosed an arrow into the darkness of the canyon. A distant grunt was heard, and a shadowy figure came tumbling down the canyon wall, rolling to a stop next to the fallen boulder. The children screamed louder.

"Raiders!" yelled a boy in the crowd.

Spears began raining down into the valley, coming within inches of the crowd. Wilma and Robin responded by shooting a series of arrows into the canyon walls.

"Holmes!" called out Pinocchio. "I need you, Doc, and Sir Dodger to take the children to the city. We will handle these pests."

Holmes and Doc hurried to the front of the group. Together, they ushered the children around the boulder and off toward the distant lights. Mark almost went with them, until a collection of shrieks filled the canyon. Rump threw his magical fireball into the sky, where it remained suspended in mid-air like a dim lamp, bright enough to expose the dozens of raiders hiding in the rocks. Rump took out his mace and accompanied Pinocchio and Humpty as they charged toward the horde entering the valley.

A spear came flying directly at Mark. He instinctively threw his hands up in a feeble attempt to block the attack. His fireball shot from his palm and struck the spear out of the way, sending the charred staff spinning into the distance. He stared at his hand, momentarily dumbfounded, and then regained his senses. Drawing the Hunter's Dagger from its sheath, he headed into the fray with his friends.

One of the raiders leapt from its perch and landed on a pile of stones near Mark. It resembled a mix of a bear and a man, with black fur and tattered cloth covering its body. Its face was hidden beneath a brown hood and a mass of shaggy black hair. The raider emitted an inhuman shriek and dove at Mark with its spear in the air. Mark ducked, forcing the raider to topple over his back and land face-first in the dirt.

"You were supposed to go with the children," said Pinocchio, dispatching the raider with his hammer. Mark yelled as another attacker snuck up behind the Wooden Soldier. Pinocchio swung his hammer around and sent the raider flying across the valley.

"You need all the help you can get!" said Mark.

Suddenly, he felt a pain in his chest. For a second, Mark thought he had been stabbed, but right away, he knew it was something else. The tightening in his chest, the hoarse breathing, the uncontrollable coughs; it was all too familiar. Tears formed in his eyes as he cursed himself for not quitting smoking earlier. He tried his best to ignore the pain and to keep fighting.

The Companions made their way down the valley as the skirmish progressed. In between coughs, Mark peeked back at Bunkertown to make sure the children were safe, but without any walls, he wondered what kept the raiders from overrunning the city. More of them kept coming from the canyon's shadows. The Companions would soon be overrun.

Another screech pierced the air, but it wasn't coming from the raiders this time. Robin pointed at the sky, where two figures descended into the valley. It was difficult to make out more than their silhouettes until they flew into the light of Rump's fireball. At that moment, Mark smiled in relief.

The two figures were none other than Scarecrow and Ugu the Maker, two members of the Royal Guard of Oz. They were mounted on a pair of griffins, majestic creatures with the golden bodies of lions and the feathered wings of enormous birds. Their heads were that of eagles: bold and confident, with stern eyes and thick beaks issuing more shrieks as they swooped into the canyon.

The raiders dropped their spears and grabbed their ears as they screamed in pain. Scarecrow steered his griffin into the valley, where its claws picked up the distracted raiders and threw them into each other. Ugu was close behind on his steed, firing green orbs of concussive energy from his hands. On the ground level, the Companions picked off any stragglers, but the griffins' screams were causing many of them to retreat into the shadows.

Return to Storyworld

Further down the valley, Doc and Holmes escorted the crowd of children past the towers marking the edge of Bunkertown. As they entered the city, the guards stationed at the top of the towers slammed their mallets into the giant bells. A series of loud gongs reverberated across the valley.

One of the raiders perched on a ledge delivered a series of sharp chirps. The rest of the attackers scurried away from the battle and melted into the shadows of the canyon. When the final raider disappeared, the warriors from Oz landed their griffins.

They both looked the same as when Mark had last visited Storyworld. Scarecrow wore a long brown cloak over a burlap tunic that draped down to his knees. More burlap covered his arms, and his hands were concealed within tattered brown leather gloves with bits of straw poking out from the gaps in the stitching. He wore a brown flat-brimmed hat pulled down over his burlap-sack face and hiding one of his eyes.

Ugu resembled an ordinary middle-aged man Mark would encounter in his own world. He wore a brown patchwork suit and a thin black belt with a glowing green gem at the buckle. His matching patchwork top hat was missing, revealing choppy blonde hair and rather large ears.

"Is that Sir Dodger and the Neverlanders I see?" asked Ugu.

"You guys are lifesavers," said Mark, shaking Scarecrow and Ugu's hands. "What're you doing here?"

There was a trumpet blast from Bunkertown. A handful of soldiers poured out of the city holding torches and ringing silver bells above their heads.

Return to Storyworld

Leading the group was Mayor Scrooge, wearing a helmet too big for him and carrying a chipped and rusted sword. Holmes and Doc were right behind him.

"Are the raiders gone?" demanded Scrooge, his large nose poking out from the slit in his helmet.

"We took care of them," replied Scarecrow. "Might you be the leader of this city?"

"Yes, I am Mayor Thaddeus Scrooge."

"I am Scarecrow, and this is Ugu. We are members of the Royal Guard of Oz. One of our members, Nick Chopper, was summoned here not too long ago, correct?"

Scrooge slipped off his helmet, revealing a deep frown. "Yes, Sir Chopper did come here. I had sent a raven to Oz asking for his assistance since we did not receive a Literary in time."

"And what happened to him?"

"He... he went off in search of a villainous Piper, and we have not seen nor heard from him since, I'm afraid."

"Wait, you mean Nick Chopper already went to the mountain?" asked Mark. "Why didn't you tell us? We could've searched for him while we were there."

"I was more concerned about getting my daughter back safely. To be frank, I didn't think twice about the tin man. Mercenaries come and go."

Scarecrow and Ugu both scowled at the mayor. Even Mark felt distaste for Scrooge and his matter-of-fact tone about Nick's disappearance.

Return to Storyworld

"Where did he go?" asked Scarecrow curtly.

Scrooge pointed across the town to the Adrictan Mountain, whose outline was faintly visible in the night sky. The Royal Guard of Oz hastily said their goodbyes to the Literary Companions, mounted their griffins, and set off. Mark was worried about what they would find in their search for Nick.

Scrooge eagerly invited the Companions to celebrate and rest in Bunkertown now that the children had been rescued, but Holmes insisted they return to Himshire as soon as possible. He didn't even try to mask the annoyance in his voice. Mark couldn't blame him.

"So be it," said Scrooge. "One of my guardsmen will guide you to our airfield. You can take one of our sky-ships, free of charge of course, as a thank you for your services. I hope we never have to deal with that Piper ever again."

"I can assure you, Mayor Scrooge," said Holmes, "he is gone for good."

Chapter 7

Developments in the Case

The Literary Companions were escorted through the city and taken to the very edge of Bunkertown's limits, to an isolated corner next to the canyon walls that was absent of any buildings. They arrived at a large sandy field, where a dozen sky-ships were docked against wooden platforms.

These ships resembled the *Titan*: small, wooden, and with two small masts stemming from the front and back of the deck. Unlike the *Titan*, these masts did not sport enormous wind-catching sails. They were instead topped with massive wooden propellers wider than the ships' hulls. Jutting out the back of the ships were smaller propellers with large metal blades.

Scrooge's guard emerged from the nearest ship and descended the rope ladder. Following him was a portly man with a light brown goatee, a weather-beaten face, and a head of messy orange hair. He wore a brown aviator cap with a pair of thick-rimmed goggles wrapped around his forehead, and a matching bomber jacket with white fur lining the sleeves and collar. Stitched into the back of his jacket was an elaborate design of what looked like a skyscraper with a glowing beacon on top.

"Gentlemen and lady," called out the man, leaping from the last rung of the rope and landing in the sand. "The name's Cap'n Burton. I'll be directin' ya' to Himshire this evenin'. Any questions 'fore we take off?"

Holmes went pale and gulped upon seeing the sky-ships. "To be honest, I'm not fond of heights, Captain."

"Ah, no need ta' worry," said Burton, waving his hand dismissively. "They tol' me 'bout your last ship being caught in a storm. That's the beauty of travelin' through the sky: if we run into a storm, we can fly o'er it. Now, let's getcha folks home. You mus' be tired of ol' Junkertown, as I like ta' call it."

"What do you call your ship?" asked Rump.

"I call 'er the *Spider*," said Burton happily. He pounded the bottom of the hull with his fist. The entire ship trembled, and the rear propeller briefly sputtered to life. Holmes groaned loudly.

It was around midnight by the time the *Spider* was ready to depart. Captain Burton yanked a lever near the front mast, triggering the top propellers to spin to life. As they picked up speed, they smoothly carried the ship into the air.

The *Spider* flew higher and higher, hovering over the other vessels lying dormant in the sand. There was a slight jolt (at which point Holmes nervously held onto the mast for dear life), and the ship resumed its easy transition into the sky. The moment it cleared the top of the canyon walls, the captain kicked a pedal near the steering helm, activating the rear propeller. The *Spider* chugged along at a steady pace, leisurely strolling into the clouds and off to Himshire.

Return to Storyworld

The past two days had taken their toll on the Literary Companions. They retired to the beds below deck with Burton promising them he'd wake them once they arrived. Mark collapsed onto the soft cot and let out a long sigh. The bed was so comfortable. He was ready to pass out.

But after an hour, sleep didn't come. Mark was wide-awake. His body ached and felt sore, and his eyelids drooped, but he simply couldn't get to sleep. His brain and body just wouldn't allow themselves to shut down. He needed something to relax, and he knew just where to get it.

Mark went above deck where he was welcomed by a cool midnight breeze. The *Spider* flew above the clouds and under the light of the half-moon. Burton stood at the helm while singing quietly to himself. At the rear of the ship, Holmes leaned on a wooden chest with his pipe in hand and his eyes closed. Mark crept up to the agent.

"Holmes?"

The agent opened one of his eyes and nodded. "Hook-Slayer."

"Mind if I join you up here?"

Holmes opened his other eye. "Do as you please." He inhaled from his pipe and puffed out a cloud of smoke. It took a while for him to notice Mark staring at him. He held up his pipe and gave a small grin. "Ah, okay. I should've known."

Mark eagerly took the pipe. The moment he inhaled, he felt the familiar relaxing sensation. He blew out the smoke and passed the pipe to Holmes.

"I needed that," said Mark. "That cannabis is magic."

"Well, I'd say it's more of herbalism, but I understand. If it wasn't for this, I don't know how I'd survive this flight."

"I'm guessing you feel better now?"

"Very much so," replied Holmes. "Imagine that: a man who faces crime and murder every day is terrified of flying."

"Don't feel too bad. A lot of people in my world are afraid of flying."

"What are you afraid of, Hook-Slayer?" inquired Holmes. "You haven't shown much fear since you've arrived. Caution, sure, but no fear."

Mark was hoping to go to bed after having a quick smoke, but he didn't expect the typically curt Holmes to be up for a conversation. He decided to stay around for this rare moment.

"To tell you the truth, I'm terrified of clowns," Mark let out a chuckle. When Holmes shrugged, Mark shook his head and resumed. "Never mind. But you know, the first time I came to Storyworld as a kid, I was scared of everything. I was a little coward."

"That's understandable. You were a child. I remember my Literary was a full-grown man by your standards, and even he had his share of scares during our adventures. I still get a little shaken up at times. Couldn't you tell from my fight with the Sandman's bodyguard?"

"Not at all. You seem pretty calm to me. How do you do it?"

The agent's response was to take a deep drag from the pipe. He blew the smoke out in a series of ringlets that floated off into the air. Mark rolled his eyes.

"You sure love weed, don't you?"

Holmes shrugged again. "It's a lot safer than what I used to do. My body was practically a petri dish of strange substances. I'm surprised I've lived this long."

"Well, weed *is* supposedly safer, but you don't want to become addicted to it."

"You can't become addicted to it! Who's been spreading this lie? You're not the first person to say that. My partner, Watson, used to tell me…"

Holmes went quiet. Mark realized this must've been a soft topic for the agent. He recalled Doc mentioning Watson's fatal encounter with the magical sand. Clearly, Holmes wasn't over his death yet.

"You miss him, don't you?" asked Mark.

"I don't want to talk about it." Holmes puffed out more smoke.

"Sometimes, it helps to talk about it," Mark said, throwing caution to the winds.

Holmes took another hit. "How? How does it help? Will it bring Watson back? Will it magically undo everything that's happened? Oh, do tell me how talking about it helps, *Mister Hook-Slayer*."

Mark was taken aback by the abrupt attitude. "Whoa, I'm just sayin—"

"You were brought here to guide us on the mission, not to act as my personal therapist."

Holmes emptied the ash from his pipe and stowed it in his jacket. He returned below deck, leaving a confused and annoyed Mark sitting alone.

"What's that about?" asked Burton, who had left the helm to join Mark.

Return to Storyworld

"I have no idea," said Mark absentmindedly. He anxiously glanced at the front of the ship.

Burton waved him off. "Nah, don't worry. It's a straight shot back to Himshire. No need for me ta' steer unless we hit a storm. So, is that fella' with the hat your host?"

"No, thankfully, he isn't. I guess technically Rump and Humpty are my hosts again, like they were last time."

"Last time was when you killed Captain Hook, wasn't it?"

Mark nodded. "I guess my reputation precedes me, eh?"

"Well, it's pretty hard not ta' spot the Hook-Slayer. I mean, ya' killed one of the most dangerous men in Storyworld. But it's a bit of a surprise ta' see ya' here again. I ain't heard of a Literary comin' to Storyworld twice. Usually, it's a one'n'done deal."

"Yeah, they explained it to me. They said how I had a magical aura that let me come back. I'm not sure what the deal is, so you'll have to ask them. Did you ever host anybody?"

"A while ago, yeah. Me, my twin brother, and our little sister hosted the same Literary. Couldn't tell ya' his name for the life o' me, though. All I 'member is that he loved peaches and chocolate."

Mark and Burton conversed throughout the night. He was much easier to talk to than Holmes. At one point, Humpty snuck onto the deck of the ship with *Dodger's Adventure* at his side. He sat down against one of the masts and began reading the book by moonlight. Mark waved to him. He couldn't tell since it was so dark, but it seemed as if Humpty had looked at him, and then buried his nose in the book without so much as a smile or a nod.

Burton spoke up. "So, Mr. Dodger, wha—"

"Can you please stop calling me that?!" said an annoyed Mark. "My name is Mark. Not Dodger. Not Sir Dodger. Not Mr. Dodger. Not Hook-Slayer. Just Mark Bishop. Dodger is this stupid nickname I gave myself in high school. And Hook-Slayer is an even dumber nickname Rump and Humpty gave me."

"Well, sorry for showin' respect there. I don' get how being called Hook-Slayer is dumb," said a slightly offended Burton.

"It just feels fake. I don't deserve that kind of name. I never could've killed Hook alone. All I did was stab him in the end. Everyone else did the work."

"I heard you did much more than that," said Burton. "Didn' you lead an assault to take back Neverland Castle? And didn' you beat a Stronghand by yourself? And I heard you did all that when you was a kid. People know who you are in Storyworld. They know you're the Hook-Slayer, Mr. Dodger... er... Mark."

"I... I don't like it," said Mark. "I get it's supposed to be an honor being called Hook-Slayer, but I don't feel comfortable going by that name. And Dodger reminds me of a bad time in my life. I tried really hard to put it behind me. I'm asking you to call me Mark from now on."

The conversation died quickly, leaving Burton and Mark sitting in awkward silence. Eventually, the captain returned to the helm. Mark wanted to apologize for giving him attitude, but instead, he leaned back in his seat and put his hands behind his head, watching the night sky transition into dawn.

Return to Storyworld

Mark somehow managed to fall asleep. He woke up hours later to see the rest of the Companions assembled on deck. Robin and Wilma were leaning over the railing and staring at the passing clouds. Humpty was still reading, now joined by Rump seated next to him. Pinocchio, Holmes, and Doc were at the front of the ship in a huddle around Burton and the helm.

It was early morning. The air was cold, the sun was past the horizon, and there was a light breeze rolling across the ship. Mark yawned and stretched. The few hours of sleep had done him good. He felt fully rejuvenated.

"We should be close by now," Burton yelled to the crew.

Mark peeked over the railing. There were dense clouds obscuring the view from the deck of the *Spider*. All he could see was an endless sea of gray and white. Burton pushed a lever controlling the propellers, forcing the ship to slow down and descend beneath the clouds. Mark rested his chin on his arms and continued gazing.

The clouds lifted, allowing him to see the world below. About a mile away was the city of Himshire. Mark recognized the funnel-like shape and the wide bay enclosed within steep cliffs. He also saw the three ironclad guard towers in the center of the bay. It might've been Mark's imagination, but for a moment, it seemed like the towers' cannons were aiming up at the ship.

"Hey, guys," Mark said quietly, lifting his head, "those towers guarding Himshire, how far can they shoot?"

Holmes joined Mark at the railing. His eyes widened to the size of saucers when they saw the towers. The agent spun around and sprinted to the front of the *Spider*.

"Go higher! Take the ship higher!" Holmes yelled at Burton.

Burton cocked his head in confusion. He was about to speak, when they heard a distant explosion, followed by a loud crash that shook the entire ship.

"Take the ship higher!" repeated Holmes.

Burton moved the lever to its earlier position, kicking the propellers to their full speed. The ship soared toward the clouds. There was another explosion in the distance, and a second cannonball struck the *Spider* with such force that it penetrated the bottom of the hull and shot out of the deck mere inches away from Rump.

"Grab onto somethin'!" yelled Burton.

The captain threw the wheel, and the ship spun to the left as it went higher. A third cannonball whistled through the air. It narrowly missed the *Spider*'s body, but it struck one of the propellers. The blade shattered, showering the deck with dozens of pieces of splintered wood.

With one of the propellers gone, the ship was now sinking through the air. Mark felt his stomach fluttering and his heart thumping in his throat. He wrapped his arms around the railing.

Burton yanked a handle attached to a chain behind the helm. There was a loud creak that came from below deck, along with the sound of a large cloth flapping in the wind. Two enormous fabric wings sprouted from the sides of the ship. The *Spider* stopped falling and began gliding smoothly through the air toward Himshire. The towers guarding the bay continued firing, but their cannonballs sailed past the incoming vessel.

Burton slid the goggles over his eyes and tightened his hands on the helm. "It's gonna be a rough landin', folks!"

The ship was no longer plummeting, but it was still heading to the ground at an uncomfortable speed. The fluttering in Mark's stomach lessened slightly, but his heartbeat was as rapid as ever. Burton steered the *Spider* toward a small patch of clear land on the edge of the city, near the border of the surrounding forest. It was going to be a painful hit.

Mark's teeth chattered as the ship collided hard with the tops of the trees on the edge of the forest. The *Spider* slid across the branches, carving a path along the treetops. The hull was strong enough to protect the crewmembers, but the thick, sharp tree limbs easily shredded the cloth wings to pieces.

Everyone onboard fell over when the ship came to an abrupt stop in a gathering of five short thick trees hunched together. Mark sat up and shook his head clear of leaves and twigs. Around him, the rest of the Companions were doing the same. Thankfully, nobody suffered any serious injuries. Rump was actually giggling.

"That was a little fun!"

"Not for my ship, it wasn't!" said Burton angrily. He tore off his goggles and threw his hands in the air with a grunt of frustration. One of the *Spider*'s propellers and its supporting mast had been torn off by the cannon fire, and the wings were entirely torn to shreds.

"Those damned towers!" said Wilma. "Don't worry, Captain. We'll get this sorted out."

Humpty reached underneath a hollow enclave on the deck and pulled out his copy of *Dodger's Adventure*.

"Good thing you didn't lose that," Mark said with a grin. Humpty ignored him.

The Companions disembarked the ship using the rope ladder. They were fortunate enough to have landed mere yards from the city limits. As they approached the gates, a troop of soldiers came out with their bows drawn. They were dressed in the same manner as Wilma, except their badges were silver.

"Halt! You're under arrest for trespassing on Himshire lands!" said one of the deputies. Once he saw Wilma, he lowered his bow. "Sheriff Tell! What are you doing with these intruders?"

"Stand down, Hawthorne! These are welcome visitors. Agent Holmes and I told you about the Literary mission. I want to know why the Bay Guards attacked our ship!"

"We're... we're sorry, Sheriff. Not every day we see sky-ships flying into Himshire. The Bay Guards are always on full alert."

Wilma huffed. "I'll have a word with 'em later. Right now, we've got work to do. I want you to gather the strongest people in the city to fetch this ship out of the trees. I want it down and repaired by tomorrow afternoon at the latest. And I want the Bay Guards' captain at the station tomorrow morning. Is that clear?"

Return to Storyworld

The deputies nodded in unison and vanished into the city. Wilma huffed angrily again, shaking her head. Robin stood behind her, doing his best to hide an impressed smile.

"While the ship is being taken down, we should go to the crime scene," declared Holmes. "We'll need to see if we can find more clues at the workshop."

Burton decided to stay behind with his ship until the townspeople came to help him pull it down. The Companions said their farewells and entered the city as Holmes steered them to the clockmaker's residence.

There was a huge change in the number of people in Himshire this morning compared to when Mark first arrived. Hundreds of citizens walked up and down the streets, conducting their everyday business. Similar to Bunkertown, there was a strong sense of melancholy in the air. Everyone appeared to be pleasant but distracted as they went on their ways. Many of them stared at Mark as he passed, and his response was to keep his head down. He was in a more relaxed mood thanks to the cannabis from last night, but he still felt off. A sense of foreboding crept into his mind.

The Companions hurried to the workshop. The surrounding area had fewer people milling about. Anyone passing by would make a point to steer clear of the workshop and walk on the opposite side of the road, as if they were afraid of a virus emanating from the building. There were now red banners on the door and windows, barring access. Holmes unhooked the banner on the entrance and ushered his team inside.

A dusty, congested smell hung in the air, burning Mark's nostrils and eyes. It was a sunny morning, but the workshop interior was dark and dank, and the only light came from the cracks in the window curtains.

Entering the largest room, Mark was amazed to see the walls covered in countless clocks. The sound of the synchronous ticking of the clocks was haunting, and Mark's sense of unease intensified as his eyes passed over the timepieces. In the center of the room were the shattered remains of what appeared to be a tall grandfather clock.

"What happened?" asked Mark.

Holmes reviewed his notes on the crime scene, highlighting the sand found under the body and the lack of apparent motives behind the killing.

"So what are we looking for here?" asked Pinocchio.

"Anything suspicious. We're at a dead-end with our clues. I was hoping we'd find something that could lead us the right way."

Mark was disappointed that Holmes, supposedly one of the best detectives in fiction, was practically admitting he was stumped by the case. Nevertheless, he listened to the agent's directions and started scouring a section of the workshop where the tables were buried underneath piles of papers.

Mark picked up one of the documents. It was a sketch of a square-framed clock with twelve separate hands and two gears at the top and bottom of the face. Another document featured a drawing of a clock that was apparently powered by the wind (at least, that's what the notations said). Mark kept digging through the images of clocks, noting how no two timepieces were the same, both in terms of aesthetics and mechanics.

Return to Storyworld

Something caught Mark's eye as he started on a new pile. There was one paper that stuck out from the rest. It was brown and wrinkly, and when he picked it up, it was soft as tissue paper, as if it had been folded and unfolded countless times. While the other documents were filled with clock designs with annotations here and there, this page consisted solely of text. Most of the writing was faded, and only small portions of various sentences were legible. There was a name signed in cursive at the bottom of the letter.

Abraham Van Helsing

"Hey, guys. I found something weird. It's a letter written by Abraham Van Helsing. Does that name ring a bell?"

"He's one of the town retirees," answered Wilma at once. "We're pretty familiar with him down at the station. He's always complaining about the lack of security in the city."

"I found this note from him." Mark brought the letter over to Holmes. "That whole table is nothing but drawings of clocks, but this was sitting on top of one of the piles. It looks out of place." He squinted and pressed his eyes up to the paper. "I can barely make out most of it. The writing is faded."

"Let me see," said Holmes. The agent carefully reviewed the document, tracing the lines with his fingers. "I can make out a handful of phrases. 'All is well... your fault...' and then he wrote, 'hope the clocks are coming along fine' as a post-script. This is useless." He tossed the letter over his shoulder.

"Well, hold on," said Mark, picking the paper back up. "Why is it on top of the other papers? This isn't exactly something you'd keep around your workshop. I think it was important to Giles. And feel how soft it is. He must've opened it and read it a bunch of times."

"We don't have time to analyze the clockmaker's personal affairs, unless they have to do with this case."

"But this could be a huge clue! Why can't we go visit Van Helsing? Maybe he knows what's going on? You said we were at a dead end, so what else are we supposed to do?"

"Are you a detective?" Holmes asked plainly.

Mark blinked. "What?"

"Are you a detective?" the agent repeated.

"No, I'm—"

"Then you don't know what you're talking about. I told you I'm leading the case, and I say we're not wasting our time going to Van Helsing's home."

Mark balled his fist, but kept a level head. "Look, you were the one saying how stuff is connected in Storyworld. What if this is one of those connections?"

"This is different. There are connections, and then there are wild assumptions. Even though you're a Literary, it doesn't mean you have this divine intuition that trumps my years of detective work. Now, if you're done distracting me, I have clues to find; real clues!" Holmes returned to inspecting the broken grandfather clock pieces.

Return to Storyworld

"What the hell is your problem?" Mark said boldly. He was tired of Holmes. The agent had been giving him attitude since he first arrived in Storyworld. It was like dealing with Hansel all over again, except this time, Mark wasn't going to stand for it.

"My problem," hissed Holmes, "is that every hour we don't solve this case is another hour a murderer runs free. I don't have time for your half-arsed assumptions and theories. We're not going to keep delaying our mission because of a Literary hunch."

"Well, maybe the case would've been solved a while ago if you were actually a good detective."

Holmes looked like he'd been slapped across the face. He approached Mark with a furious glare in his eyes.

"Care to say that again?" said the agent.

"Why did you need me here in the first place if you're not going to listen to my advice?" asked Mark. "Clearly, you need help, no matter how good of a detective you think you are."

"Solving a case takes time and diligence. You don't understand the first thing about detective work. It's not as easy as running into a fight, waving a dagger around. Maybe you're right. Maybe there was no point bringing you on this case…"

"And maybe if you knew what you were doing, the case would've been solved before your partner was killed."

The punch came out of nowhere. One moment, Mark was looking

Holmes in the face; the next thing he knew, he was knocked into the workshop table. Doc and Wilma held Holmes back as Rump and Robin helped Mark to his feet.

"Don't you ever speak about Watson!" roared Holmes. "Just because you're the Hook-Slayer doesn't mean you can say what you want without consequences!"

Mark didn't respond. He could taste blood on his lips.

"You both need to calm down," said Pinocchio, stepping between them. "Sir Dodger, that response was unnecessary and uncalled for. Agent Holmes, if you lay another hand on the Literary, I'll break it. Is that understood?"

Neither Mark nor Holmes spoke, though the agent relaxed and stopped fighting against his restraints. Pinocchio swiveled his head between them.

"I want you two to shake hands and to put this behind you." Again, there was no response. Pinocchio grunted. "If you do not settle this right now, King Humpty and I will handle it our own way."

Holmes snorted. "I think he's too distracted to do anything of the sort."

Their heads turned to Humpty, who was reading the last pages of *Dodger's Adventure*. When he looked up, he blushed deeply and clapped the book shut.

"My apologies, what were we talking about?"

It had been a long time since Mark heard Humpty talk, and immediately, he caught a different tone in his voice. Humpty always had a shrill, irritating way of speaking that was powerful enough to stand out and catch people's attention.

Return to Storyworld

Now, he spoke in a calm, monotone voice, but it sounded unnatural and forced.

"King Humpty, what is the matter with you?" asked Pinocchio.

"I said I was sorry," said Humpty, holding his monotone voice, but with a slightly higher volume. "I did not mean to be distracted. I was just engrossed in my reading."

"Reading? READING?!" exploded Pinocchio. Mark had never seen the Wooden Soldier lose his temper in such a manner. His eyebrows spun so fast they resembled miniature propellers. "We are in the middle of a murder investigation and you are reading?!"

"There is no need to yell, General."

Pinocchio's anger was taken over by pure bewilderment. He looked at Humpty like he was possessed. "You... something is wrong with you," he whispered.

"I am perfectly fine."

"No, you are not. You are not the same person who has stood by me all these years. You are not the King Humpty I know."

"Obviously, I am different. I am no longer the same nuisance who was once your second-in-command."

"What do you mean?" asked Pinocchio slowly.

"None of you have ever been honest with me, have you? I thought I was a respected member of Neverland. The truth is, I was nothing more than a bothersome twit."

"Where did you get such a ridiculous notion?" asked Rump.

Return to Storyworld

Humpty didn't answer. Mark saw his hands fidgeting over the cover of the book. A sudden realization dawned on him. Humpty's coldness and reclusiveness over the last couple of days finally made sense.

When Mark wrote *Dodger's Adventure*, every detail, every tiny knick, every little character flaw had been transferred onto the pages, including Humpty's strong personality. Mark had considered his attitude as bossy and annoying when he first ventured into Storyworld, and he didn't hold back when including these details in his book.

"Humpty, I'm sorry," said Mark. Everyone stared at him as he bowed his head in shame. "I was a kid. I was dumb. I shouldn't have written that stuff about you. You're not annoying or irritating. You're a great leader. I wasn't mature enough to appreciate it."

"I am a joke," said Humpty. "You said it yourself in these pages."

"I never called you a joke! I made you into a hero! I wrote about you winning the drinking contest with the giants, fighting those bounty hunters in Oz, saving Princess Tinkerbell—"

"You made numerous remarks about the silliness of my egg body! You blatantly commented on my annoying voice and irritating demeanor! I was portrayed as a fool!" A single tear silently fell from Humpty's eyes. "And you wrote of our personal conversation outside the inn, where I admitted my feelings about Princess Tinkerbell. How could you reveal that? That was personal!"

"Humpty," said Mark. He was going to explain how nobody knew Humpty was a real person, which is why it shouldn't matter what other Literaries thought about him. He was just another fictional character to the Literary world. But Mark realized that saying this might only make him feel worse.

Silence once again fell over the Companions. Mark sat down in front of the unlit fireplace with his head in his hands. He heard Humpty open the book and resume his reading without another word.

"Let's keep searching for clues," Holmes said dryly. Mark couldn't see him, but he could tell the agent was giving him a dirty glare. Robin, Rump, Wilma, and Pinocchio joined Holmes on his search. Doc came over and sat next to Mark.

"Are you okay?" he whispered.

"You should be asking Humpty, not me," said Mark.

"He will be fine. But you seem a little tense."

"I'm actually really tense," Mark said in an unintentionally snappy tone. The pleasant effects of the cannabis had worn off, returning him to his anxious, grouchy, and depressed self.

Doc pulled his flask out of his jacket and offered it. "Drink. It will help you relax."

Mark didn't need telling twice. He gladly took the flask and drank a quick gulp. The contents had a bitter, stinging taste, much stronger than whiskey, yet it was strangely soothing as it went down his throat. Mark coughed and handed back the flask.

"Good job, Doc. That's heavy stuff."

"I am a man who knows his alcohol," replied Doc, draining the remnants of the flask. Smacking his lips, he said, "Refreshing. I have not had a sip of this in weeks. I was starting to miss it. Remind me to make another batch soon."

"I never figured you to be much of a booze expert. When did you learn to make that?"

"To tell you the truth, I was not trying to make a leisurely beverage when I created it. It started out as a remedy for my amnesia. Then I realized that it may not be doing its intended job, but it has quite the delectable flavor."

"Wait, amnesia?" asked Mark.

"Yes, I suffered a head injury when I was a teenager." Doc brushed aside the hair above his left ear to reveal a long thin scar and a slight indentation in his skull.

"Yikes," said Mark, cringing.

"Oh, it does not hurt. But I *am* curious about what happened. The earliest I can remember is waking up in the medical center with a throbbing headache and absolutely no recollection of my past, aside from my name."

"That must be tough. You don't remember anything about your past life?"

"According to the orderlies at the medical center, I was found on the building steps with some nasty injuries, including this nasty gash on my head. My best educated guess is that I was robbed. Maybe it was for the best I don't remember." Doc let out a grave chuckle.

"But as I was saying, that incident inspired me to create this drink you just sampled. When I was released from the hospital, I chose to pursue an education in chemistry and medicine. My plan was to invent a potion that could help me regain my memory, and I figured I could use it on others who have suffered from amnesia as well. Unfortunately, my endeavors have been moot, and while this is a delicious drink," Doc shook the empty flask in his hand, "it is nowhere near beneficial for my condition. In fact, you could say it probably makes it worse."

"What do you mean?"

"Well, it is the strangest thing. Sometimes, when I drink this potion, I tend to get a bit carried away and black out for hours at a time. Luckily, I always make it to my bed safe and sound, oddly refreshed."

"You black out?" asked Mark uneasily. "Are you sure it's a good idea to be drinking it now? The last thing we need is you passing out when we're on a case."

Doc waved his hand. "Wilma drank that night on the Isle of Twilight and she was fine. I figured a little sip now wouldn't hurt. Do not worry about me. I am a doctor. I know how much my body can sustain."

"You know, I've been wanting to ask you for a long time. What's your full name? Which doctor are you? Are you Doctor Faust?"

"No, no," said Doc with a shake of his head. He extended his hand and said, "Doctor Henry Jekyll, at your service."

Chapter 8

Bear and the Herotians

It took a moment for the name to register in Mark's mind.

Doctor Jekyll.

Mark's jaw dropped. Thousands of thoughts and ideas clicked together in his mind. The pieces of the case were coming together. The revelation was so overwhelming that he felt lightheaded.

"Are you okay, Sir Dodger?" asked Doc.

The color had rushed out of Mark's face as he began breathing heavily. Turning to the fireplace, he retched into the hearth. The Companions ceased in their search at the sounds of the heaving. Pinocchio came over and knelt next to him.

"Are you okay? What happened?"

"I-I do not know!" stammered Doc.

"He's dangerous!" Mark sputtered in between retches. "Don't trust him!"

Doc stood up, a look of horror and confusion on his face. As he opened his mouth to speak, he suddenly grabbed at his chest and gave an inhuman roar. His body began to transform. Brown hair emerged from his skin, covering his entire body, while thick claws sprouted from his fingertips and pierced through his gloves. He bent over and clutched his stomach, revealing an enormous hunch bursting through the back of his coat. His brown hair accumulated in a thick mane around his head, and his roars transitioned into a high-pitched cackling as his teeth sharpened into fangs. The glasses fell off his face, revealing glowing yellow eyes.

"Mr. Hyde!" said Mark.

"That's my name," replied the transformed Doc with a grin. A pair of enormous black wings unfolded from his hunch. Hyde flapped them once, sending a huge burst of air across the workshop. The wind picked up the papers on the tables and threw them about, temporarily blinding the Companions.

"Don't let him get away!" called out Pinocchio.

Hyde made a break for the window, but Holmes pinned him to the wall.

"We need to restrain him!" yelled the agent, putting Hyde in a chokehold.

Pinocchio raised his hammer, but Hyde flicked him aside with one of his wings. Humpty and Rump approached him from both sides in an attempt to flank him, only to be deflected by the wings as well.

Holmes and his opponent had their arms locked around each other in a tight embrace. Hyde opened his mouth wide, as if he was about to swallow the agent's head whole, when two arrows zoomed across the workshop and pierced his wings. Holmes shot his leg out and kicked Hyde in the stomach with the heel of his boot, which sent him flying into the wall. Wilma hurried over and threw a pair of clasps onto Hyde's wrists, and then tied a length of rope around his wings so they couldn't move.

"Get him up! I want to question him!" said Holmes. He was breathing heavily and his face was red.

"I don't think he'll talk," said Mark.

"Then we're going to need to be persuasive," said Holmes, cracking his knuckles.

Mark and Pinocchio lifted Hyde off the ground and threw him in a vacant chair in the corner. Wilma and Rob stood on either side of him with their bows aimed at his head. Hyde sat motionless, grinning eerily with his eyes focused straight ahead. Mark found it unsettling how Doc's original face was recognizable beneath the transformation.

"Can anyone explain what is going on and what happened to our friend here?" asked Pinocchio.

"It was the name that gave it away," explained Mark, taking a seat across from Hyde. "Doc's Literary wrote a story about him, where he drank this potion that transformed him into a monster. Every time he drank from his flask, he thought he was blacking out, when he was actually transforming into Mr. Hyde over here."

"The Piper must've been working with Hyde," said Holmes, not taking his eyes off Hyde. "One of the children from Bunkertown told us how she saw a shadow of a man talking to the Piper. Her description of that shadow matches the features of this… thing."

"And he must've flown to the Sandman's island and stole his magical sand," added Mark.

Return to Storyworld

Hyde chuckled and licked his lips. Pinocchio thumped him on the back of the head with butt of his hammer.

Wilma gasped. "That's why the Sandman pointed at me! Remember when I stuck him with an arrow? Doc came into the clearing behind me. The Sandman musta' recognized him!"

"So this Hyde character is the one responsible for Dickory's murder, and then some," concluded Holmes.

"But wait," said Wilma. "A couple things still don't make sense. I drank his potion too, that night on the island, but I didn't turn."

"Don't you remember? You were violently sick the next morning. You probably purged it from your system."

"But that was hours later. What about now? He just drank the potion and it turned him in seconds. Shouldn't it have done the same for me?"

"Me too," said Mark. He faintly clutched at his chest, worried that he might suddenly transform as well.

Holmes was silent for a beat, scrutinizing Wilma and Mark with narrowed eyes. He crossed his arms over his chest, and his expression suddenly lit up.

"That's it!" He drew his pipe from his jacket and kissed it. "Cannabis, you are a miracle! The night before we landed on the Isle of Twilight, you and I smoked, remember? What if the cannabis negated the effects of the potion and forced your body to expel it?"

"Are you really saying that weed saved us?" Mark asked unbelievingly.

Return to Storyworld

"I'm not about to go into the science of cannabis and Doc's potion, but when you look at everything together, it makes the most sense. We can review it later. But for now…"

Holmes pulled up a chair in front of Hyde and stared into his yellow eyes. "So you flew to Bunkertown, met with Peter the Piper, went to the Isle of Twilight, took the sand, and revisited Himshire to kill the clockmaker. My question is, why? Why such a convoluted plan? What was the point of it all?"

Hyde didn't answer. He kept staring straight ahead, retaining his creepy smile. His breathing was disturbingly loud and raspy, like his lungs were filled with ash. His low chuckling was even more unsettling.

Holmes inched closer to him. "What was to gain? Why did you kill Giles Dickory?"

No answer again. Holmes took off his jacket.

"Tell me what the point of all this was. You killed the clockmaker and you killed my partner and best friend."

Hyde laughed loudly. Holmes leapt from his chair and tackled Hyde from his seat. It took the combined effort of Mark, Wilma, and Robin to pull him off. The whole time, Hyde was laughing hysterically, rolling around under the agent's grasp.

"He's still Doc! He doesn't know what he's doing! He's our friend!" pleaded Mark.

"That thing is not my friend!" cried Holmes. "My only friend was murdered by this creature!"

Return to Storyworld

"You cannot hold him accountable for his actions when he is under the potion's influence," said Pinocchio firmly.

"Rump, don't you have a spell or a potion that can reverse this?"

Before Rump could answer, Holmes firmly stated, "We're not changing him back until we get answers!"

"Aside from torture, I do not see how we can make him talk," replied Pinocchio.

Holmes scowled at Hyde and flexed his fingers, but Pinocchio held his arm out.

"We are not torturing anybody! I do not care whether you are the leader of this mission; I refuse to resort to such inhumane tactics. We will find another solution."

"A truth potion!" called a voice from the doorway.

The Companions looked up. Standing at the entrance of the workshop was a skinny man in a brown and dark blue velvet suit. He had shiny cheeks peppered with freckles and a pointy nose sitting below a pair of large blue eyes and a crown of curly blond hair.

Wilma scoffed. "This is a closed crime scene, Owlglass. Get out of here, or I'll throw you in the stocks again!"

The man called Owlglass took a step back so that he was no longer inside the building. "See! Not intruding or nothing!"

"Excuse me while I deal with this idiot," Wilma said. As she went to detain the man, he threw his hands up.

"Wait, wait! I'm here to help you! I heard you talking to that creepy guy! You need a truth potion!"

Wilma ignored his pleas as she bent his arms around his back. Owlglass howled in pain.

"Hang on," said Mark. "What do you know about a truth potion?"

As Wilma held his arm in a painful position, Owlglass said, "There's a magic school, a bit of a walk away. The potions master can give you a batch of his truth serum. One drop on the tongue and you'll be singing like a harpy!"

"Don't believe this one," said Wilma. "Nothing more than a liar and a cheap prankster. He just got out of jail for tricking a blind man into buying an 'exotic headless singing bird' a month ago."

Owlglass bit his lip, holding back his snickers. Wilma bent his arm back further.

"Where do we find this magic school? Is it in Himshire?" asked Mark.

Pinocchio's eyebrows twitched. "I am not sure of this, Sir Dodger. He does not seem trustworthy, according to Sheriff Tell's words. What kind of deviant tricks a blind man?"

"We keep hitting dead-ends," Mark whispered, "and I think we're getting desperate. What if this guy's telling the truth?"

"And what if he is not?" asked Pinocchio.

Their eyes locked in an intense gaze. Throughout his time in Storyworld, Mark knew he could always rely on Pinocchio to back him up; even now, when Humpty could hardly look at him. He hated going against the Wooden Soldier's wishes, but listening to Owlglass might be their best choice.

"The school is on the other side of the Meyern Woods," called out Owlglass. "I'll gladly take you there, if you pay me a gold piece per person."

"I swear," said Wilma through gritted teeth, "if this is another one of your scams…"

"Why can't you ever trust me?" said Owlglass, frowning.

"Because the last time I trusted you, you let two dozen chickens loose in the town hall, you rancid codpiece!"

"You have to admit that was pretty funny…"

"Stop!" Mark called out. "I say we check out the magic school and see if this truth potion is real. Holmes, what do you think?"

The agent hadn't taken his eyes off Hyde since he transformed. His response was a half-hearted grunt.

"I am not sure of this, Sir Dodger," said Pinocchio apprehensively.

Mark approached Owlglass. "We don't appreciate being tricked or being lied to. We've had enough trouble already. If you're messing with us…"

"Yes, yes, I know the deal," said Owlglass, rolling his eyes. "You'll toss me back in my cell, won't you, Sheriff?"

"Hah! You'd be so lucky! If you're pulling another one of your pranks, I'll tie you to a tree and turn your arse into a pin-cushion!" Wilma said fiercely, letting go of Owlglass.

"Now, take us to the magic school," ordered Mark."

Return to Storyworld

The Literary Companions left the workshop and accompanied Owlglass to the woods. There was a brief delay as they decided what to do with Hyde. They wanted to keep an eye on him, but they also didn't want to split up. Therefore, they agreed to bring him along on the journey.

Hyde's hands were handcuffed and his wings were bound, and he now had a rope tied around his neck as well. Holmes pulled the rope behind him while Wilma and Robin walked on either side with their bows ready. Hyde growled as he was dragged along. He was no longer smiling or laughing. Instead, he bitterly leered at Holmes. Mark thought he caught a tiny grin on the agent's face as he yanked on the leash every now and again.

As they entered the Meyern Woods, the Companions passed Captain Burton and a troop of men and women standing around a now-dismounted *Spider* leaning against a tall sprawling oak. The damage to the ship was worse from the outside. The captain waved his arms around, pointing at the scratches and yelling at a deputy frantically jotting down notes. Nobody acknowledged the Companions as they wandered into the trees.

Mark was hesitant about going into the woods after the experience on the Isle of Twilight. Fortunately, the foliage and trees in the Meyern Woods were not as dense, allowing plenty of sunlight to shine through, yet still providing ample shade to make the entire area feel cool and refreshing.

Owlglass led the Companions through the woods. There was no path or clearly defined route, so they had to weave in and out of trees, rocks, vines, and other natural obstructions. Twice, Owlglass stopped at a random tree, looked around, and then took a sharp turn to the left or right. The entire time, he was humming an off-beat tune and clapping his hands loudly.

"Not much farther now!" he called out. "Or is it further? It's farther, isn't it? I want to think it's further…"

"Shut up," Mark muttered.

The trees were spaced far enough apart for the Companions to walk through, but their higher, thicker branches were tightly wrapped around each other. Soon, the Companions found themselves underneath a natural ceiling of tangled branches intertwined so closely that hardly any light could penetrate.

Adding to the haunting darkness was the dense fog settling over the woods. It started off floating over the dirt, reaching up to Mark's knees, but as the Companions ventured further, it became more abundant and overwhelming. It was getting difficult to see in the distance, and Mark had trouble keeping an eye on Owlglass.

"This is as far as we are going!" said Pinocchio, prompting the Companions to stop.

"But we're almost there!" pleaded Owlglass.

"We can hardly see anything in this forest, and frankly, it does not seem like you know where you are going. I do not think we will find any magic school in this fog."

"This fog is part of the school's defenses! It's a super secret school. They don't want nobody wandering into their midst. But it's clearing now!"

As if by magic, the fog did indeed clear, but only within the immediate vicinity. Mark and the Companions were now standing at the center of a wide patch of dirt devoid of plant-life; no trees, no branches, no leaves, no grass. It was like all life in this part of the forest had been wiped from existence.

"Well, where is it?" demanded Pinocchio.

"It's here, and there, and everywhere!" Owlglass stated happily.

"I knew this was a waste of time!" said Wilma.

Mark was livid, but he was too embarrassed to say anything. He refused to meet Pinocchio's eyes.

"Let's get this idiot back to Himshire before I beat him senseless," said the sheriff.

The Companions turned to leave, when suddenly, the woods went deathly silent. Up until this moment, there were sounds of crickets chirping, branches settling, and the wind blowing across the treetops. All those sounds ended when Owlglass spread his arms out wide and faced the Companions.

A skeletal hand erupted from the ground, joined by another one beside it. A second pair of hands sprouted up on the other side of the clearing. Then another. A garden of hands emerged around the field, accompanied by the sounds of groaning voices and crumbling dirt. The Companions gathered in a tight huddle and stood back-to-back as Owlglass smiled at them.

The hands clawed their way out of the ground. The noise of dirt being scratched away combined with the sounds of the bony fingers creaking in unison made Mark's hair stand on end. His palms grew sweaty on the Hunter's Dagger.

One by one, more skeletons in rusty armor emerged, shaking dirt from their bodies and flexing their bony joints. Mark's heart beat faster as the closest skeleton came out from the dirt. Its bones were enormous white logs connected together by thick joints resembling pale stones. It wore a dark iron helmet that protected its entire head, except for the empty eye sockets and the discolored jawbone with missing teeth.

More skeletons appeared, carrying swords, axes, spears, and half-broken shields. One particular figure stood out among the rest as it burst from the patch of land in front of Pinocchio.

This skeleton was at least eight feet in height, towering over the Wooden Soldier. It wore no armor aside from metal shin-plates, rusted gauntlets, and a gray loincloth. Its chest was wide, and its visible ribcage was big enough to encase Rump if he were curled into a ball. Out of all the skeletons, this one was the freshest and had retained most of its skin, which was a mixture of a moldy gray and green, like it had been left to rot in water for eons. Waxy gray skin stretched tightly over its large skull, and its lips had rotted away, displaying a set of chipped teeth. Wisps of gray hair matted with dirt clods popped out of its exposed cranium.

The giant skeleton wielded a sword as large as its body, and just as decayed and rotted. When it raised its blade in the air, the other skeletons formed a circle around the Companions. Every step they took and every movement they made was accompanied by the eerie cracking sounds of their old bones.

Owlglass approached the giant skeleton. "I brought you the goodies, Bear!"

"So you have," croaked the giant, his mouth clicking with each syllable.

"Can I have my payments now?"

Bear lifted his sword and sliced it across the air in one fluid motion. There was a brief pause, and then Owlglass's head toppled off and rolled on the ground, a grin permanently etched on his face.

The skeletons roared in laughter, creating a symphony of clicking sounds with their jaws. Bear lightly tipped Owlglass's still-standing body aside and approached Pinocchio. The general did not blink nor show signs of fear, but his hands tightened on the grip of his hammer.

"You have a Literary," said Bear.

"It does not concern you who is in my party," replied the Wooden Soldier.

"It *does* concern me. If one were to slay a Literary, they would be granted omniscient abilities. That Literary's death can give me unmatchable power, especially considering he is the Hook-Slayer. I want that power."

"If you want him, you will have to go through us," stated Pinocchio. Rump tugged Mark into the center of the group.

"Do not think you are a threat to us, Pinocchio," said Bear calmly. "We know who you are as well, and we are fully aware of your feats. Though you lead one of the strongest military arms in the realm, it does not mean you are a match for me and my army of Herotians."

"Shall we test this theory of yours?" asked Pinocchio, raising his hammer to his chest.

Bear examined the weapon. "The hammer of the Midnight Marauder. A formidable weapon, but no match for my Hrunting."

"The sword so powerful that six Stronghands could not carry it," quoted Pinocchio.

Bear nodded. "Now, submit the Literary to me, or—"

Two arrows flew over Pinocchio's shoulder and sailed into Bear's head.

"You want him?" said Robin, preparing to fire again. "Come get him!"

Bear calmly removed both arrows and tossed them away, making Robin's smirk vanish.

"Oh, damn," muttered the archer.

Bear bellowed so loudly the entire clearing shook. His army of Herotians yelled in unison and charged at his command.

Mark dove dagger-first at a thick Herotian running at him. The blade went between two of the skeleton's ribs, not having any effect on it. The Herotian laughed and lifted a rusted axe. Holmes appeared behind it, grabbed the arm holding the axe, and twisted it in its socket. A disturbingly loud crack was heard as the shoulder splintered apart, separating the arm from the torso. Holmes threw the arm to the ground, but he didn't see the Herotian behind him with another blade in its remaining hand. Mark shouldered the agent out of the way and swung his dagger, decapitating the skeleton. When he took a step back, he accidentally stepped on the skull and crushed it into pieces. The Herotian's body crumpled.

"The heads! Destroy the heads!" yelled Mark.

Holmes swore loudly. Mark turned and saw Hyde's wings burst from their bindings. As he took flight, one of the Herotians came at him with its sword raised. Hyde responded by grabbing its skull with his bound hands and squeezing it to dust. He took off as the Herotian's body fell.

"We'll worry about him later!" Mark reassured Holmes.

More Herotians engaged the Companions in battle. Wilma and Robin sheathed their bows and armed themselves with their daggers. Any skeletons that came near them received a swift stab through the head. Rump, whose height kept him from reaching above the Herotians' torso, ran around swiping at the skeletons' knees with his mace. Once they fell, he would crush their heads with his weapon or stomp on them with both his feet.

For a moment, it seemed like Humpty was not going to fight as he clutched the copy of *Dodger's Adventure* to his chest. Then the king stuffed the book down the front of his shirt and unsheathed both of his swords. With lightning-fast reflexes, he carved his way through a column of Herotians about to flank Rump. One skeleton tried to sneak up on him with a spear, until Holmes came to the rescue and obliterated its head with a downward smash of his elbow.

Mark's chest started to tighten. *No, not now*, he thought, kicking a fallen Herotian's skull into pieces. He fought against the fierce cough fighting its way up his throat. Another Herotian was charging at him, swinging its sword wildly above its head. Mark raised his dagger, ready to defend himself, but he couldn't hold it in any longer. He doubled over in a series of massive coughs as the Herotian bore down on him.

Someone vaulted over his back. Mark quickly looked up as Humpty bowled into the skeleton. He yelled as he punched the Herotian's skull into the dirt. Mark coughed out his thanks, but Humpty returned to battle without a word.

Pinocchio and Bear were locked in intense combat. Bear's attacks were vastly different than any of the Neverland warriors' fighting tactics. Whereas Pinocchio and Humpty relied on nimble dodging and swift reflexes to outwit their opponents, Bear's entire strategy was based on pure aggression. He seemed to be putting his entire strength and the weight of Hrunting into every single attack. This would throw him off balance, allowing Pinocchio to strike him with the hammer, but the Herotian's tough bones hardly took any damage.

Bear also didn't mind collateral damage. Occasionally, one of his Herotians would wander too closely to the fight, only to be battered away by their leader's vicious swings. Bear was almost defeating more of his own soldiers than the Companions were, which Pinocchio used to his own advantage. He enticed Bear to attack him, and then leapt out of the way at the last second, letting the sword behead three adjacent Herotians.

The fight caught Mark's attention. He felt a sense of déjà vu. It was strangely reminiscent of another battle he witnessed ten years ago.

"Watch out, Sir Dodger!" called Pinocchio.

Mark didn't realize how close he was to the combatants until Bear slashed Hrunting in a circular arc that threatened to take off his head. He ducked, allowing the corroded blade to skim mere inches over his hair. When he stood up, he didn't notice Bear continuing the swing. Mark threw the dagger up in defense as Hrunting came soaring back at him. Pinocchio swung his hammer down, forcing the point of Hrunting's blade to the ground. Unfortunately, Pinocchio was a split-second too late; Bear's sword struck the Hunter's Dagger so hard that it cracked into two pieces and knocked Mark onto his back.

Bear stared into the Pinocchio's eyes and released a loud roar. Pinocchio grabbed the Herotian's lower jaw and yanked it off his skull. Bear let go of his sword and grabbed at his mouth. The Wooden Soldier swung his hammer down with all his might onto his opponent's skull, crushing it into fragments. Bear's headless body sank to its knees.

"Are you okay, Sir Dodger?" asked Pinocchio

Mark pointed over his shoulder and yelled, "Look OUT!"

It was too late. Bear's headless corpse rose from its knees and latched its hands tightly onto Pinocchio's upper arms. He tried to kick his way free, but Bear's hold was too strong. Mark was paralyzed with fright and watched in horror as the scene unfolded.

Bear tightened the grip on Pinocchio's arms, splintering them to pieces. The Wooden Soldier cried out and made one last attempt to wriggle free of the grip, but it was no use. It was at that moment Mark saw something in Pinocchio's eyes that he had never seen before: hopelessness.

"Dodger..." he said gravely.

Bear dropped Pinocchio, then opened his arms wide and clapped them fiercely together on his head, crushing it into dust. His lifeless body collapsed to the dirt.

"NO!" cried Mark.

Time slowed down at that point. The field went quiet, though the

Return to Storyworld

Companions were still battling the Herotians. Mark couldn't grasp where he was or what was happening. He could only stare at Pinocchio's fallen body.

The headless Bear bent down to pick up Hrunting. Nearby, Humpty had fallen to his knees, his face frozen in shock. Rump, however, didn't look sad or terrified. Mark had never seen this expression on the alchemist's face, but he knew what it was: pure, bottomless rage.

Bear had retrieved Hrunting and was now slowly advancing on Mark. Rump threw down his mace and removed every single vial from his belt. He took them all and pressed them together in his hands. The glass shattered, and multicolored liquids and blood seeped from the alchemist's hands. He closed his eyes as Bear was readying his sword.

When Rump's eyes burst open, they had become a shocking white. He threw his hands up to the sky and formed a large ball of cackling white energy in his palms. Bear raised his sword for one final strike, and Rump threw the energy ball at him.

A blinding light enveloped the area, so bright that Mark had to close his eyes as a thunderous roar pounded in his ears.

In an instant, the roaring stopped completely, and the woods reverted to their original tranquil state. Mark opened his eyes to see the fog had cleared. The field was dark and littered with the bodies of Herotians. Humpty, and Rump were huddled around the body of Pinocchio as Holmes and Wilma stood by, looking on solemnly. There was no sign of Bear. All that was left was a shard of rusted metal and a small pile of dust.

Return to Storyworld

Mark sat with his friends and stared at what was left of Pinocchio. No words were said, and everybody's face had the same look of hopelessness that Mark saw in Pinocchio's eyes as he said his last word.

Chapter 9

Revealing the Past

"I… I cannot believe he is gone," Humpty said quietly.

The Literary Companions had taken the time to dig a grave for their fallen friend. Wilma asked if they wanted to have a convoy deliver his body home so he could be laid to rest in Neverland. Humpty and Rump said Pinocchio had told them long ago how he wanted to be buried where he was slain if he ever died in battle; so the Companions spent hours digging a grave in that field.

Nobody cared about the case at this point. It didn't matter if they were behind schedule, or if they had run out of clues, or the fact that Hyde had escaped in the midst of battle. Pinocchio was dead, and he deserved the proper respects.

Once they laid the Wooden Soldier inside his grave, Mark went to place the war hammer on his chest, but Rump stopped him.

"You lost your dagger in battle. Hold onto the hammer."

"I… I can't. I wouldn't feel right taking it."

"General Pinocchio acquired the weapon from another defeated warrior many years ago. Consider it an inheritance," assured Humpty.

"No, I don't deserv—"

"Enough!" snapped Rump. "You'll take the hammer as your own! You earned it, and you have as much right to it as Pinocchio did."

Mark didn't answer and merely glared at Rump. He dropped the hammer carelessly into the grave. The alchemist looked furious, but it was Humpty who grabbed Mark by the collar of his shirt.

"Listen, Sir Dodger! You might think I am annoying and irritating, but I do not care anymore! As King of Neverland, I order you to take the hammer out of the grave and to bring it with you as your own weapon."

Mark broke free from Humpty's grasp and grabbed him by his own collar. The other Companions stood up, and Robin reached for an arrow, but Humpty held his hand up to stop them.

"I told you I'm not a hero or the Hook-Slayer or whatever you expect me to be, you idiot," said Mark through gritted teeth. "I'm a screw-up! I'm not taking Pinocchio's hammer. It was my fault he died."

"It was *our* fault," corrected Humpty in a calm tone. "We are as much to blame as you are."

Mark dropped Humpty and swore to himself. He walked back over to the grave and sat down, burying his head in his hands. He felt numb, and his head was swimming.

Rump knelt next to Mark. "What happened since your last trip to Storyworld?"

"What do you mean?" mumbled Mark, not lifting his head.

"Something has happened to you; something hurting you inside. I don't need magic to tell me you've been in pain since you arrived in Storyworld a few days ago. Why are you taking the blame for Pinocchio's death? Why all the guilt?"

Mark sighed. "Do you guys remember how you found me in my old house a couple days ago? I came back because… because my parents died. I stopped talking to them ten years ago. I never got to say goodbye. We faded out of each other's lives, and it was my fault. It was all my fault."

A single tear rolled down Mark's cheek. Aside from Amy, he had never told anyone about his relationship with his parents. He was afraid it would hurt him too much. But he had to say it now. He had to experience that pain. He deserved it.

"It was my fault," he repeated, "just like it was my fault what happened with my wife."

"You were married?" asked Humpty.

Mark nodded. "To a great girl, named Amy. She was amazing. We had this… connection, right off the bat. We were made for each other. I mean, we were in love. Simple as that. But I went and screwed it up.

"This one day, I got a call from this girl I knew in college. She asked me to come help her out with a book signing. One thing led to another, and the next thing I knew, we were kissing. I… I cheated on my wife!"

Mark expected to see disgusted frowns and scowls from the Companions, but instead, he was met with curious gazes.

"What happened then? Did you tell your wife?" asked Rump.

"Of course I did. I told her exactly what happened. I knew I messed up, but the damage was done."

"And did she leave you?"

"No. Worse. She forgave me."

"Well, now I'm confused. It sounds like she understood it was a mistake."

"No, it wasn't a mistake. It was a disaster. My wife trusted me. She was good to me, and I betrayed her trust. Then, when she forgave me, it felt worse. It made me mad that she'd let it go. I didn't deserve her.

"I figured the best way to avoid hurting her again was to kick myself out of her life. I was running away from my problems again, just like I did when I was a kid and I moved out of my parents' house."

There was silence. None of the Companions said anything, though Rump patted Mark on the shoulder. It was a surprise when Wilma came over and sat with them as well.

"Mistakes happen, in both our worlds. It's not about your mistakes; it's about learning from them. Sounds to me like you sure learned from your mistake, so why let it hang over your head?"

Mark didn't answer. He merely stared into Pinocchio's grave.

"If anyone knows about mistakes, it'd be me," said Wilma. "Did you know I never said goodbye to my brother 'fore he left for Neverland? I had to say my farewells to his body when we buried him. Not a day goes by where I don't think about poor John or my stubbornness."

"What happened between you two?" asked Mark.

"We were never that close to begin with. We got into an argument one day, and my big mouth told him I didn't want to see him again. That was the same day he left to join Neverland. We... we never really spoke again." Wilma wiped her eye on her sleeve. "You can imagine how I felt when I heard about his death."

"But it was a mistake what you said to him. You didn't really mean that."

"Exactly. A mistake, a dumb one at that. We all make 'em. And not letting go of those mistakes leads to regret. We can't let that hang over our heads forever. We move on. We try to become better people. It's hard to move on when you're too busy dwellin' on the past."

"She's right," added Holmes, his hands buried in his pockets. "I'll admit, I haven't been myself lately. Ever since Watson died, it's been like walking through a haze. It's interfering with the way I think, and it's been hurting my detective work. I should've known Jekyll was the culprit."

"He was your partner," said Rump. "Why would you suspect him?"

"He was an associate and nothing more!" Holmes said forcefully. "Watson is the only man I ever truly considered a worthy partner. He was a better man than any of us. He deserves vengeance."

"Is that why we're all on this case?" asked Mark. "Because you want justice for Watson?"

Holmes nodded. "I owe him my life. If it weren't for him, I would've died at the hands of Professor Moriarty at Richter Falls. After my wife died and my son abandoned me, Watson stayed by my side. But I don't think he knew how much I appreciated him.

"I regret not letting Watson know how great a friend he was, and I regret not being able to save him. But regret is a nasty disease. I should know better than to let it affect me so."

Rump shrugged. "If I had a gold piece for every mistake I've made and every regret from my youth, I'd have enough money to buy my own kingdom."

"I have to agree with them," said Robin. "You're being too hard on yourself, Sir Dodger. We've all made mistakes, some grave and some minor. Do I have to remind you of all the things I regret from when I was a rogue in Neverwood Forest?"

"Or that time in weapons training when you misfired your arrow and struck General Pinocchio in the hindquarters?" commented Humpty.

Robin scowled at Humpty, who sat there with a straight face. After a few seconds of silence, he cracked a wide smile and let out a laugh. The other Companions joined in one-by-one, and they all proceeded to laugh. Mark gave a half-hearted smile. He felt slightly better. This was the first time he had opened up about everything that had gone on in his life since he and Amy separated. It was almost therapeutic.

"You are a good person, Sir Dodger," Humpty said to Mark quietly once the laughter had died down. "No matter what mistakes you have made in the past, you have the power to do good. We believe in you."

Mark merely nodded and gave a another small smile.

"Now, I think it's time we get back to the mission, eh?" said Wilma.

"But we're at a dead end," Mark said, his spirits dampening. "Hyde got away, and we don't have any other clues from the workshop."

Return to Storyworld

"On the contrary, you found a very important clue, my good sir," said Holmes. He pulled out the ancient letter Mark found earlier. "I think we should listen to your lead and pay a visit to Abraham Van Helsing. He could shed some light on the case."

"Then let us stop dawdling and start doing!" called out Humpty. The Companions were mildly surprised at the king's unexpected burst of positivity. He met their confused stares and said, "Why are you looking at me so strangely? We have a mission to complete!"

The Literary Companions finished burying Pinocchio (after Mark had taken the war hammer out of the grave), gave one final salute to the Wooden Soldier, and left the clearing in a hurry. The bodies of the dead Herotians had begun crumbling and decaying into dust, and the stench was overwhelming. Humpty unsheathed his swords and carved through the forest with the Companions close behind.

A light shone in between the trees roughly a half-mile ahead. Humpty quickened his pace and wove in and out of trees as they became more spaced apart. Suddenly, he stopped in his tracks. As Mark caught up to him, he dropped his swords.

"What's the matter?" asked Mark, skidding to a halt. Humpty was as pale as a ghost. Mark followed his gaze and saw a horrific scene on the edge of the woods.

Dozens of corpses lay around the damaged hull of the *Spider*. They were

Return to Storyworld

the bodies of the Himshire citizens who had come to pull the ship down. Scattered among the group was a handful of Himshire's deputies, all with claw marks across their chests and faces. The *Spider* itself had been torn to shreds. All that was left was the frame of the hull and pieces of the railings. The masts and wings had been ripped off the ship and broken into dozens of pieces. The back propeller lay in the middle of three bodies with half its blades missing.

"Captain Burton!" cried out Robin.

The Companions ran to the front of the ship where the captain's corpse was slouched against the hull. His jacket had been shredded open, revealing bloody scratches along his arms and chest.

"Hyde! Hyde did this!" growled Holmes.

"Where do you think he went?"

Holmes pointed to the semi-destroyed *Spider* and said, "He took the time to wreck the sky-ship, meaning he doesn't want us following him. He also knows we're aware of his partnering with the Piper. He's heading to the Adrictan Mountain."

"We gotta get there before him!" declared Mark.

"Without a ship?" said Robin. "There's no way we can catch up to a man who can fly. And we don't even know if he's truly going to that mountain. There are millions of places he could be."

Holmes couldn't answer; neither could Mark.

"He has a point," stated Rump. "I think we should follow the earlier lead and meet with Van Helsing first. He might be our strongest clue at this time."

Return to Storyworld

Mark attempted to keep his frustration from getting to him. More people were dying in Hyde's wake, and he could be anywhere, wreaking more havoc. But Rump was right. Their best course of action would be to see what Van Helsing had to say.

"Fine. Let's go see him."

Wilma led the Companions through the city to a small sectioned-off district close to the shipyard. Along the way, she stopped a passing deputy and informed him of the situation with the *Spider*. The shocked deputy hurried off to gather a team to investigate the scene.

"What's Van Helsing like?" asked Mark as they walked down the cobblestone path.

"He keeps to himself in his cottage. Only time I've talked to him is when he came to the station askin' for more security. Old Abe is a paranoid one..."

"What do you know of him in the Literary world?" asked Holmes.

"I don't remember much, but I think he had something to do with vampires." The color drained out of Mark's face. "You don't think we're going to be dealing with vampires, are we?"

"Very unlikely. The last of the vampire herds vanished in the Dawn-Break Migration years ago. They haven't been seen in these parts since."

"Around this bend," said Wilma, pointing at a curve in the road ahead. The Companions walked down the street and arrived at a dead end, where they were greeted by a tiny hovel wedged in between a pair of three-story buildings.

Holmes knocked on the door three times. There was no answer. Wilma knocked next, stating her name and title. The door creaked open an inch. A gray eye peered through the crack.

"What is it, Sheriff?" came the voice of an elderly man.

"Can you open the door, Abe? We have some questions for ya'."

The gray eye blinked twice. The door swung open, revealing a short middle-aged man. He had combed-over brown hair with signs of gray in various spots, and a patchy five o'clock shadow with a matching color scheme. There was a deep dimple in the middle of his round chin and two more in his cheeks. His flat nose, pinned-back ears, and tiny puckered mouth along with his protruding belly made him look pig-like. He wore brown wool pants and a matching vest over his white button-down shirt, and his small feet were tucked into black slippers. He stepped aside and welcomed the Companions into his home.

There was a heavy odor lingering in the air that smelled like a mix of sweat and smoke. Mark was impressed by the assortment of what was apparently vampire-hunting memorabilia decorating the building. Van Helsing's collection included a line of wooden stakes of varying sizes, a miniature crossbow, blood-stained daggers, chipped axes and swords, a torn cloak with frayed edges, shrunken heads with large fangs and no eyes, and finally, a pale, rotted corpse nailed to the wall by its hands and feet with its head concealed in a metal mask with a padlock on its side An overgrown crossbow loaded with an arrow the size of a javelin sat nearby, aimed directly at the creature's chest.

"Why do you keep the body here if you're paranoid?" asked Wilma.

Return to Storyworld

"It's a relic from my adventures. Then again, it never hurts to be prepared," wheezed Van Helsing.

"You take pride in your past work, no?" Holmes asked matter-of-factly. He picked up a nearby journal and skimmed through it.

"Well, not everyone can say they defeated Lord Dracula. Of course I would take pride in such a feat." Van Helsing seated himself and crossed his legs. "So, what can I do for you?"

Mark was going to ask about the letter they found in the workshop, but Holmes shushed him. The agent narrowed his eyes at Van Helsing as he spoke.

"You heard the town clockmaker, Giles Dickory, was murdered recently."

"Yes, yes, it's very sad. I planned to buy a clock from him."

"Really? Did you happen to have any other relation to Mr. Dickory other than as a customer?"

Van Helsing blinked. "What? What do you mean? What relation? I might've met him in the marketplace or tavern, but other than that, I have no—"

"Mr. Van Helsing," said Holmes, "you understand lying during an investigation is illegal, especially when it revolves around a murder case."

Van Helsing now looked offended. "I beg your pardon! What grounds do you have to be making such accusations?"

Holmes produced the letter from the workshop. Van Helsing instantly went as pale as the corpse on the wall.

"No idea what that is," he said in a poor attempt to keep his voice calm.

"I don't have the patience for this, Van Helsing! The handwriting on this letter is yours. I matched it to the writing inside your journal."

"I have no idea where that letter came from!" Van Helsing said indignantly. "I wanted to buy a clock from Dickory! Why do I care who killed him?"

"You're wearing a watch and you have a perfectly functioning clock next to your bed," said Holmes. "You have no need for a clock, especially one of Dickory's expensive handcrafted pieces. Now, for the last time, what do you know about Dickory's dea—"

"Look out!" shouted Mark.

Holmes had already grabbed Van Helsing's wrist. He attempted to pry a long dagger from the old man's grip. Mark went to help as well, but he noticed something odd. Van Helsing wasn't trying to attack the agent; he was aiming the blade at his own neck and struggling to stab himself. Holmes managed to yank it out of his fingers and threw it aside.

"This won't be simple for either of us," huffed Holmes. He pulled a pair of metal clasps from his belt and threw them over Van Helsing's wrists.

"No, please! Please don't ask me again!" wailed the man.

"Tell us, or we throw you in a cell for obstruction of justice!" said Wilma.

"Then take me to prison!" begged Van Helsing. "Take me to prison, or execute me. Just please, don't make me tell you!" He threw himself on the ground and began to cry.

Wilma and Holmes were baffled, as were the other Companions. Van

Helsing sobbed and repeated his pleas over and over. Mark knelt down next to the man.

"You're afraid of something, or someone, aren't you? Is that why you can't tell us?"

After a pause, Van Helsing nodded, tears flowing from his eyes.

"Is it Mr. Hyde?" Mark asked.

At the mention of the name, Van Helsing stopped sobbing. "You... you know of him?"

"Yeah. He's been on our case, but we've known him as Doctor Jekyll. He changed into Mr. Hyde and escaped a couple of hours ago. We want to know how he tied into the clockmaker's murder."

The horror in Van Helsing's face intensified. Mark knew this man held the information they needed.

"Whatever it is, we can help you," reassured Mark. "We don't want to see anybody else get hurt. We can probably stop Hyde if you tell us what you know."

Van Helsing spoke in a quivering voice. "My family has to be protected. He threatened to kill them if I said anything."

"I can get a team of deputies here in five minutes," said Wilma. "They'll guard your family night and day."

"They're not in Himshire. They're in my home city, Olympia. They have no idea of the danger I put them in." He took a deep breath. "I will tell you what I know, but you must promise me one thing."

"Name it."

Return to Storyworld

"If I tell you, you must not put me in jail. I need to go to Olympia to be with my family. Once I reveal everything, they will no longer be safe."

Wilma looked uncertain for a moment, but she eventually said, "Fine, I won't arrest you. You have my word as Sheriff of Himshire. But your information better be useful."

Van Helsing gave a sigh of both relief and exhaustion. He sat back in his chair and allowed Holmes to unlock his clasps. Once his hands were free, he sighed again and placed them on his lap.

"Doctor Jekyll, Giles Dickory, and I have a long history together."

Chapter 10

The Confession

"Prior to my adventures as a vampire hunter, I was a scientist," began Van Helsing. "A scientist with a keen interest in the study of the human body. I had always been fascinated with our unique anatomy and how we came to be, so I made it my goal to find out all about life.

"When I attended the Barzdath Academy of Science, I met a man named Giles Dickory, who shared my interest in the concept of life, albeit in a different manner. Giles was the son of a clockmaker, and he believed that life moved similarly to a clock. He wanted to learn more about what made humans tick, so to speak. So together, we studied topics such as anatomy, physiology, biology, and countless other subjects revolving around life.

"During our schooling, we also took extensive philosophy and history classes. We learned about the creation of existence and the Builder. I assume you know about the concept of the life-force?"

Mark glanced at Rump and Humpty before nodding at Van Helsing to resume.

"Our professor taught us how magickers and alchemists have attempted to replicate the process in the past, and how they've failed in their endeavors. At the time of our education, the most recent person to attempt this magic was a being dubbed the Sandman."

The Literary Companions gasped in unison.

Van Helsing gave a dark smile. "You're aware of this man, yes? We learned how the Sandman was chased from his home when a rumor had spread that he almost cracked the forbidden Builder formula, the ability to manipulate the life-force. Rather than wait around to be arrested, he escaped to the Isle of Twilight, where he resides to this day."

"When you say manipulate the life-force..." said Mark.

"I mean exactly that," responded Van Helsing. "The Builder could create life, end life, and essentially control the life-force as he pleased."

Van Helsing paused for a moment to peek out the window, then resumed.

"Giles and I idolized the Sandman for supposedly deducing the legendary formula. We wanted to be Builders as well. We wanted to control life, and in order to do that, we needed that magic sand.

"Luck was with us, for Giles was graced with the presence of a Literary. The three of us, along with our assistant, Henry, ventured to the Isle of Twilight to retrieve our prize.

"There was some... trouble... acquiring the sand," Van Helsing, said in a bitter tone. "The Sandman wasn't very welcoming of visitors, and he warned us how the sand itself wasn't enough to complete the Builder formula. We offered to bring him with us to assist in the experiment, but he was very dismissive and sent us away. But our Literary snuck back later that night to steal a batch of sand.

Return to Storyworld

"Now that we had the magic ingredient, we assumed the hardest part was over. All we needed was a test subject: a corpse. But this proved to be more difficult to procure than the sand. We went to local morgues and graveyards asking for cadavers to use for our experiment, but we were shooed away when we didn't tell them our plans. We were also struggling to find building materials, like wood and metal, and a suitable workshop. Things were getting bleak, but once again, luck found us.

"We were leaving the graveyard, distraught, when a dwarf approached us, claiming he had overheard our predicament. He told us how he and his brothers lived in a nearby mountain filled with the corpses of lost travelers and treasure-hunters. This mountainous graveyard was practically ripe for the picking. There were also plenty of metals to be mined and collected from the caverns, which was why the dwarf and his brethren had settled there. We had found a place to set up our workshop!"

Something about this story sounded uncomfortably familiar to Mark. He leaned in and listened more intently as Van Helsing shifted in his seat and returned to the story.

"Giles, his Literary, myself, and Henry went to the Adrictan Mountain, near the trade settlement of Bunkertown—"

The Companions gasped again.

"Ah, you've heard of that as well. Then you know about the cave-master, Peter the Piper, yes? He told us how he had lived in the mountain for a long time, and that he had become a sort-of leader to the dwarves. They did as he commanded, and in exchange, he taught them special kinds of magic. An unusual dynamic, but we were not about to question our hosts.

"Peter welcomed us to his home and told us he'd be happy to lend us the mountain, but in exchange, we had to tell them exactly what we were planning. We initially kept our experiment a very close-guarded secret since it's highly illegal to practice life-force magic. At that time, the only people who knew what we were up to were myself, Giles, Henry, and our Literary, and it should've remained that way. But we went against our instincts and told the Piper as payment for his hospitality.

"It took us months to complete the construction of our workshop, even with the dwarves' assistance. Once that was set up, we found a suitable corpse from one of the caverns, pieced it together the best we could with metal and cloth, and we officially had our test subject. Now we just needed to give it life!"

A knot formed in Mark's stomach. Each sentence of the story was like a step on a ladder, and each step made him more anxious. He beckoned Van Helsing to go on with his tale.

"We prepared the revival apparatus and placed the magic sand on the body, assuming it would instantly bring it to life. You can imagine our disappointment when nothing happened. Giles and I returned to our blueprints and conducted another month's worth of research. Wouldn't you believe it, our solution came in the form of a lightning storm.

"Giles noted how lightning carried a surge of energy with it, and that energy might have been exactly what we needed to spark our creation to life. But our workshop was in a poor location. We were bound within the mountain, with no access to the sky. Henry suggested we travel to the Dronos Caves, up in the mountains near Arcadia. These were the highest peaks in the region, and they were sure to get us close to the lightning.

"Because we no longer needed their services, we bid farewell to Peter and his dwarves. But that wouldn't be the last we heard of them.

"We found a perfect spot to assemble our apparatus for our second attempt at the experiment. My fear was that we were too close to the city of Arcadia. I didn't want anyone wandering into the area and stumbling upon our experiment, or else we would be arrested. Little did we know, we were about to have much bigger problems."

Van Helsing took a deep breath. "The experiment... it worked. After weeks of waiting, a storm settled in. Lightning struck the top of our machine, and our creature came to life. It was outstanding. We had created a living, sentient being."

Mark noticed Van Helsing's eyes starting to water. "Something bad happened, didn't it? Something really bad."

Van Helsing nodded. "It was horrible. Peter and the dwarves had followed us. They were spying on our experiment. The moment our creation came to life, they surrounded us and said they were going to take it back to the Adrictan Mountain, for whatever reason.

"When the dwarves attacked us, it must've triggered a defense mechanism in the creature. It broke free from its restraints and went berserk. It was a truly terrible and fearsome sight. Imagine the mentality of an infant combined with the strength of ten rampaging Stronghands.

"In the midst of this episode, our assistant was struck in the head by a large rock, supposedly killing him. Then our creature escaped the cavern, and when it went outside, it must've been attracted to the lights and sounds coming from Arcadia at the bottom of the mountain. We were unable to stop it from charging down the valley and running amok in the city.

"Hundreds of people died in the rampage. Men, women and children fell prey to the monster. Had it not been for the combined effort of Giles, his Literary, and myself, we never would've been able to stop it. Sadly, by the time the creature was slain, the damage had been done.

"Giles took full responsibility for the incident and forbade me from ever telling anybody the truth. Rather than submit himself to the authorities, he escaped Arcadia and decided to pursue a new life in Himshire under a new name and a new identity."

"Wait, what was his new name?" asked Mark.

"Sorry," said Van Helsing. "Giles Dickory *was* his new name. His real name was Victor Frankenstein."

Mark was the only person who gasped this time.

"Before he left," continued Van Helsing, "he wanted to make sure he settled his affairs first. He and I went up to the cavern to destroy the machine for good. While we were up there, we discovered that Henry had survived the attack, albeit with significant brain damage. He woke up with no recollection of what happened, and Giles decided it best to keep it that way. He said he would take Henry with him to Himshire, where he could start a new life and not be burdened by the same guilt that plagued Giles and myself. Giles told me he left Henry at the medical center with a note stating his full name."

"Henry Jekyll," said Mark. The Companions gasped a third time. "This definitely explains a lot."

"There is more," admitted Van Helsing. "What I am about to tell you is the reason I requested immunity from legal ramifications, at least until I can make sure my family is safe. I am partially responsible for the death of Giles Dickory."

There was a moment of silence. Van Helsing looked like he was about to sob again, but he held his composure. He spoke in a calm and steady voice.

"Giles and I kept in touch over the years, as you can tell from that letter. I found out about his residency in Himshire, and that he had once again taken up clock-making for a living. At the same time, he secretly kept an eye on Henry, who had gone on to become a chemist and a doctor. After spending many years hunting vampires and hosting my own Literary, I too moved to Himshire to be closer to my old friend, and to also keep watch over Henry from afar.

"My first night here, I heard an intruder lurking in this room. I came out to investigate and found what I thought was a demon. But upon closer inspection, I recognized the familiar face behind the mane of hair, the sharpened fangs, and the yellow eyes. The man called himself Mr. Hyde, but I knew he was really Henry Jekyll underneath.

"Hyde told me he remembered me. He said he had developed a cure for his amnesia, but the problem was that it transformed him into the monster I saw before me. The potion he drank not only unlocked his memories, but it unlocked a beast within him as well.

"Every once in a while, Hyde would sneak down my chimney or break the lock on my door and talk to me about how his memories were returning little by little each night. He also informed me how, the more memories that came back, the more the monster took over. He told me how he was not restrained by fear, ethics, law, or conscience. According to Hyde, when a man is not bound by these factors, he can unleash chaos. And that is what he believed himself to be: chaos incarnate.

"He said that when he reverted to Jekyll, he had no recollection of his time as Hyde, but Hyde knew exactly what happened as Jekyll. They were two completely separate people. Jekyll kept drinking the potion and unintentionally becoming Hyde. The more he drank, the more control Hyde had over the body, and the more control Hyde had over the body, the more chaos he could wreak.

"My nights often consisted of Hyde telling me of the crimes he committed. In the beginning, it was quite tame. He told me how he was simply scaring unsuspecting citizens around Himshire. Then he informed me he was getting bored, so he went to other cities to wreak more havoc, such as slaughtering animals and destroying buildings with people inside. Each visit, he would tell me a story that was more evil and more brutal than the last."

"And you didn't think to report any of this?" asked an agitated Wilma.

"He was protecting his family," said Mark, answering for Van Helsing.

Return to Storyworld

"Hyde knew about his family, because Jekyll knew about them."

Van Helsing nodded. "Hyde said he remembered everything about our past lives in Olympia. I had told Henry about my children and ex-wife residing there. Though I haven't seen them in years, I love them deeply, and I could never forgive myself if anything happened to them. Hyde said he would kill them if I ever revealed his secret."

"What's this got to do with the clockmaker's murder?" asked Wilma.

"Hyde thirsted for more chaos. It was becoming an addiction to him, and addicts are never satiated. They keep injecting more and more in hope of satisfying their appetite. With Hyde, he was desperate for the ultimate chaos. That was when he recalled the incident with our creation, when he first lost his memory. The massacre in Arcadia was one of the most terrible events in the city's history. Hyde wanted to replicate that event. In order to do this, he would have to conduct the experiment again."

"Oh, no," said Holmes silently, placing his hands on his temples. "That's the case. This explains everything now. Hyde went to visit the Piper and the dwarves for help on this project. The factory was already set up in the Adrictan Mountain, and they had the necessary supplies. That's why the Piper must've hypnotized the children from Bunkertown. He needed help with the construction. Then Hyde flew to the Isle of Twilight to steal the Sandman's magic sand. Once this was done, he came back to Himshire and killed the clockmaker. But how did he know Giles was actually Victor Frankenstein unless..." The agent cast a look of horror at Van Helsing. "You told Hyde his real name! You betrayed your friend!"

"I told you he threatened my family!" replied Van Helsing. "I had no choice! But I didn't tell him where to find the documents!"

Holmes narrowed his eyes. "What documents?"

"The blueprints to build the monster and the plans to operate the apparatus that would give it life. There was a certain configuration needed to harness the precise amount of energy and channel it into the creature. I lied and told Hyde I had no idea what Giles did with it. Without those directions, he shouldn't be able to do anything."

"And Giles destroyed those plans, correct?" asked Holmes.

"Well, not necessarily," said Van Helsing, fidgeting with his fingers. "He refused to destroy them after the massacre. He said he wanted to hold onto them for scientific value. But no need to worry!" Van Helsing added when Holmes leered at him. "The plans are safe and secure. I told Giles to stow them away to prevent them from being found by anyone. He said he was building the perfect hiding place for them. I can assure you they're safe!"

The Companions took a moment to sigh in relief, except for Mark. He had gone pale.

"Where was he hiding the plans?" asked Mark, but the sick feeling in his stomach told him he already knew.

"They were going to be sealed away in a grandfather clock he'd been constructing."

Chapter 11

A Race Against Time

"We're going after him!" said Holmes, storming out of the house.

"We don't even know where he is!" replied Mark.

"He's going to the Adrictan Mountain to meet the Piper and the dwarves, and we're going to beat him there!"

"How? We don't have a ship or any way to get to Bunkertown, and we don't have a plan. So what the hell do you expect us to do once we get there, *if* we can get there?"

"The first thing on my agenda is to break every bone in that monster's body. Then, I'm going to tear his wings off!"

"You need to calm down, Agent," said Humpty as he and the other Companions emerged from Van Helsing's home. "Your personal qualms are affecting your ability to think rationally. First and foremost, we need to find a way to Bunkertown."

"Does Himshire have any sky-ships?" asked Mark.

"None," said Holmes. "All we have are sailing ships, but those won't do us any good. They're too slow. Hyde has a massive head start."

Holmes was right. How many hours had it been since Hyde escaped? The sun was already hovering over the horizon and getting ready to set. The Companions had spent too much time at Van Helsing's home. Hyde could be at the Adrictan Mountain already.

"I *may* have a way," said Rump quietly, his hand resting on the single vial in his belt that wasn't empty. It contained a black, smoky substance similar to the Asher-detection spell.

"What is it?" asked Mark.

Humpty's eyes widened. "The teleportation spell? Do you think it will work?"

Mark eyed the potion apprehensively. He recalled Rump first mentioning the spell ten years ago. At the time, the alchemist had used it to transport himself and an enemy to another location, but the magic was botched, and the person teleporting with Rump was supposedly killed.

"Are you sure about this, Rump? Last time I was here, you said it wasn't safe to use that stuff."

"That's why I haven't brought it up until now. I kept it for an extreme emergency, in case we had absolutely no other options left."

"Well, I think it's safe to say we're out of options."

"Are you absolutely sure?" asked Rump, holding the vial cautiously.

The Companions nervously glanced at one another.

"Look, everyone," said Mark. "I'm not good at this speech thing, and we're running out of time, so I'll keep it short. We've got no other choice. I'm scared of what that teleportation spell can do to us, but I'm more scared of what

Return to Storyworld

Hyde and the Piper are planning. We need to take this chance."

Humpty nodded. "He is right. I am willing to take this chance."

"Eh, I'm not one to shy away from a little danger," said Wilma.

"Well, someone needs to protect this team," said Robin with a grin.

"I'm desperate to settle the score with Mr. Hyde," uttered Holmes.

"Very well," said Rump, a tiny smile forming as he uncorked the vial. "Once this potion touches the ground, it'll create a powerful vortex, which will let us travel through time and space. We should arrive at the Adrictan Mountain instantaneously. Upon stepping into the vortex, your task is to concentrate on the destination. All your thoughts must be directed at a specific place. I cannot stress that enough!"

"That doesn't sound too encouraging," muttered Robin.

Rump ignored the comment and said, "I think a good meeting place would be that ledge above the cavern overseeing the factory. Like I said: focus entirely on that location. As long as you can picture it in your mind's eye, you should be fine. Does everybody understand?"

The Companions nodded. Mark was doubtful, but he knew this was the only way. He pushed away the pessimism in his mind and focused on the ledge inside the cavern.

Rump poured the potion onto the ground, where the smoky substance swirled around in a miniature tornado. It soon grew into an enormous funnel that towered over the Companions. Mark's mind battled against the increasing anxiety by focusing on the image of the ledge.

"See you on the other side!" said the alchemist cheerfully. With that, he held onto his helmet and dove into the vortex, his body vanishing amidst the swirling black clouds.

"I'm... I'm not too sure of this," Robin said cautiously.

Wilma grinned at him. "And here I thought you were one of the brave ones." She nudged him out of the way, hunched her shoulders, and entered the vortex.

"Might as well get it over with, Lox," said Humpty, beckoning the archer to follow him into the whirlwind.

Holmes didn't say anything and simply nodded to Mark as he dove into the spell. Mark was the last person remaining. Focusing on his destination, he gripped the war hammer tightly, closed his eyes, and ran.

The sensation of teleporting was bizarre. Mark found himself floating in a dark void. It didn't feel like he was traveling hundreds of miles across time and space, but he could still sense he was leaving Himshire. The darkness and emptiness of the void was so haunting that it prevented him from properly concentrating on his destination. There wasn't any sound, making the experience even more daunting.

The overwhelming emptiness permeated Mark's mind to the point that he couldn't picture the cavern anymore. Instead, he was flooded by a myriad of thoughts, emotions, and memories. One particular memory played in front of his eyes like a movie.

Mark was seated at his writing desk in the den of his and Amy's old apartment in Philadelphia. There were torn scraps of paper and broken pencils scattered around the desk. Mark had his head buried in his hands. Amy sat in a chair next to his desk, sobbing softly.

"It's okay," she said, reaching out to rub Mark's back, but he shrugged her off.

"No, it's not okay. I'm leaving. You can keep the apartment. I'll cover the rent. I'm gonna find a place downtown." Mark wasn't crying anymore. He wasn't sure he had any tears left.

"Please, Mark. It was a mistake. I told you I forgive you!"

"No, you don't understand. I'll pack my things and be out of here by tonight."

"You don't have to leave!" pleaded Amy. "Can't we move on? Why are you beating yourself up for it?"

"You don't deserve what I did to you, Amy," said Mark in quivering voice. "You deserve someone who'll treat you better, not a scumbag like me. I'm no better than my parents…"

The vision distorted, and it was replaced by a new memory of when Mark was a teenager. It was right after he had gotten back from Storyworld and confronted his parents in the kitchen.

"I'm sick and tired of hearing you two!" said the teenage Mark. "I never did anything to deserve what you guys put me through for the past eighteen years. I don't get what's wrong with you! Why can't you be normal, supportive parents? You're like these two miserable people who have to constantly fight and take your bad moods out on each other and on me. I'm done with it. I'm moving out on my birthday, and until then, I don't want you talking to me, and I better not hear any fighting anymore either!"

The memories shifted again. This time, the scene was from a dream he had experienced during the first night he slept in Storyworld.

Mark was alone, sprinting through a forest. Behind him, he could hear someone yelling at him in a voice that sounded similar to his father. When he looked back, there was a dark figure chasing him with the Hunter's Rifle in his hand. Mark tripped, falling face-first to the hard dirt. The pursuer's footsteps drew closer. Mark flipped over. He couldn't make out the stranger's face. There was a cloak over their head. They pointed the rifle at Mark's heart and squeezed the trigger.

The visions stopped abruptly. Mark could no longer sense he was traveling. The void encircled him, rendering him immobile. He couldn't move his body or blink his eyes.

"There is something very special about you, Mark Bishop," said an echoing voice.

Mark was frozen in place. He couldn't see where the words came from, but they sounded very close, like they were being spoken directly into his ear.

"Who said that? Where am I?"

"You are between here and there, in the middle of the start and the end, the center of the from and the to."

Mark rolled his eyes. "Listen, I'm not in the mood for jokes or riddles or whatever you're doing. Can you just shoot me out at the Adrictan Mountain, whoever you are? I can't deal with this."

The voice chuckled. "You Literaries always speak in such strange ways, I must say. Luckily, I am capable of peering into the very depths of your mind to comprehend your thoughts. Everything you have known, seen, felt, heard, or experienced is shared with me at this moment."

"Good luck dealing with all that. It's a mess."

"You lead an interesting life. Full of twists and turns, ups and downs. Yet you always press on. Nothing can deter you. Like the Literaries before you, you have the makings of a true hero."

"I'm no hero; I'm a screw up," admitted Mark.

"Your friends and countless others would agree with me that you are indeed a hero. I see massive potential in you, and I believe you will succeed in your mission, Hook-Slayer."

Mark's frustration turned to anger. "Do you even know what's going on? Read my mind and find out. We don't know if we'll get to the Piper or Hyde in time. What if they're already finished building that monster? What if it's on a killing spree across Storyworld? We have no plan and no clue what we're up against."

"I can assure you the answers will come with time. You will soon know everything you must. For now, I am sending you on your way. But first, I must give you this."

A long gray object materialized in front of Mark. He could now move his arms, and he reached out to grab the bottom of the object. There was a flash, and his hand wrapped around the handle of a long sword with a shiny silver blade.

"This is the Grand Sword," said the voice. "A powerful weapon for your quest."

A patch of light finally shone through the dark void. Mark felt himself moving again. The light became larger and larger as he zoomed in its direction. He could see the Companions on the ledge of the cavern.

In an instant, Mark was hurled from the void and thrown onto the ledge. It took a moment for him to regain his senses.

"Where were you? Did you concentrate on the destination like I told you?" asked Rump frantically.

"Yeah, sorry. I got a little side—"

"Where did that sword come from?" asked Humpty.

The Grand Sword was lying near Mark's hand, its blade encased within a thick sheath wrapped in royal blue cloth.

"Yeah, about that. I'll explain later. Did you guys find anything?"

"No, I think we're the only ones here," said Holmes.

The ominous light that previously illuminated the cavern had dulled slightly, but it was bright enough for them to see the motionless factory. The conveyor belts and levers were dormant; not one sound came from the machinery except for the creak of a pulley or the settling of a platform.

The Companions followed the spiraling staircase down into the depths of the cavern, and then crossed over a walkway to a wide metal platform sitting at the center of the factory next to an enclosed room. Numerous metal slides led into this room; Mark recalled the hypnotized children dropping scraps of metal down them the other day.

"Should we go in there?" suggested Mark, nodding at the room. "There were kids dropping metal into those chutes. If we're going to find anything, it'll be in there."

There was small doorway blocked by an iron gate with thick iron bars and a solid padlock. With a massive strike from the war hammer, the Companions broke the lock and wrenched the gate open. They slowly entered one by one, their weapons ready in case there were any unexpected surprises.

The light from the cavern walls poured into the room with them, allowing them to see everything inside. There were tables lining the walls, all of them hidden under stacks of documents and notebooks, much like in Dickory's workshop. The floor was covered in chunks of metal and wood, broken tools, torn scraps of clothing, and piles of paper. The chute openings in the walls had wire carriages underneath them filled with more pieces of metal and wood.

Holmes pointed to the center of the room, where an enormous table was surrounded by even more shards of jagged metal and bloody rags. Lying on this table was a massive body, covered from head to toe in a dirty gray blanket.

"Is that it? Is that the monster?" asked Robin.

"Hyde must not have arrived yet," said Holmes, relieved.

"So what do we do now?" said Mark.

"We need to find the blueprints Van Helsing mentioned. Without them,

Return to Storyworld

Hyde shouldn't be able to resurrect that monster. Start looking!"

The Companions split up around the room and searched through the tables. Mark approached the closest table and rifled through a stack of papers. They were filled with calculations, sketches, and random notes here and there. Out of the corner of his eye, he caught Rump about to peak underneath the blanket.

"Hey, don't mess with that!"

Rump let go of the blanket. "I was just curious."

"I know, but... it's ... don't mess with that, okay?"

Mark felt more and more uncomfortable being in the same room as the corpse. He tried not to stare at it.

"Stop fooling around," commanded Holmes, "and get back to searching for those blueprints!"

"They might not even be here..." Mark began, but his attention was drawn to the edges of a black ragged cloth draped over his table. He looked at the other tables and saw how his was the only one covered. It seemed out of place.

There were hundreds of pieces of parchment stacked on the table. Mark started tossing them off to the side. The Companions stopped what they were doing to watch him feverishly digging to get to the cloth underneath.

As the last piece of paper was tossed aside, Mark noticed there was an image emblazoned on the underside of the cloth. He lifted a corner and flipped it over. The moment he laid it back on the table and saw the picture of the skull and crossbones, his heart dropped into the pit of his stomach.

It was the Jolly Roger: the symbol of Captain Hook.

Return to Storyworld

Chapter 11

The Final Piece

"Oh, no," said Mark.

"Correct me if I'm wrong," said Holmes, his face pale, "but isn't that the sign of Captain Hook of Barbaria?"

The Literary Companions all had the same terrified look in their eyes as they gazed at the Jolly Roger.

Mark's throat was dry as a bone. "Hyde stole the plans from Giles to bring Hook back to life," he choked out.

Someone grabbed Mark's arm and squeezed it tightly. It was Robin, who was staring at the corpse under the blanket with absolute terror in his eyes. One by one, the rest of the Companions faced the table. Mark half-expected the corpse to sit up and tear the cloth off its face, revealing the haunting red eyes of Captain Hook.

"We need to destroy that body!" said Humpty.

"We need to find those blueprints, or else Hyde could revive anyone," replied Holmes.

"I wish there was a way we could destroy this entire room," mumbled Rump. "If I had my fire potion left, we could torch the place."

Return to Storyworld

Mark froze, as did Holmes. They both looked at each other and grinned. Holmes snapped his fingers, igniting his finger-flame. He placed his hand next to the closest stack of documents and made them burst into flame. Mark and the other Companions rushed to grab whatever papers they could and piled them on the fire and the corpse.

"This place should burn like a tinderbox," said Holmes, dusting his hands.

"Then let's get out of here!" said Mark.

As the Companions made for the exit, the iron gate swung closed, and a thick iron bar slid out from the side and jammed it shut.

The Companions stopped. Humpty reached out and forcefully shook the bars. When they wouldn't budge, he rammed it with his shoulder.

"What happened? Who shut the gate?" asked Mark in a panic.

Humpty took the war hammer and smashed it on the bars as hard as he could. The weapon had no effect aside from leaving a few shallow dents.

"That won't work," hissed a deep voice. Hyde stepped out from the side of the doorway, the broken handcuffs still clasped around his wrists.

"You!" shouted Holmes.

"Me." Hyde cackled and licked his lips. "Hot in there?"

Holmes pressed up to the gate. "Smile all you want! We torched your documents *and* the body! You won't be bringing anybody back from the dead!"

Someone nearby clicked their tongue. From the other side of the doorway appeared Peter the Piper, looking worse for the wear. His hat was gone and his clothes were torn and dirty. He had multiple scratches and bruises all over his face.

"You burned our workshop," said the Piper with a deep frown. "You know, it took us a long time to build it. No matter, we didn't leave any valuables in there." He looked beyond the Companions at the growing flames.

As Hyde laughed, Mark looked back at the fire as well. The blanket had fallen off the table to reveal that the corpse was in fact a bunch of carefully placed rocks and piles of dirty rags.

Mark heard a deep rumbling echoing within the cavern. Troops of dwarves in multicolored robes started emerging from around the factory. A group of green-robed dwarves descended the spiral staircase. Another gang of yellow-robed dwarves appeared from behind the Piper. Several red-robed dwarves climbed up a ladder by the Piper's feet. Soon enough, there was a small army of colorfully dressed dwarves assembled behind the Piper and Hyde.

"Go to the caves and begin setting up," the Piper ordered Hyde. He handed him a folded piece of paper. "We will meet you there."

Hyde took the parchment and put it inside his jacket. He then faced Holmes. "Too bad you didn't get to avenge your friend. Pity."

Holmes didn't say a word. He continued glaring silently. Hyde cocked his head. He stepped forward and opened his mouth to speak again when Holmes grabbed him by the shoulders and pulled his head into the bars. Hyde broke free from his grasp and hissed loudly while spreading his wings. The dwarves behind him jeered and laughed.

"Now, now!" said the Piper, stepping between them. "Stop fighting, children! We don't have time to waste. Let us be on our way."

Hyde growled and gave one last sneer at Holmes and the Companions before flying away.

"Goodbye," said the Piper. He grabbed a lever above the doorway and pulled it down, sliding a metal sheet in front of the gate and sealing the Companions within the room. The echoing footsteps and laughter of the dwarf army faded away.

"Any ideas on getting out?" asked Mark, trying to keep his voice calm. The heat in the room was getting intense, and the smoke was now gathering in thicker plumes. "Do we have any more of the teleportation potion?"

Rump held the vial up to his eyes and closely studied the smoky liquid inside. Mark wasn't sure if it was the encroaching flames or the intense heat, but it seemed like the alchemist had gone extremely pale.

"There... there isn't enough," he whispered. "One of us won't be able to teleport."

"What? Why?"

"I'm—I'm sorry. There's not enough for the six of us."

"No, there's gotta be something you can do. None of us are being left behind!"

Rump apologetically held his hands up, defeated. Mark wanted to scream at him, tell him that he's lying, but deep down, he knew the truth. One of them was not leaving.

Humpty snatched the vial from Rump's fingers and threw it. A vortex

Return to Storyworld

opened up in front of them, this one significantly smaller than the portal from earlier.

"Go to Bunkertown and raise the alarm," declared Humpty. "Maybe you can stop the Piper and Hyde while they escape."

"No!" said Mark.

"You cannot do this!" cried Rump.

"That is an order!" demanded Humpty. "I will find another way out!"

Rump nodded solemnly and beckoned everyone to the vortex.

"No, Humpty, you can't do this!" pleaded Mark. "There's gotta be another way!"

Wilma and Holmes grabbed Mark by the arms and hauled him toward the portal. Rump called out for Robin, but the archer refused to move. Humpty grabbed Robin's arm and dragged him toward the vortex.

"Forgive me, Your Highness!" Robin elbowed Humpty in the abdomen, forcing him to double over and clutch his stomach. The archer pushed him into the other Companions, sending them all into the portal together.

The five of them traveled through the void. Unlike the last journey, which was a smooth and quiet ride, Mark was now overwhelmed by the dizzying amount of color flashing in front of his eyes and roaring wind filling his ears. The Companions clung to each other as they twirled through time and space. Mark put all his effort into focusing on Bunkertown, but he was distracted by Robin's selfless act. The same man who once tried to mug him in the Neverwood Forest had just sacrificed his life to save him.

Return to Storyworld

The void expelled the Companions onto a patch of soft dirt. Everybody stayed on the ground motionless, with the occasional groan and whimper. Mark couldn't move. Deep down inside, he knew something had gone terribly wrong.

"That didn't go as well as the first journey," groaned Rump.

The Companions rose to their feet, except for Humpty, who stayed on his knees, staring at the ground dejectedly.

"Robin…" he whispered. "I should have been the one to sacrifice myself for the mission. I am the King of Neverland. It is my responsibility!"

Mark put his hand on Humpty's shoulder. "I'm sure he got out of the room. There had to be another way out…"

"This… this isn't Bunkertown!" Holmes yelled.

Mark didn't notice right away. They were in the middle of a dirt path surrounded by tall trees. It was strangely familiar. At first, Mark assumed they were back on the Isle of Twilight, but the trees were not as clumped together, and the area wasn't as dark or humid. The sky was clearly visible above the treetops, and judging by the slight purple bordering the distant horizon, it was sunset.

"What'd you do, Stiltskin?" asked Holmes.

"I'm not sure! My potion should've taken us directly to Bunkertown!"

"No, we're in the Neverwood Forest," said Mark quietly when he saw a familiar set of towers in the distance.

Holmes went from confused to livid. "Why are we in Neverwood? Do you have any idea how far we are from Bunkertown?"

"It's my fault. I was distracted. I was thinking of the time Robin tried to rob us. It was in this area. I guess my memory messed with my concentration and I must've brought you guys with me. I'm... I'm sorry."

"Do you realize what you've done?!"

"I said I was sorry! I got distracted!"

"Holmes, you must calm down!" said Rump. "This might be beneficial for us. If we're truly in Neverwood, then we should be near Neverland Castle. We can restock before we go to Bunkertown."

"It's too late for that. Hyde and the Piper will be long gone by then," said Holmes.

"Then what do we do?"

Holmes pulled a parchment from his jacket and unfolded it, revealing an intricate map. "We head them off at the Dronos Caves."

"How did you—" Mark said, but he remembered Holmes grabbing Hyde in the mountain. "You swiped the map?"

"A trick I learned from the Irregulars," Holmes muttered, peering over the document. "Arcadia isn't far from Bunkertown. Even without this map, Hyde will get there soon, and who knows how long until Piper and the dwarves arrive? But even if we get there first..." The agent went pale.

"We beat Hook once, we can beat him again!" Humpty said.

"This is different," said Mark, shaking his head. "Remember how Van Helsing said the monster attacked Arcadia? Hook was already a monster to begin with. Now that he's rebuilt with metal and magic, who knows what he can do? And then there's the Piper, Hyde, and those dwarves to worry about. How will the five of us stand any chance?"

There was a moment of silence as the Companions were at a loss as to what to do. Mark's eyes fell on Humpty, who absentmindedly rolled Pinocchio's hammer in his hand as he pondered. He recalled something he had heard on the Isle of Twilight.

… he was a fantastic warrior and possibly the greatest combatant I had ever seen. He singlehandedly held off a hundred pirates with nothing but this hammer at his side. Like I said, quite the fighter…

"What if we fight fire with fire?" suggested Mark. "If the Piper and Hyde can raise people from the dead, why can't we?"

Holmes narrowed his eyes. "You want us to resurrect someone? That is highly illegal, not to mention exceptionally difficult. I don't believe any of us are capable of such a feat."

"The workshop is already set up, and Rump, you're one of the smartest alchemists in Storyworld. Can't you figure out how to do it?"

"I appreciate the compliments, Sir Dodger, but we lack one important ingredient: the magic sand. And I'm nowhere near intelligent enough to decipher that formula anytime soon."

"Actually," Holmes said, drawing a vial from his pocket, "I still have this bit of sand from the crime scene."

Mark was now feeling hopeful. "This could work…"

"But we don't have a body," reasoned Rump. "Who do you intend on raising that would be strong enough to change the tide of the battle?"

Return to Storyworld

"The guy who used to own that weapon." Mark pointed at Pinocchio's hammer. "The Midnight Marauder."

"Are you mad?!" said Humpty, his eyes practically popping out of his head. "Not only do you want to break one of the highest laws in magic, but you want to revive that scoundrel? Absolutely not! He was a vile, despicable—"

"— fierce and nigh-undefeatable warrior," finished Rump in a tone of growing excitement. "Sir Dodger is correct, Humpty. If there's anyone who can stop Hook, it would be the Marauder. It's a viable option, and frankly, the best one we have."

"We do not need to resort to resurrecting anyone! As I said before, we killed Hook once, we can surly defeat him again, without that crook's assistance!"

"Hook is not the same person as last time," reasoned Rump. "He is undoubtedly going to be stronger, and much angrier. Us five alone do not have a chance."

Humpty grabbed the alchemist by his shoulders. "Do you not remember what the Marauder did? King Gabriel, rest his soul, would be outraged that we even *spoke* about resurrecting that rogue. And how do we know if it will even work?"

"Do you have any other options?" asked Holmes.

Humpty struggled to think of something else to say, but in the end, he simply crossed his arms and huffed loudly. "Fine. I am not happy about this, but so be it."

"Very good!" said Rump, clapping his hands together.

Return to Storyworld

"I hope this Marauder's body is close by," said Holmes. "We don't have much time to spare."

Humpty grunted. "It is here, in this forest."

The Literary Companions decided to split up. Humpty (reluctantly) agreed to lead Mark to the Midnight Marauder's burial site while Rump, Wilma, and Holmes went to Neverland Castle to hurriedly brew a new teleportation potion. They were to meet back at the site in an hour. Rump led the sheriff and the agent down the path toward Neverland Castle as Humpty steered Mark into the trees.

The journey through the Neverwood Forest was less brutal than traversing the Isle of Twilight's thick foliage, but Mark's level of discomfort was just as high. He felt a combination of anxiety, nervousness, excitement, and fear. In an attempt to distract himself, he asked Humpty to fill him in on the Marauder's history.

"He was the head of a team of mercenaries," he explained with a hint of distaste in his voice. "They were not aligned to any particular kingdom and instead hired out their services to anybody willing to pay. They ventured across Storyworld, allegedly saving hundreds of towns and kingdoms from destruction.

"The Marauder's history is murky. Legend has it he accidentally killed his own Literary, which granted him immortality and superior abilities. He was so regretful of his actions that he dedicated the rest of his life to seeking atonement."

"If he killed a Literary and became immortal," asked Mark, "then how was he killed? Isn't the whole thing about immortality that you *can't* die?"

"Immortality and invincibility are two different things, Sir Dodger. It was possible to defeat him, but it took the combined efforts of Neverland's greatest soldiers to subdue him."

Mark stopped in his tracks. "Wait, what do you mean by that?"

"Well, when Hook first attacked Neverland many, many years ago, the Marauder was there to assist with the kingdom's defenses. Unfortunately, we found out he was as much of an evil being as Captain Hook. It was he who essentially handed the kingdom over to the pirates, betraying us all."

"What? He was a traitor?"

Humpty frowned at him. "Why do you think I am so adamantly against his resurrection? The Marauder betrayed Neverland, and thus he was to be executed. It was not an easy feat, I can tell you. King Gabriel, myself, Pinocchio, Rumpelstiltskin, and a handful of other warriors had to work together to defeat him in this very forest.

"I thought you were aware of this, Sir Dodger. It is understandable if you no longer wish to resurrect the Marauder. But now is the time to make that decision."

Humpty pushed a branch to the side, revealing a clearing past the trees. In the center of this clearing was an enormous wooden crate with bronze clasps around the edges and a metal band wrapped around the center.

When Mark didn't respond, Humpty said, "Ultimately, this is your choice. Shall we revive the Midnight Marauder?"

Return to Storyworld

Mark had to let this information sink in. The fact the Marauder was a traitor to Neverland was now making him rethink his decision. Did they really want the assistance of a man who apparently almost destroyed Neverland? Mark glanced at the crate and realized that they had no other choice. He sighed deeply, then nodded.

"Yeah, let's bring him back."

Humpty and Mark struggled to bring the casket to the Companions' meeting point. It was a lot heavier than they expected. They decided it was easiest to push it along the ground through the forest, where its enormous size carved through the foliage. They arrived at the rendezvous at the same time as Rump, Holmes, and Wilma. Compared to Humpty and Mark's disheveled appearances, the rest of the Companions looked refreshed and ready for a new adventure.

Rump's bandoleer had been filled with a fresh batch of multicolored potions, and he had changed out of his ragged tunic into a black armored chest plate with the Neverland crest on it. Holmes also sported a thin animal-hide chest plate underneath his jacket along with a pair of matching gauntlets. Wilma's quiver was fully stocked with arrows, and she had also acquired a brand new bow. This one had a sleeker, more defined design with edges that flared outward and a green fabric wrapped around the center.

"Do you have the map?" asked Rump, holding a new vial of black smoke.

Holmes placed the parchment on top of the casket and ordered the Companions to circle around it.

Return to Storyworld

"Do you think we can teleport by going off a picture?" asked Humpty.

"It's not so much about the image, but rather the concentration. Focus on this point." Rump pointed at a dot with the hastily drawn word *Dronos* underneath it. "Think about this location. Let your imagination fill in the gaps. The spell should work, so long as nobody gets distracted this time."

With one final nod of approval from the Companions, Rump emptied the contents of the vial out onto the casket. For the third time, a swirling vortex of black smoke emerged from the liquid, starting as a small tornado, then growing into an enormous whirlwind. The Companions latched onto the casket as the spell sucked them up and cast them into the dark void.

Mark spun through the darkness, holding onto the casket with one hand and pinning the map down with the other. He kept his gaze locked on the sketch and refused to let his mind wander.

Dronos, Dronos, Dronos, he said over and over in his mind. He thought repeating the name over and over would help his concentration. The howling wind pressed against his ears and eyes, but he wouldn't be distracted this time.

In a heartbeat, the Companions were pitched out of the darkness and tossed onto a patch of gravel and dirt. The casket was the last thing to come out of the void, crashing to the ground mere inches from Mark's outstretched hand

"We made it!" Rump said joyously.

The Companions had landed on the edge of a high mountain crag overlooking a steep incline and a deep valley. Behind them, there was a wide opening in the rock face that led into a dark cave. Peering over the edge of the nearby cliff, Mark saw hundreds of tiny lights peppering the darkness at the bottom of the valley.

"Enough dawdling; let's get the casket to the laboratory," said Holmes.

Nobody spoke as they carried the casket through the caves. The lump in Mark's throat was growing bigger with each step they took, hoping against hope that their plan would work. The fate of Storyworld was resting on their shoulders, and they couldn't afford a single error. Mark wanted to say something to boost everyone's morale, but he couldn't think of anything that would even convince himself. So the Companions walked in silence, following Rump and the light from his spell.

The Companions exited the main tunnel and entered an enormous cavern, roughly the same size as the one inside the Adrictan Mountain. The walls sloped inward the higher they went and reached at least fifty yards into the sky. It was like they were standing within a giant volcanic crater.

The light from the moon barely illuminated the cavern, so Rump threw his fireball into the air to brighten up the area. At the center of the cavern stood a collection of instruments that must have been the remnants of Frankenstein and Van Helsing's old lab. There was a long metal slab on four legs standing within a shallow pit, and beside it was a metal tower with buttons and gauges across the front. Poking out of the top of this tower was a long metal rod that extended above the cavern's walls and into the sky, where it ended in a round knob.

Mark was surprised at the small, simple design of the old lab. Besides the table, the tower, and a stack of wooden crates piled next to them, there was

Return to Storyworld

nothing else noteworthy in the cavern; large boulders, gravel, dirt, and shards of wood and metal here and there.

"Let's get the coffin over to the table," murmured Mark. This place gave him the chills.

The Companions heaved the casket over to the apparatus and dropped it next to the metal slab. Mark got a better look at the tower and saw that it was full of dozens of knobs, buttons, levers, and gauges. He hoped Rump could figure it out.

The biggest problem was opening the Marauder's coffin. The metal clasps sealing it shut were unbreakable, and the wood itself was impenetrable. Every Companion attempted to break through, but nobody was successful, including Rump and his spells. The casket might as well have been a steel vault.

"Don't worry," reassured Rump. "We'll find a way t—"

A large shadow swarmed over the area. The Companions raised their heads to the sky as a giant black shape flew over the cavern's opening. Mark gasped when he realized he had seen this flying object before.

"Is that a magic carpet?"

"It's them! We're out of time!" said Wilma.

"What do we do now?" asked Mark.

Holmes rubbed his chin and looked around the lab. "I might have an idea."

Return to Storyworld

Chapter 13

Fighting Fire with Fire

The magic carpet soared across the sky like a dark, silent cloud. Peter sat at the front with his legs crossed and his hands resting on his knees. His eyes were closed, and he hummed a slow melodic tune. It wasn't the same as playing his flute, but he needed to hear music to keep himself content. He also needed something to drown out the irritating grumbling and grunting behind him.

Along with his seven usual dwarf cohorts, Peter shared the carpet with a troop of twenty additional dwarf alchemists and two hundred surly pirates. On one side sat the dwarves in their colored robes and hats with belts of potions wrapped around their waists. On the other side sat the pirates dressed in their traditional garbs of torn rags, moldy animal pelt clothing, rum-soaked bandanas, crusty eye-patches, and chipped and bloodied weaponry. The pirates' odor was overwhelming, which was why the dwarves had piled onto the far side of the carpet, occasionally tossing disgusted scowls over at their fellow passengers.

"Why are they here anyway?" Peter heard one dwarf whisper to another. "Do we really need them? Their smell is awful!"

"They insisted on coming along," replied the second dwarf. "They wanted to see the resurrection for themselves."

Return to Storyworld

At the center of the magic carpet, dividing the two factions, was an enormous coffin made out of pitch-black metal with gold clasps around the edges. Every time a dwarf so much as glanced at it, the pirates would gnash their teeth and protectively put their arms on top of the lid, as if they were afraid someone would steal it from them.

"We'll be needing their help, in due time," Peter said to the dwarves behind him, his eyes remaining closed. The answer seemed to satisfy them since they said no more.

Peter agreed that the pirates' stench was unbearable, but they were absolutely crucial for this experiment. After what happened the last time, with Frankenstein's creation going on a rampage upon its resurrection, it was important to take the proper precautions. Once Hook was revived, there was no telling how he would react. His mind might go haywire as well, and they wouldn't want him running amok. Frankenstein's original creation may have been fierce, but Hook will put it to shame with his power once he's brought to life.

That was why the pirates were there. They needed to act as safeguards. Peter believed the pirates would be able to control their master upon his resurrection, or they could act as fodder in case he does fly into a rage. Peter wished he still had the Bunkertown children under his control. He could've used them for additional shielding.

The carpet slowed down. Peter opened his eyes as a crowd of tall mountain peaks drew closer. In the distance, he saw the familiar antenna poking out of a wide crater. They had arrived at the Dronos Caves.

Return to Storyworld

Peter commanded the carpet to land by the edge of the mountainside, next to the cave entrance. The moment the carpet touched down, he signaled to his followers. A team of pirates positioned themselves around the giant coffin and lifted it onto their shoulders while four dwarves lit fires at the tops of their walking staffs.

Peter waved them off. "Go on ahead. I need to wait for Hyde. He should've been here by now."

The fire-wielding dwarves led the procession into the caves with their staffs held high. Peter's eyes followed the coffin as it was carried into the darkness. He couldn't help but smile. In less than an hour, Captain Hook will be alive again.

Peter cast a glimpse down the mountainside. Far below, he could see the distant city of Arcadia, a collection of hundreds of buildings and lights on a stretch of grassy plains. The city looked relatively peaceful and quiet, but small figures were seen walking from one building to another. Soon enough, if everything went according to plan, Arcadia would be nothing but embers and rubble by the morning.

It was impossible for Peter to feel empathy. Such feelings had been squashed out of him at a young age, when he was a street rat in Bunkertown. He learned that the only person he should worry about was himself. He didn't care what happened to anyone else as long as he got what he wanted. And he was going to get his revenge. Bunkertown was going to burn.

A black form came hurdling from the sky above him. Peter squinted and recognized the familiar wings, hunched back, and mane of hair. Hyde did not speak as he landed.

"I thought you would've been here already," said Peter.

"Lost the map," growled Hyde.

Peter rolled his eyes. "No matter. Let's get inside."

The two entered the caves and caught up to the dwarves and pirates.

"Once Hook is revived," Peter explained to Hyde in a whisper, "and once we're sure we have control over him, we'll let him loose in Arcadia to gauge his power. Then we will take him to Bunkertown."

They soon arrived at Frankenstein's old laboratory. The area was shrouded in near-pitch-black darkness, except for the sliver of moonlight shining through the hole up above. Peter barked an order, and the leading dwarves ran forward with their staffs, which they planted around the perimeter of the cavern. Their fire lit up the area, revealing the desolate revival apparatus.

"You sure it still works?" asked a dwarf.

"Set up the body," was Peter's response.

The pirates hauled the coffin to the table while the dwarves gathered around the equipment. One of the dwarves fiddled with the tower. Reading from a wrinkled old parchment given to him by the Piper, the black-robed dwarf pulled a lever by the tower base. The tower issued a dull roar as it powered up. The dwarf's hands danced across the panel on the side of the tower, twisting dials and turning knobs as the needles within the gauges swung between numbers.

"Put the body on the table," commanded Peter.

Return to Storyworld

The coffin was carried over to the station. One of the pirates took a key hanging from his necklace and placed it into a concealed outlet on the side of the casket. There was a loud click, and the gold clasps around the edge of the coffin lid popped open. Five other pirates helped slide the lid aside.

Peter had never seen the infamous pirate leader before, but he had heard stories of him. He marveled at the terrifyingly large size of Hook's corpse, impressed with how menacing he appeared even in death. He was tall, broad-shouldered, and barrel-chested, and legend had it that he possessed extremely potent Stronghand blood.

The dwarves had patched up the old wounds in Hook's body with thick slivers of metal fused into his skin. His left arm and right leg, both of which were lost in battle ten years ago, were replaced with new metal appendages that had been taken from the tin man of Oz. The rest of his body was melted down and forged into a shiny, sickle-shaped hook, which was welded onto the stump of Hook's right wrist and secured by a thick metal band.

Hook's head was shaved of its greasy black hair and replaced with a thick metal sheet forged into the top of his skull. The dwarves also wrapped a metal collar around his neck: a crucial detail according to Frankenstein's blueprints. The final addition to the body was a hidden metal shield built into Hook's chest, reinforcing his torso and protecting his heart.

Peter grinned with excitement. It had taken weeks to forge the exact combination of metals into the best material for Hook's resurrection. His dwarves had done a superb job with rebuilding the body. He wished the pirates had done more, though. Their meager contribution was to dress up their old leader in a dirty black shirt bearing the Jolly Roger and a matching pair of ragged pants. Regardless, Peter was happy with how it turned out. He was confident the pirate captain would not fall to a common Literary again.

The pirates gently placed Hook's corpse onto the table. A dwarf in yellow robes consumed a potion from his belt and held his hands up to the sky. The night was cloudless when they first arrived at the caves, but when the dwarf lifted his arms, a collection of thick black clouds rolled in, obscuring the moon and stars. Seconds later, there was a bolt of lightning accompanied by a thunderous roar that shook the very foundation of the Dronos Caves.

"Keep it controlled," advised Peter.

A dwarf in a blue robe approached the table holding a belt with a green gem in the buckle and a long sword much bigger than his body. These were two more useful tools acquired by Oz soldiers who were unfortunate enough to happen upon the Adrictan Mountain. The dwarf wrapped the belt around Hook's waist and placed the hilt of the sword in his metallic hand. When these items were in place, he opened a compartment at the bottom of the tower and pulled out two wires ending in metal clamps. He went to connect the clamps to the collar around Hook's neck.

"Wait a moment!"

Peter gently pulled Hook's mouth open to reveal jagged, sharp, metal teeth, and emptied a bottle of sand onto his tongue.

"Is that all?" asked the dwarf holding the wires.

"As long as you followed the directions and set everything correctly, we should be fine," said Peter.

"Get on with it!" growled Hyde.

As the dwarf went to connect the wire, a light whistling sound echoed across the cavern, followed by a dull thud. Peter's eyes found the blue-robed dwarf, who fell to his knees with an arrow in his chest.

A fireball came from behind a boulder and landed in the center of a group of pirates. It exploded forcefully, sending men flying across the cavern.

Mark heard the Piper yell, "Ambush!" and the sounds of dwarves and pirates screaming as thunder crashed overhead. Another fireball soared through the air and took out a pair of dwarves nearby. From where he was hiding, Mark could only see small sections of the cavern, but the shouts and flashes of color were all too clear.

A troop of dwarves began shooting blasts of various colored orbs across the cavern. A beam of blue light struck the ground in front of Mark's hiding spot, leaving behind a smoking crater. He gulped and tightened his grip on the Grand Sword.

More spells were thrown around the area. Mark could faintly see Wilma crouching behind a boulder and rapidly firing arrows at the dwarves and pirates. As soon as they went to attack her, Rump tossed one of his spells from the other side of the cavern, drawing attention away from the sheriff as she ran for new cover. Then Wilma would start shooting again as Rump sought a new vantage point. Everything was going according to plan. Dwarves and pirates were falling left and right.

"Useless!" growled Hyde. Mark watched him leap into the air and grab onto the antenna. His yellow eyes scanned the cavern. "There you are!"

For a moment, Mark panicked, thinking Hyde had found him, but the creature dove off the pole and flew right past. He was going after Rump, who was chugging a new bottle of potion. With his claws outstretched, Hyde dove toward him.

Holmes leaped from behind a crate and tackled Hyde out of the air. The agent used one hand to hold the monster down by his neck while he repeatedly punched him in the face with the other. Hyde roared and flapped his wings, forcefully tossing Holmes away. As he took flight again, Holmes grabbed onto his shoulders. The two began soaring around the cavern, brawling in mid-flight.

Down below, a squad of pirates ran toward Rump's hiding spot. Wilma fired an arrow to catch their attention, but they seemed to have caught on to their bait-and-switch game. Rump unhooked his mace from his belt, ready to meet the enemies coming at him.

As the pirates ran behind the revival tower, Mark stuck the Grand Sword out from his hiding spot behind the crates, striking one of them in the ankle and causing him to fall over. The tightly packed group tripped over one another and landed in a small pile. Mark hopped out from behind the crates and struck a pirate in the face with the end of his sword's handle while stabbing another in the side. An elbow came up and hit Mark in the temple, knocking him to the ground.

Return to Storyworld

Mark blinked several times. His vision was blurry from the hit, but he could still see the shapes of pirates surrounding him. Humpty popped out from one of the crates with both his swords at the ready. He yelled loudly and dive-bombed two pirates. Mark seized the momentary distraction to attack another pirate as Humpty handled the rest.

Hyde flew close to the ground while holding Holmes out in front of him, dragging his back against the gravel. The agent's jacket blocked most of the damage, but he grimaced as the jagged stones scraped his body. At one point, the two combatants flew through a horde of dwarves who were converging on Wilma. Hyde's wings clipped three of the dwarves' heads as Holmes sent his elbow into the skulls of two more. Wilma disposed of the remaining attackers with her bow and arrow.

A dwarf in a red robe ran at Mark with both his hands holding enormous fireballs. Mark prepared to swing his sword when a blue ball of energy whizzed past his ear and struck the dwarf's belt, which erupted in a shower of sparks and flames. Rump skipped toward Mark and Humpty, tossing more blasts around the cavern. Wilma joined them, launching arrows from her quiver so fast she was able to reload her bow before her previous arrow could hit its target.

"There're too many!" panted Mark.

"We need to revive the Marauder now!" said Rump.

"How?!"

The Marauder's casket was lying next to the revival tower, where it blended in with the other crates. On the other side of the tower, the Piper connected the cables to Hook's metal collar.

"NO!"

Mark broke away from the Companions and sprinted toward the revival station. He lifted his blade high in the air and dove at the Piper's back. The Piper nimbly ducked away as the Grand Sword came down on top of Hook's metal arm, where it harmlessly bounced off. Mark spun on the spot and was greeted with a punch across the face by the Piper. He grimaced and grabbed at his jaw, but remained standing.

The Piper picked up an axe. "I owe you for destroying my flute, Hook-Slayer. That wasn't very nice."

"Oh, shut up," said Mark, swinging the sword again. The attack went too wide, throwing him off-balance. The Piper swiped the axe at his side. Mark felt a sting crawl up his ribs, but he ignored it and reversed his swing. The pommel of his sword came around and clubbed the Piper across the face, causing him to tumble into the dirt.

Mark checked his side. The blade had cut through his shirt and left a nasty gash on his ribs, but it didn't seem too deep. Luckily, his adrenaline rush slightly dulled the pain. Deep in the pit of his chest, he was starting to feel the familiar tightening sensation again.

The Piper wiped his bloody mouth on his sleeve. He snarled at Mark, but then smiled widely and gazed over his shoulder. "It's too late."

Another dwarf in yellow robes had disengaged from the battle and stood on the revival tower with his hands in the air. A series of thunderclaps rumbled the cavern. Bolts of white lightning shot across the sky and struck the metal knob at the top of the antenna.

"Throw the switch!" yelled the Piper.

At the Piper's command, the dwarf pulled a lever on the side of the tower as another lightning bolt struck the antenna.

At first, nothing happened except Hook's body jolting like it had been shocked. Then an ear-shattering roar filled the cavern.

Mark's eyes were glued to the table. The corpse that had been stiff and lifeless moments ago was now beginning to move. Its fingers were flexing, and its shoulders were rolling in their sockets as its head moved side to side. The body shot up into a sitting position, roaring into the sky. The head slowly rotated to face Mark, its red eyes focusing on him as its lips slithered into a smile.

Captain Hook had returned.

Chapter 14

Blood and Gravel

The pirates cheered as their revived leader rose from the table. The moment Hook's feet touched the ground, the entire cavern shook, and chunks of gravel and dirt crumbled from the walls. Although the dwarves did not cheer as the pirates did, they did share a look of shock and awe. A wide smile crossed the Piper's face.

Hook's red eyes did not leave Mark as he walked toward him. His footsteps were so heavy they left indentations in the ground, and each step kicked up a large cloud of rock and dust. The lightning continued overhead, but Hook's stomping put the thunder to shame. His one arm swung back and forth, the new hook gleaming in the torchlight. His metallic arm dragged the long sword along the gravel behind him.

Humpty slayed his two dwarf opponents and made a mad dash across the cavern. He slid across the gravel, slicing his swords at Hook's ankles. There was a sound of scraping metal as the blades grazed the pirate's prosthetics, not leaving a single scratch. Hook cocked his metal foot and launched a kick that caught Humpty under his ribs and sent him careening through the air.

Return to Storyworld

Rump came charging across the cavern with a fireball in his hand. He wound up and tossed the spell at Hook. The flame singed a small hole through his shirt, but it didn't do any damage to the metal shell around the captain's torso.

Hook spun around just as Rump was leaping off a boulder with his mace held high. The green gem at the center of his belt fired an orb of energy at the alchemist, striking him out of the air.

Wilma grabbed three arrows from her quiver and fired them at the same time. Two of the arrows became stuck in Hook's thigh and the other bounced off the metal plate in his head. Wilma threw her bow on her back and armed herself with the short dagger from her boot.

Hook swiped his sword at the sheriff's neck, missing by mere inches. Wilma stabbed her dagger upward into his forearm. At the same time, she kicked the two arrows deeper into Hook's leg. Hook merely laughed as he grabbed her by the leg and hurled her away.

Mark found himself backed up against the wall, unable to say a word as Hook approached him. He tried to yell for help, but no noise came out.

The Piper ran up to Hook, pulling a cloth out from under his shirt. He unfolded it and held it up. It was a flag bearing the Jolly Roger.

"Do you know who you are?" said the Piper, pausing between each word as if he was talking to a small child. "Do you *remember* who you are?"

Hook shoved past the Piper and kept walking without a word. The Piper scowled and moved to block his path, this time practically shoving the flag into Hook's face.

Return to Storyworld

"I have revived you, and therefore, I am your master! I command you to do as I sa—"

The Piper never finished his sentence. The pirate captain stabbed him in the stomach with his new hook and lifted him off the ground.

"No one commands me," Hook said in a metallic voice. He threw the Piper's body away.

A loud cheer came from the pirates as the dwarves watched in horror at their master's death. They all loudly whispered to each other.

"He killed Peter!"

"Captain Hook killed him!"

"Peter's dead!"

"I am nobody's servant!" Hook kicked the Piper's body. "You now fight for me, or die!"

The remaining dwarves looked at one another, and then fell to their knees, bowing to Hook. The pirates joined in as well. Mark was frozen in place. He looked at his fallen friends, hoping one of them would get up and fight, but nobody moved.

A loud yell came from one of the tunnels. Hyde and Holmes came flying back into the cavern, both their faces bruised and bloodied. They exchanged several more punches before Hyde disengaged from Holmes and threw him to the ground.

"Pest!" said Hyde, perching on a nearby boulder. His mouth cracked into an enormous smile when he laid eyes on the revived Hook.

Return to Storyworld

Holmes struggled to stand. One of his eyes was swollen shut, and there was a large gaping wound above his cheekbone. He slowly looked up at Hook leering at him. Surprisingly, the agent chuckled.

"So, the legendary Captain Hook has returned. I didn't think it could be done, but here you are." Holmes stood up, wobbling slightly. Hook towered over him by at least a foot. "I see you've gotten upgrades, eh? Extra weaponry, a metal plate around the chest to protect the heart, and a tough skullcap for protecting the brain. I'm impressed with the work they've done. You're a regular walking fortress, aren't you? But no castle is impenetrable. There's bound to be a soft spot. My guess, it's at the base of your neck. Am I correct?"

Hook moved his metal arm, as if he were about to strike.

Holmes held his hand up. "Well, I guess there's one way to find out." He dropped his hand.

Two arrows whistled through the air and struck the back of Hook's neck, forcing him to his knees. Mark regained his senses and looked to Wilma, but she wasn't the one who shot the arrows.

Standing at the entrance to one of the tunnels was Robin, his face blackened with soot.

The pirates gasped as their leader fell to his hands and knees. For a moment, it seemed like he was about to keel over. Holmes approached him with a satisfied smirk.

"Guess I was right," said the agent.

Hook looked up with an angry glare in his eye. "No, you were not." He swiped at the agent's legs, tripping him. At the same time, he fired another green blast of energy at Robin, knocking him into the wall.

Hook picked up Holmes by the throat and growled, "Did you really think a pair of arrows could stop me?"

Holmes struggled against the iron grip. As he gasped for air, it almost sounded like he was laughing.

"No, but.... they.... distracted you."

For a moment, Hook looked confused. He glanced over his shoulder and immediately yelled, "Stop the Literary!"

Mark ducked the two pirates that flanked him and hurdled over a third. He grabbed the cables from the revival tower and jumped atop the Marauder's casket.

As lightning crackled overhead, the pirate army converged on Mark. Hook threw Holmes aside and charged forward. Hyde leapt from his perch and dove at the Literary as well.

A single bolt of lightning struck the ball at the top of the antenna. Time seemed to slow down as the electricity traveled down the metal rod. Trusting his instincts, Mark took the Grand Sword and stabbed it down into the coffin, miraculously penetrating the wood and sinking into the Marauder's body.

Mark found himself on a white platform amongst a black void, reminiscent of his journey through the teleportation spell earlier. He wasn't sure how he got here, and he thought he must've been dreaming. Then he remembered that he was in the middle of a battle and had stabbed the Grand Sword through the Marauder's casket. Something must've happened to send him into this strange void. All he could see was his own body and the white platform underneath him. Everything else was darkness. Was he dead?

"That was a very brave thing you did, Mark Bishop," said a disembodied voice.

"Am I dead?" asked Mark.

"You are not dead."

"Am I dreaming?"

"You are not dreaming."

"Then where am I?"

The voice didn't answer. There was the sound of footsteps echoing across the floor. Mark spun around, trying to determine where they were coming from, but he couldn't see anything except blackness.

A tall man materialized out of thin air, approaching Mark with his hands behind his back. He had dark black hair, brown eyes, and a rough-skinned face with a small nose and small chin. He wore golden sandals laced up his shins, and matching bracelets wrapped around his forearms. A sleeveless black toga covered his torso down to his knees, and he had a red sash tied around his waist.

"Are you the Midnight Marauder?" asked Mark as the man approached him.

"I was, long ago," he admitted with a hint of sorrow in his voice.

"We need your help."

Return to Storyworld

The Marauder gave a pained smile. "Sadly, I cannot help you. I cannot return to Storyworld."

"What? Why not?"

"I am not wanted, nor needed."

"What's that supposed to mean? We need you!"

The Marauder beckoned Mark with his finger. "Walk with me."

The two trekked across the platform, their footsteps echoing loudly in the void.

"You have heard of my deed," said the Marauder. "You know what I did, both good and bad."

"The bad doesn't matter now! We need you for good! They said you're the best warrior that ever existed. We can't fight Hook without you."

"Yes, you can. You do not need my help. You already have the power to defeat him once and for all."

"No, we don't! We're outnumbered and we don—"

"No, I mean you personally, Mark Bishop. You are the one with the power."

Mark stared at him blankly and said, "I don't get it."

"Remember how I said you were not like your predecessors?"

Mark was about to respond when the Marauder nodded.

"Yes, that was I who spoke to you earlier, and it was I who presented you with the Grand Sword. I meant every word I said to you in the void. You hold more power than anyone who has ever come into this world."

Return to Storyworld

"How's that possible?" Mark asked. "I'm a normal guy from Philadelphia. There's nothing special about me. And I don't know why you thought I deserved the sword, or why everyone thinks I was worthy to carry your hammer. Don't you know anything about me? I cheated on my wife. I stopped talking to my parents. I'm not a hero or whatever you expect me to be."

"Do you remember your encounter with the Forever Witch?" asked the Marauder.

Mark cocked his head. "Yeah, I remember her. How did you—"

"You proved yourself different the moment you resisted her charms," pressed the Marauder.

"How?"

"The Forever Witch was a powerful magicker who inhabited Storyworld for eons. She was known for her unique power to seduce anyone she chooses. Nobody could resist her charm, including myself."

"She got to you?!" Mark asked incredulously.

"Yes, she enticed me long ago. But unlike her other victims, she did not kill me. She had a special fondness for me, and she decided to keep me imprisoned as her pet for years. Then, a Literary came to save me from her spell. Unfortunately, a terrible scuffle broke out, and I accidentally killed the Literary.

"What I did was terrible. The effects from his death broke me free from the Witch's magic, and I was able to escape from her home. I committed my life to making the world a better place. My goal was to eradicate evil so that no Literary would ever need to be summoned or harmed again."

Return to Storyworld

Mark was silent. They walked across the white platform, further venturing into the void. No matter how far they traveled, there was no end in sight.

"If the Forever Witch couldn't charm me," said Mark, "what about the siren? Didn't you see what happened? I nearly drowned when that siren tried to lure me off the ship."

"You were tempted by the siren because you lost your innocence and faith in yourself. Your personality has changed much since you were a teenager. While you are now much more confident, you also lost touch with what made you such a hero in your adolescence."

The Marauder's words were not registering in Mark's mind. Everything made sense, but it didn't sit well within his conscience. Something was off.

Tell me, have you ever felt out of place in your own world?" asked the Marauder.

Mark had to think about this for a moment. He nodded and said, "When I was a kid, definitely. That was regular teenage angst, though. Every kid goes through that."

"And you felt a strange comfort when you traveled to this world and went on adventures with Humpty Dumpty and Rumpelstiltskin, correct?"

"A little bit. I think it was because I made a difference here. In my world, people treated me horribly. It was always my parents yelling at me, or this jerk giving me a hard time at school. When I was in Storyworld, I was taking down giants and fighting bounty hunters. I actually mattered here. It was kind of exciting, but I don't know if you could consider it 'comfortable'…"

Return to Storyworld

"That was another thing that made you stand out from your previous Literaries, Mark Bishop. You adapted to this world very quickly when you first arrived. From what I have witnessed in the past, most Literaries have a hard time coming to terms with their summoning. The first two or three days after they arrived, they were too preoccupied gathering their thoughts and absorbing their surroundings. Not only did you immediately come to accept this strange new world, but you also demonstrated a strong proficiency in your abilities."

"Like how?"

"You defeated a troll, a Jabberwocky, a legion of bounty hunters, a Stronghand, and the notorious Captain Hook, all when you were a teenager!"

"It was luck, or other people helping me," reasoned Mark.

"No, it was inner power," countered the Marauder. "How many times must I remind you? You possess a power unlike any other. I would never have given you the Grand Sword if I did not think you were a hero who deserved it."

Despite everything he was saying, the Marauder's words didn't resonate with Mark. He couldn't accept it. He absentmindedly rubbed the back of his hand, remembering when he punched the mirror a few nights ago.

"I don't feel like a hero. I hurt the people that mattered the most in my life…"

"Nobody is perfect. You simply made mistakes, and you have learned from them. One of the greatest things about you Literaries is that you can identify your mistakes and use your knowledge to better yourselves. You would be surprised at how rare that trait is in Storyworld. Yet Literaries spend too much time worrying about errors they have made in the past. There is no point in dwelling on the ruins of your past when you can easily construct a bright future."

"You don't underst—"

"I *do* understand! I have made many mistakes in my past, some petty and some extraordinary. My whole life as a mercenary revolved around my desperate desire to make up for a past mistake. It was not until I passed from my mortal body and ascended to this current state that I learned the importance of moving on. You cannot wait as long as I did. Let go of the past and embrace the present, so that you can control the future. Let it go."

These last three words slowly washed over Mark like a cold wave, freeing him from the depression and other negative feelings plaguing his mind for years. He realized the Marauder's words were true: he couldn't hold onto his past mistakes. Dwelling on them prolonged his misery. It was time to truly let go.

The Marauder clapped Mark on the shoulder. "Now, there are other matters for you to attend to."

The two finally reached the end of the white platform. The Marauder nudged his head over the edge. Mark was astounded to see that they had an aerial view of Frankenstein's laboratory. The battle between the Literary Companions and the pirates and dwarves was still raging on, but none of the tiny figures were moving. They were like little statues, frozen in time and space. Even the clouds in the sky were motionless. A miniature version of Mark stood on top of the Marauder's casket, holding the cables and the Grand Sword.

"As I stated, I cannot come with you. You will have to fight the battle on your own," declared the Marauder.

"We don't stand a chance without you."

The Marauder frowned. "You still doubt yourself, and I cannot change that. What I *can* change is your experience with this world. If you wish, I can send you home."

"You mean back to my own world?"

"Correct. I can send you home and you will have no memory of this trip. You will return to the exact moment before Humpty and Rumpelstiltskin visited you. It will be as if you never left, but the effects of our previous conversation will linger in your mind. The lesson will remain, but the experience will vanish."

"What'll happen to my friends? They're fighting down there…"

"Unfortunately, you will be leaving them behind at this very moment. They will not remember you being part of their group. Their memories will be wiped of your visit."

"And Hook?"

The Marauder blinked. "They will fight him alone."

Mark observed the battle below, his mind a whirlwind of thoughts. If he left now, he could work on rebuilding his life back home, starting with reconciling with Amy and organizing funeral arrangements for his parents. On the other hand, he would be abandoning the Companions. If he were given this option ten years ago, he probably would've said yes and asked to go home without so much as a second thought.

But that wasn't who Mark was today. Even if the odds were piled against him and his friends, and even if he was facing possible death in the battle, he couldn't leave the Literary Companions. He refused to take the easy way out.

"Send me back to Storyworld."

The Marauder smiled. "All you need to do is take the first step."

Mark drew in a deep breath, his heart thumping and his fingers tingling. Raising his foot in the air, he leaned forward and let himself fall off the platform and into the black void.

The Marauder watched as Mark descended to Storyworld, his body encased in a glowing white and yellow aura. He then stepped off the platform and followed.

Chapter 14

Evening the Odds

The entire cavern shook violently, causing everyone to fall, including Captain Hook. The revival table and tower were both destroyed in a flash of white light when the antenna was struck by the last lightning bolt. All that was left was a thick cloud of smoke and dust. Sections of the walls crumbled away, kicking up more dust around the edge of the cavern.

Mark opened his eyes and found himself kneeling in the smoke, his palms pressed against the ground and the Grand Sword planted in the gravel next to his hand. Panting heavily, he noticed that his breathing had changed. He no longer had the thick rasp he adopted from years of smoking. Now, every breath he took was like a strong wind gushing through his lungs. His vision and hearing improved as well. He could identify every individual piece of gravel on the ground, and he could hear the tiniest movements as the pebbles shifted.

As he rose, Mark was shocked at how much taller he felt. He examined his body and discovered he had undergone a major transformation. He was now wearing a black toga, golden sandals, and matching golden wristbands; the same outfit as the Midnight Marauder. His arms became much more muscular, and when he flexed his fingers, he could feel pure strength coursing through his body.

Return to Storyworld

There was a growl behind him. Mark turned to see Hyde leering at him through the smoke. He launched himself at the Literary. Mark instinctively shot his hand out and grabbed Hyde by the throat, holding him effortlessly at arm's length. He then cocked his other arm and crashed his fist into Hyde's face. Hyde went hurtling through the air and crashed into the wall, where he left a body-sized crater.

Everybody else in the cavern stood up, marveling at the Literary in disbelief. The only person not stunned by Mark's transformation was Captain Hook, who let another roar erupt from his mouth. Their eyes met, and for a brief moment, Mark thought he caught a hint of fear in the captain's gaze.

Hook stomped at him, his sword at the ready. Mark's instincts kept him rooted to the spot as he came closer. As Hook swung his weapon, Mark ducked at the last second, feeling the breeze from the blade as it flew over his head. He sprung up and caught Hook with a devastating punch underneath his chin, throwing him flat on his back.

The pirates and dwarves yelled as the Literary Companions cheered. The combatants rose with renewed vigor. As Hook's minions charged at Mark, the Companions moved in to intercept them.

Rump swallowed another potion that coated his hands in black auras. He grabbed two passing dwarves by the napes of their robes, lifted them over his head, and hurled them over the battlements. Humpty barreled through a throng of pirates, stabbing and hacking at anything in his way. Robin and Wilma stood back-to-back, shooting off arrows in rapid succession.

Return to Storyworld

Two pirates approached Mark's sides in an attempt to flank him while another came up in front of him. Mark swiftly picked up the Grand Sword just as the three pirates converged on him. He stabbed the two attackers on the side and kicked the pirate in front of him in the chest, sending him flying into a boulder.

Hook stood up, his eyes burning redder than ever. The captain leveled his sword again and charged with a mountainous roar. Mark did the same and the two clashed in the center of the cavern in a vicious sword fight.

Hyde wedged himself out of the cavern wall, shaking his head vigorously and moaning. As he regained his senses, he saw the alchemist in front of him with his back turned. He growled and flew at him with his claws bared.

"Look out!"

Humpty shouldered Rump out of the way. Hyde sank his claws into Humpty's chest, pinning him to the ground.

Hyde cackled. "It seems your reign is over, King Humpty."

Humpty grinned. "I disagree, Mr. Hyde."

In a flash, Humpty swiped both his swords behind Hyde's back. Hyde let out a bloodcurdling shriek. His wings fell in a mangled, bloody mess. He grabbed at the bloody stumps on his back, howling in pain. Humpty twirled his swords with a smile.

"No, King Humpty," said a voice. "He's mine."

Holmes approached them, a manic gleam in his eye. The agent had discarded his jacket and hat, leaving only his bloodstained tunic and pants. Humpty nodded and joined Rump as he took on another squad of pirates.

Return to Storyworld

Hyde stopped whimpering. Forcing a grin, he said, "I don't fear you."

"You should," replied Holmes.

Baring his teeth, Hyde sprinted at the agent.

Mark and Hook continued their sword fight, showing no signs of exhaustion or relenting in their fury; in fact, the more swings they took at each other, the more vicious their fight became. Hook alternated between ferociously swinging his sword and swiping his hook, but Mark blocked and parried everything that came his way. Every once in a while, another pirate or dwarf would attempt to swarm them, only to be kicked or punched aside. Twice, an unlucky dwarf came too close to Hook's sword and suffered a brutal death.

Hook gave one particularly heavy swipe of his sword that missed Mark by a hair and caught him off-balance. Mark brought his knee up and slammed it into his opponent's chin, briefly dazing him. In that split-second the captain lost his focus, Mark grabbed a hold of his metallic wrist and gave it a quick twist. There was a sickening crunch as Hook's metal hand broke off his arm and fell to the ground, still clutching the long sword.

The pained shriek echoed around the cavern, but Hook didn't falter in his attacks. When Mark went to slice at him with the Grand Sword, the pirate captain caught it in the crook of his hook and pinned it to the ground. Mark took one of his hands off the hilt and punched at his face, but it was blocked by the stump of Hook's metal arm. The two combatants stared at each other, breathing heavily, as they were locked in this stalemate. Hook's belt buckle glowed with a green light. It released a concussive force that struck Mark in the chest and tossed him on his back, forcing him to drop the Grand Sword.

Though he possessed the power of the Midnight Marauder, Mark could still sense pain. The blast felt like a cannonball shot at his chest. Hook approached him, the green gem glowing again. The buckle fired another spell, but something came flying through the air, intercepting the blast, and landing in front of Mark. It was the Marauder's hammer.

Before Hook had a chance to attack again, Mark kicked him in the chest, throwing him backward into the rubble of the decimated revival apparatus.

"Help me!" shouted the downed Hook. A handful of pirates and dwarves swarmed at Mark. He grabbed two of the pirates by their heads and tossed them aside as Wilma, Robin, and Rump handled the rest.

"Go after Hook!" ordered Rump. "We'll handle everything here!"

Hook was retreating down one of the tunnels with a gang of minions. Mark grabbed Pinocchio's hammer and the Grand Sword and pursued him.

"Hook!" Mark yelled down the tunnel. The Dronos Caves were dark, but his heightened senses made it easier for him to navigate the passages. He could hear the pirates' yells along with Hook's stomping footsteps.

Following his senses, Mark happened upon a light breeze coming from a narrow tunnel. He could see the faint light of the exit in the distance. He also saw the silhouette of a small group of pirates running, Hook's prominent figure towering above the rest.

Mark ran down the tunnel. The pirates were near the exit, but he was close behind. Dropping the Grand Sword, he took the hammer in both hands and flung it with all his strength. The weapon soared down the tunnel and made a heavy clanking sound as it struck Hook with such force that it sent him face-first into the ground.

The pirates stopped and spun around to see the Literary approaching them with the Grand Sword in his hands. They quickly lifted their leader to his feet.

"You're going to die here tonight!" grunted Hook. With that, he led his men in a charge.

Mark slayed three of the pirates with a wide swing of his sword, and sent his elbow into the skull of another. In a moment of panic, Hook shoved his remaining minion at Mark, who backhanded him across the face and knocked him out cold.

Hook's breathing was shallow and ragged. His hunched shoulders relaxed slightly, and he managed to produce a sneer. Examining the Literary up and down, he said, "So, how did you become the Midnight Marauder?"

Mark hesitated. "I guess he wanted to give me a helping hand."

"Hah!" The captain swung his hook, missing Mark as he leaned backwards. He quickly pivoted and kicked him in the chest. "It will take much more than muscles and a sword to defeat me!"

The kick knocked the wind out of him, but Mark quickly recovered as Hook loomed over him.

"I don't need them," Mark said, grabbing his chest. "I did it when I was seventeen years old."

"Well, this time, your friends are not here to help you."

Return to Storyworld

Hook swung his hook down at Mark's head. With a loud yell, Mark threw his hand up. The hook tore through his palm, but stopped inches away from his face. Captain Hook's jaw dropped.

The pain in his hand was unbearable, but Mark held strong. He glared at Hook as he slowly rose. With another yell, he drew back his other fist and delivered a mighty punch at Hook's chest, denting the protective metal plate and launching him down the tunnel.

Hook tumbled across the gravel and skidded to a halt against a fallen boulder. He groaned and wheezed as he clutched at the deep dent in his chest. He attempted to stand, but failed. His breathing became shallower with each passing second. Mark picked up Pinocchio's hammer and walked up to him.

With blood dripping from the corner of his mouth, Hook scowled up at the Literary and wheezed, "Go… ahead. Strike me down. Just like… just like when you were a child. You think you are… better… than me? No… no. You are weak. You are… inferior."

Mark stopped in his tracks. Lowering his weapons, he said, "You know, you're right. I *am* weak. But I'm trying to become stronger. That's why I'm walking away this time."

Hook's red eyes narrowed. "What?"

"Your heartbeat changed." Mark said, staring at Hook's chest. "I can hear it. It was pumping like a machine minutes ago. Now, it's barely moving. You're going to die soon anyway. I'm not going to attack a dying man." Mark turned and walked away.

Return to Storyworld

Hook growled. "No! No! Don't you walk away!" He leaned heavily against the boulder. "How dare you turn your back on me?!"

The gem in his belt buckle fired a green burst of energy. Mark leaned to his side, letting the blast soar over his shoulder, and in one fluid motion, he threw Pinocchio's hammer at a large stalactite hovering over Hook's head.

There was a dull rumble as the rock formation broke from the ceiling. Hook didn't have a chance to react as the enormous rock came crashing down on top of him.

Chapter 15

Farewells

When Mark returned to the cavern, he found that the fight was over, with the Companions reigning victorious. Robin, Wilma, and Rump were dragging the bodies into the center of the cavern, where they had constructed a makeshift fire pit.

"Sir Dodger!" called out Rump as he entered the cavern.

The Companions stopped what they were doing and gathered around him, gawking at his transformed body.

"How did this happen?" asked Humpty.

"It's a long story, and I'm not even sure even I understand it," said Mark. He saw the claw marks on Humpty's shirt and asked, "How did *that* happen?"

Humpty chuckled and said, "I would attribute this to a combination of both good and bad luck." He reached into his shirt and revealed the semi-destroyed copy of *Dodger's Adventure to Storyworld*. There were four deep claw marks in the top half of the book.

"I'm really glad I didn't listen to my agent's advice about trimming a couple chapters," Mark said with a smirk.

Humpty gingerly held the book out. "My apologies."

Return to Storyworld

"It's fine. Keep it," replied Mark.

"What happened to your hand?" Rump said.

Mark had torn a scrap of cloth from the bottom of his toga and wrapped it around his punctured hand, but the blood had soaked through and began dripping. Rump didn't wait for a response and handed him a healing potion. In seconds, the wound was healed.

Taking a deep breath, Mark declared, "Hook's dead. It's over. We won."

There was a beat, and the Companions gave a loud cheer. Their yells of delight echoed off the cavern walls as they congratulated one another. The only one not celebrating was Holmes, who sat on a nearby rock, staring at the corpse of Hyde, whose head was twisted completely around.

"I didn't want to kill him," Holmes said sadly. "You were right. He didn't have control over his actions as Hyde. I killed an innocent man."

"You had no choice," said Mark.

Holmes frowned. "There's always a choice. I was too consumed in my need for vengeance. We could've saved Doc." He walked away.

Mark wanted to say something, but Robin came up to him and clapped him on the back.

"Sorry I couldn't make it here sooner, Sir Dodger. I hope you lot weren't in too much trouble before I arrived."

Mark gave a weak smile. "We're glad you're okay, Robin. How did you escape the Adrictan Mountain anyway?"

The archer wiped the sweat from his brow and said, "Remember how the

Bunkertown children were dropping scraps of metal down those chutes? It was tough, but I was able to crawl out of one of them. When I got out, I saw that Hyde and the Piper had left already, and I'll admit I was lost in that mountain. I wandered for a bit and found a trio of griffins chained up in the lower tunnels. I released two and rode the other one here."

"How did you know where to find us?"

Robin's tone turned somber. "When I found the griffins, their masters' bodies were nearby. They belonged to the Royal Guard of Oz."

Mark now realized where Hook's magic belt and long sword had come from. He felt a sad twinge in the pit of his stomach. The Companions shared a brief moment of silence for the fallen Oz warriors.

"It's a shame," said Robin, shaking his head. "But the good news is that, in death, they were still helpful. I found a map in the griffin's saddle and learned that the Dronos Caves were not too far east. I flew here as fast as I could."

Humpty approached Robin. "Very noble of you, Lox. You came to our aid at the most dire of moments. General Pinocchio would be proud of your selflessness. With his recent passing, maybe I will consider putting you in charge of the Neverland Military Arm."

"Really?" said Robin, beaming.

"Yes," said Humpty, "but if you ever lay your hands on me in a violent manner ever again, I will break both your arms and throw you in the dungeons. Understood?"

"Fair enough," Robin said nervously.

Return to Storyworld

Humpty grinned and playfully shoved the archer.

Mark smiled at Robin as well. "Thanks for coming back to save us. You're a hero."

"No, Sir Dodger. You're the hero of this story."

Mark rolled his eyes. "For the last time, my name is—"

"Mark Bishop," stated Humpty. "But you have to accept the fact that you will always be known to us as Dodger Hook-Slayer."

"How about Dodger Twice-Hook-Slayer?" proposed Rump. Humpty smacked him in the back of the head.

Mark shrugged with a smile, accepting his permanent Storyworld title.

"Now that the case is closed and the mystery solved," said Rump, "do you want to return to your own world?"

Mark hesitated. It was time for him to go home to rebuild his life. But he was feeling conflicted. There was something in his mind that was making him think twice about returning. He remembered what the Marauder said about how he felt more comfortable in Storyworld. Mark knew he was right, but deep down inside, he also knew he ultimately belonged in his own world. He had to get back to Amy and to the rest of the things that mattered in his life.

Before he left, Mark and the Companions finished with the disposal of the bodies. What was left of Hook's body was cast into the fire pit in the center of the laboratory along with the bodies of the Piper, Hyde, the pirates, and the dwarves. After all the bodies had been accounted for, the Companions ventured outside the Dronos Caves and stood on the ledge of the cliff overlooking the valley. In front of them, the sun was peeking over the horizon, and behind them, smoke issued from the open rooftop of Frankenstein's laboratory.

A griffin was grazing outside the exit. Robin approached the creature and stroked its mane. He then frowned at the Companions and said, "Er, I don't think we'll all fit on this one griffin."

"No need for concern. I found this on the Piper's persona," declared Rump, producing a playing-card-sized object from his pocket. Ignoring Holmes and Wilma's confusion, he placed the object on the ground, where it expanded into a large, hovering carpet.

"I'll take the griffin to Oz and inform the Wizard-King of his fallen guardsmen," said Robin.

"I'll go with you," said Wilma. Robin raised an eyebrow, but she scoffed at him. "Simmer down, hero. You're going to need my protection in case you get yourself into a new mess of trouble."

Mark shook Wilma and Robin's hands as they exchanged goodbyes. The archers mounted the griffin, said their final farewells to the Companions, and then took off into the sunrise.

"Humpty," Mark said, "I didn't get a chance to say this already, but I just want to tell you I'm really, really sorry. I'm sorry I made you out to be such a pain in my book. You're not like that at all. You're an awesome leader."

Humpty smiled. "I think I should be sorry for ruining your book. But honestly, it is fine. People have often told me I am a shrewd and sometimes overbearing commander. It has worked for me thus far in life, so I see no point in changing my habits. If people find it to be bothersome or annoying, well, then they are either too young or too immature to appreciate a true leader."

Mark returned the smile and said, "I deserved that. I promise I'll give you the proper treatment in the sequel. And I'm sorry about Pinocchio's death."

"You must stop apologizing, especially for things that are not your fault. General Pinocchio died in battle. He would not have wanted to die any other way."

Mark nodded and shook Humpty's hand.

"I guess I should apologize to you too, Mr. Bishop," said Holmes, extending his hand. "I was a bit rude when we first met. That was unnecessary. You're a fine gentleman, if I say so myself. If you weren't so adamant about going back to your own world, I'd invite you to join the Himshire Investigators. You have a knack for detective work."

"You're a good man, Holmes," said Mark, taking the agent's hand. "And I think you're smart enough to handle it on your own."

"I appreciate the kind words, but I'm nothing without a partner to balance me out. Maybe I'll reconnect with my son, Bruce. Rumor has it that he's become quite the detective himself. It'd be nice to keep it in the family…"

Rump didn't shake Mark's hand and instead gave him a big hug that lifted him in the air. When he put him down, he pulled a potion from his belt.

"Are you ready?"

Mark nodded. Rump threw the potion on the ground, forming a massive black portal. Mark gave one last smile at Humpty, Rump, and Holmes. There was a tiny tear in his eye as he gave a final smile to his friends.

Return to Storyworld

Suddenly, the Companions' expressions went from sadness, to absolute horror. Humpty reached out and clamped both his hands on the Literary's wrist. Mark was confused as to what was happening, until a pair of black skeletal hands appeared from behind him and wrapped themselves around his body.

Holmes and Rump grabbed onto Mark's wrist as well, and the three of them held on with all their might, but the arms encasing his body proved to be much stronger. With a sharp tug, Mark's hands broke free from the Companions' grasp, and he was sucked into the portal. The last thing he saw was the Grand Sword falling out of his hands and the Companions shouting for him.

It had to be a nightmare.

This was all Mark kept thinking over and over again as he sat in the dark confines of his prison. When he woke up, he had to pinch himself hard to prove he was just having a really bad dream. Any minute now, he would wake up in his condo, or his hotel, or even in Neverland Castle. All he wanted was to be somewhere familiar. The moment he opened his eyes and saw that he was imprisoned within a small metal cage in a dimly lit room, he knew it had to be one big nightmare.

The chain shackled around Mark's left leg prevented him from getting too far from the center of his prison. He had tried to break free, but realized his heightened senses and physical strength were now gone. He no longer possessed the abilities of the Midnight Marauder. He was back to his normal, average-strength self.

Return to Storyworld

A nearby door creaked open. Mark twitched at the sound and shuffled over to the far corner of his cage.

"Who's there?!" he asked.

The door creaked again, followed by the muffled sound of the lock clicking shut. For a moment, Mark believed it was the wind playing with the door. Then he heard raspy breathing coming from in front of him. The darkness obscured anything beyond his cage. All he could see were the metal bars sealing him in.

The room went completely silent. Mark let out a long sigh of relief, but quickly sucked it back in when the black skeletal hands latched around the bars. His heart beat so fast it was about to burst out of his chest. A pair of shocking white eyes popped out of the darkness.

"Dodger... Hook-Slayer..." wheezed a raspy voice. "Mark... Bishop..."

"Are you sure about this, Rumpelstiltskin?"

"We have no choice. Who else can we trust for this mission? Now open the door! It's becoming cramped in here!"

Humpty reached for the handle and wedged the door open, causing him and Rump to spill out onto a wooden floor. The room was pitch-black, but the lights came on moments after the two Neverlanders emerged from the doorway. They heard the barking of an animal, and then a shrill scream that turned into a shocked gasp.

"Humpty?! Rump?! What are you guys doing here?!"

Return to Storyworld

The duo attempted to regain their composure. They were sore, battered, and bruised, having come directly from an intense battle, but they had no time to waste. Humpty gave a slight bow and launched into his speech.

"Lady Gallows, I know our presence here is unusual and unexpect—"

"You're damn right it's unexpected! How did you get here anyway? I thought only Literaries could travel to Storyworld, not the other way around!"

"It's a long story and we don't have time to explain," said Rump, panting. "There's been an emergency in Storyworld and we need your help!"

Lady Gallows shook her head, her eyes wide in horror. "What? No! Why do you need my help? I already paid my dues to Neverland. There's still a scar on my back from that fight with the Monkey King."

"Please!" begged Humpty. "We can explain along the way, but it is imperative that we set off now. Time is of the essence and another Literary's life is at stake! Do you have the Nimbus Staff?"

"Yeah, I do, but—"

"Then let us make haste!" Humpty brandished his arm into the doorway behind him. Lady Gallows refused to move and crossed her arms.

"Listen, I'm not going anywhere. At least not until you two tell me why you're here."

Humpty's cheeks went red and he grabbed his temples. Rump was flustered as well, but he calmed down enough to explain.

"We had just concluded a long, exhausting case with another Literary and we were sending him home, when someone, or something, kidnapped him. He has been captured and we have no clue where he is. As King Humpty said, time is of the essence and we cannot wait for another Literary to arrive on their own. You're the only person who can help us find and rescue Sir Dodger."

Lady Gallows went pale, as if she was about to faint. But then she reached behind her ear and pulled out a small wooden needle. In a flash, it expanded into a tall walking staff with golden ringlets on each end.

"Sir Dodger," said Lady Gallows, her voice quivering, "was his real name Mark Bishop?"

"Yes!" exclaimed Rump. "You know of him?!"

Lady Gallows whispered, "He's my husband."